P.M. BLOOMFIELD

Angus Finch and the Ghosts of Everwood

Cover design by P.M. Bloomfield

Originally published as Here Be Dragons under the pen name Jane Baker in January 2023. This revised and rewritten edition is published as Angus Finch and the Ghosts of Everwood in 2025.

First Edition
2025

Turning Page Press
turningpagepress.com
Australia

To the hopeless and the helpless. May you find your dragon.
And to my family. As ever, as always.

It does not do to leave a live dragon out of your calculations, if you live near him.

J.R.R Tolkien, The Hobbit

an ordinary life

You would think I'd be used to being punched in the stomach by now, but I really wasn't. It hurt just as badly as the first time. I gasped for breath and fell to my knees, ever the weakest link at this hellhole known as high school. What kind of sadistic freak thought that shoving a bunch of hormone-infested, pimple-faced, pubescent monsters into a single location all day long was a good idea? I mean, think about it. Where else in life are you surrounded by people *exactly* the same age as you? Where else in life are you forced to sit in a seat all day long and listen to people who've never actually experienced anything gab on about crap they've only ever read about for eight hours straight? How did anyone think we'd make it to graduation unscathed?

I don't know. Maybe being the school punching bag has just soured me towards the whole institution.

Highschool looked fine for people like the wild-eyed jerk who just forced lunch up into the back of my throat. He certainly seemed to be enjoying himself. I tried not to dwell on the fact I was haplessly a part of perpetuating a stereotype. The star athlete of the school, beating up the guy who gets A's in everything. Just for once, I would have liked for it to be different. There was a whole slew of different people here. Artists, punk rockers, goths, musicians. I mean, anyone can get beaten up by the *jock*. Just once I'd like to say, "Yeah, this black eye came from the tuba player. He's got a real mean streak." At least then it would be a little more interesting.

For good measure, Neal Bateman, my eternal tormentor, unzipped my bag and tipped the contents on the floor.

"Have fun collecting your stuff, loser," Neal laughed, impressed by his own archaic commitment to bullying. He aimed squarely for the section of my ribs that protected my liver and then kicked hard, reminding me why he was the captain of the rugby team.

Loser? Really? Do people still say that?

I caught my breath, clutching my sides, as Neal and his posse walked away. I watched them slap each other's backs, proud of what they had accomplished and wondered how much longer it would be until I graduated, to the day, hour, minute. It took me a few moments before I could get up, during which time my fellow peers of what was generally acknowledged to be the worst high school in England, walked right on around me, unaware or unmoved by my pathetic state. I brought myself to my knees and stuffed my belongings back into my bag. At least I found the book I'd been looking for. I had no idea it was at the bottom of my bag. Zipping it closed, I threw it over my shoulder and rose to my feet, taking off slowly down the hallway, trying to pretend that I hadn't just been on the floor in agony moments earlier.

Outside, it was raining heavily, not a surprise for autumn in England. Or anytime in England, actually. I hurried as fast as my bruised ribs would allow. My bus would be waiting at the stop by now and if I didn't make it, there wouldn't be another one.

I loped down the steps and caught sight of my bus waiting loyally at its station and breathed a sigh of relief. As I looked both ways to cross the road, however, the bus pulled out of its stop and groaned down the road, oblivious to my frantic waving and pleas for mercy.

"Excellent," I moaned to myself, shivering as a chill sprinted up my spine. I was now thoroughly drenched, and my floppy dark hair was sticking to my forehead and neck in great clumps.

I shoved my hands into my pockets and started on the lengthy walk home. My mother would pepper me with questions when I walked in the door sopping wet, while reminding me how dangerous it could be to catch a chill. She would then talk about my Uncle James and how, after he got caught out in the rain, he got terribly sick and was never the same again. We almost never saw him now; I wasn't even sure I could remember him.

I sighed and wondered if I could make it home before her if I ran. I looked at my watch and decided that it was worth a shot to avoid yet another lecture about Uncle James.

I took off at as fast a pace as my aching sides would allow. My feet slapped the flooded pavement, causing splashes and ripples with every footfall. I felt like I was going to be sick. Bile rose and burned my throat, but I kept running, only mildly concerned about internal bleeding or critical injuries.

As my eyes caught sight of fathers and mothers with their children, and teenagers huddling under the eaves of the fish and chip shop to take shelter from the rain, I felt the familiar pang of angst about why I couldn't just be like everybody else. It seemed to me that everyone around me had a purpose, or plans, or at least a whole family unit that made sense. I was a single child to a mother who refused to speak of my father, referring to him only as The Man. We lived with my peculiar grandfather, George, who had been with us ever since my grandmother died. I loved him, of course, but he was no replacement for a father. He was half bonkers, always muttering under his breath about things I could never understand.

Boyfriends had girlfriends, and kids had mates, and husbands had wives, but I felt like an outsider looking into a world that didn't really want me or even seem to have a place for me. I didn't really have any friends to speak of other than my dog Roger, and to be quite honest, he wasn't the most astounding conversationalist.

I was, in the purest sense of the word, a complete nobody. I was such a nobody that I could have been anybody and nobody would care.

I watched a pretty, blonde girl tuck a curl behind her ear and smile coyly as a guy reached for her waist and pulled her close. I wondered what that felt like because I had never even come close to having a girlfriend. At the last party I was invited to, when I was at the universally embarrassing age of thirteen, I was involved in a game of truth or dare, and it went exactly the way one might expect. When Amber Pots was dared to kiss me in the closet, I thought my chance had finally come. But when we got in there, she asked if we could not and say we did. Apparently, she didn't want her first kiss to be with someone like me. With that, my life as the nerd in a coming-of-age movie – probably about someone else – was complete. How cliché.

I was too caught up in a moment that wasn't my own to notice the man standing in front of me. I ran directly into him, smacking my head on his chest.

It was like hitting a brick wall. I bounced backwards and fell to the ground, knocking my head impossibly hard on the pavement. My entire world began to spin, and I wondered for a moment if I had died, and this is what it feels like to have your soul untangle itself from your body.

Thick hands were suddenly on my shoulders, yanking me to my feet. I tried to focus on the face in front of me, but my eyes were blurred. His face looked like it belonged in an oil painting, smudged and indistinct everywhere that mattered.

"Sorry," I managed to mutter. "I wasn't looking where I was going."

"Angus. Angus! Listen," the voice belonging to the blurry face in front of me was hushed and desperate. "They'll be coming for you tonight. You need to be ready. Everything is about to change. Trust them. You're safe with them. Angus, are you listening?"

My head was spinning, and I felt a surge of anger. I wanted him to let me go. I stumbled as my legs wobbled underneath me.

"Angus, remember what I said. Be ready. Trust." The rain dribbled off his head and onto my face, splashing my cheeks.

I dropped to the ground, unable to hold myself up, and somewhere in the back of my mind, I realized the man had let go of my shoulders. I held my head between my hands to steady myself and closed my eyes, waiting for the moment of dizziness and nausea to pass. When it finally did, and I felt as though I could stand without falling, I looked up to see the man I had inadvertently attacked, but he was gone.

I looked around, but no one seemed to fit the voice that had been urging me to listen. I stood up shakily and placed one tentative foot in front of the other, in the direction of home. I swiftly gave up on the idea of running or beating my mother home and resigned myself to the lecture I would no doubt receive.

As I started to walk down the path, eyes now firmly in front of me, I replayed the strange encounter on a loop, trying to extract more detail, like juice from an orange. Who was that man? He knew my name, but I didn't recognise his voice. What did he mean? If someone was coming for me tonight, I had no intention of trusting them, particularly on the word of a stranger I bumped into – *literally* – on the street.

What kind of deranged weirdo does that? I brushed my hair out of my face and decided to forget about the strange encounter. As I forcefully shoved the thoughts out of my mind, one last tantalising tidbit remained.

He knew my name…

When I finally arrived home, I felt cold to the bone, as the rain had not eased. I fumbled at the front door with my key, missing the keyhole multiple times. I all but fell inside the door, tripping on my own feet. I groaned angrily as I closed the door, then removed my shoes and trudged towards the stairs to my room, hoping to go unseen.

"Angus Cillian Finch!" My mother's voice felt like arrows in my back.

Oh no. The dreaded middle name.

I stopped on the first step and turned to see her staring at me in abject horror. "Yes, Mum?"

I watched as her anger melted into concern. "What on this green earth has happened to you?"

I must have looked as bad as I felt. "It's a long story," I murmured.

"Then you better get ready to tell it!" she snipped.

"I had another run-in with Neal Bateman, and he made me miss the bus. Then I ran into someone – literally, ran into him – and fell. I knocked my head very hard and I'm feeling quite rubbish, so if we could skip the lecture about walking home in the rain, I would be forever indebted to you."

My mother was like a human lie detector. There was rarely anything worth lying to her about because she would always know, somehow scope out the truth, and punish me eternally for failing to tell the truth. So, now I settled for brutal honesty. She seemed to appreciate it.

"That Neal Bateman is a complete scoundrel!" she boomed. "When are you going to let me speak to someone about that little worm-child? I could call the principal, or even his mother, and have this put to an end immediately."

"That's simply not how it works, Mother," I moaned. "Were you to call anyone, I would be punished even further by him and his band of brutes. It's fine. I'm fine. It's the way of the world. Positively Shakespearean. You should be proud. I'm living literature."

"You certainly are *not* fine. Come here." She turned away and gestured for me to follow her into the kitchen.

There were benefits to having a nurse as your mother, but there were also downsides. Sitting at the dining table, dripping water onto the linoleum, as she shone a torch into both eyes, while maintaining a perpetually irritated glare, would perhaps not have happened to someone whose mum didn't work fifty hours a week in the public healthcare system.

"How hard did you hit your head?" she asked.

"Very," I replied.

"Did you lose consciousness?"

"No."

"Experience dizziness?"

"Yes."

"How long did it take you to regain your senses?"

"A few minutes, maybe."

She pulled back from her inspection and stared at me for a long moment. Her large brown eyes were perfectly round, sitting snugly into a circular face. We shared that trait, but the resemblance stopped there. I had a square jaw with high cheekbones, and she had peach-coloured cheeks and a mess of auburn ringlets. She was quite pretty, but she had a sternness about her that made her intimidating. To me, at least. If I were good-looking, I would have been friends with Neal, not beaten to a pulp by him. *Average* was my middle name. More than that, there was a mysterious ethnicity that my face reflected, but my Mum was clueless as to its origins since my father had been notoriously closed-lipped about his past. My features weren't prominent enough for me to confidently say *exactly* where my heritage came from. It was a question only The Man could answer.

I began to feel awkward as she glared at me, as if searching my soul for answers. "Paging Nurse Bethany Finch. Paging Nurse Finch." I put on my best loudspeaker voice, hoping to shake her from her seriousness so she would let me out of her sight long enough for me to change into something warm and crash land on my bed with a book and a headache.

"You are to go shower, get warm, and rest. I will be up every thirty minutes to check on you until I am satisfied."

"Wonderful," I sighed, getting up from the chair. "Can't imagine a better way to spend the evening."

She watched me until I was out of sight and up the stairs. Perched on the top step was Roger, ever eager for my attention, though somewhat inhibited by age to show too much enthusiasm. I scratched his ear and headed for the bathroom as he lumbered behind me, a faithful follower. I closed the door to the bathroom behind us, stripped, and launched myself into the shower as Roger curled his little Terrier body onto the pile of wet clothes.

I tried to empty my mind, but I still couldn't quite shake the uneasiness I felt about my encounter with that strange man. What had he meant? How did he know my name?

I shoved my head under the water in the hopes of drowning my thoughts. I felt the water pour down the sides of my face, then watched as they fell to their ultimate demise as they swirled down the drain into the abyss.

Walking into my room, a towel wrapped around my waist, I stopped at the door to assess the situation. An unmade bed with crumpled blue sheets, a cluttered wooden desk with a faded map of the world printed on the top, and an old dresser were the stars of the show. The mess that stretched from the door to the far window and a leaning pile of books on the floor played supporting roles.

I picked up a shirt from a clean pile of clothes at the end of the bed and slipped it on. Discarding the towel, I slid into a pair of jeans. Removing the book at the top of the pile, I threw myself onto the bed and drowned in the thick bedding for a moment, before opening the book and picking up where I left off.

At least it was Friday. I didn't have to go back to school for two entire days, and the peace of the thought filled me with a lightness I didn't expect after the kind of day I had suffered through in relative silence.

There was a knock at my door, so I called out to grant entrance to whoever was there. I had expected it to be Mum, but when the door swung open, it was Grandpa George who stood on the threshold. He was bent and weathered as if permanently looking down at something on the floor. His eyes were almost as deeply set into his face as the lines around his mouth and across his forehead. His lips were cemented into a cheeky, boyish grin that always made me wonder what he was like when he was my age.

"Hey, Grandpa," I said, putting my book down and sitting up. "How's it going?"

"The wind's not right today," he said, shaking his head. "Something feels a bit different."

"I see," I replied. "The wind. Is there anything you would like me to do to make you feel better about it? I could give it a stern talking to for you."

"Don't be ridiculous, boy," he replied, waving his hand dismissively. "You can't control the wind."

"This is true. But for you, I would try." I would do anything for the old badger, strange as he was.

"I know you would," he answered. "That's why I'm leaving everything to you in my will."

I put the book down beside me, unprepared for how uncomfortable the thought of him dying made me. "Don't be silly, Grandpa. You're never going to die."

Grandpa looked around, then scuttled into my room and sat on the end of the bed. "Of course not. I intend to fake my death one day soon and go on an adventure. I have to get away from your mother."

"Right," I said slowly, nodding calmly at him the same way I would an escapee from a mental institution. "Very interesting plan. Uh, was it just the wind and the will you wanted to talk to me about, or?'

Grandpa shook his head. "Don't be daft. I've already said too much. Your mother sent me to fetch you. There are people at the door to see you."

unexpected guests

I swung my legs over the side of my bed. "Uh, who are they?" I asked tentatively. My stomach lurched unexpectedly.

"No idea. Men in strange getup." Grandpa's eyes shifted to the left, then the right. He leaned in close and whispered, "I think it's people from the government. Not the normal government. The *real* government. The one no one knows about. I'd be careful if I were you. They always want to know your business. Always watching you with those infernal cameras. Orwell said it, and we won't listen. Nasty beasts, the lot of them."

I swallowed hard. The encounter with the stranger this afternoon replayed in my mind, and I shuddered.

They'll be coming for you tonight.

I told myself to calm down and stood to my feet. "Let's go find out, shall we?"

Grandpa saluted me like a soldier and nodded firmly. "You just give me the signal if you need me, lad, and I'll step right in. I'll go find my walking stick, so I have something to hit them with."

I patted his shoulder. "Will do, Grandpa. Best forget the stick, though."

I walked past him towards the stairwell and slowly descended. I wasn't quite sure what the 'signal' was, but if these men were here with malicious intent, I was sure I could think of something. I wasn't sure quite how much help Grandpa would be, though.

I peered around the banister to see Mum sitting at the table with three men. Grandpa was right. Their clothes were quite strange. They were each dressed in heavy brown woollen cloaks, with linen shirts, black pants and brown boots. They looked like elves that had escaped from the pages of *The Lord of the Rings*. Papers were situated neatly on the table, along with a large cream-coloured envelope and a silver pen that sat ominously in the very centre of the pile.

Everything is about to change.

I shook away the thought and descended the stairs with forced nonchalance.

"Ah, Angus," Mum said, "there you are. These men are here to speak with you."

"What about?" I asked.

Mum ushered me over to the table. "Why don't you sit down and listen to them?"

I pulled out the chair and sat down with a thump. "All right."

Mum beamed. "I'll get us all some tea."

Of course. You're not really British until you pull out a pot of tea in uncomfortable situations.

I stared blankly at the men as Mum left, my lips pulled back tightly over my teeth, not sure what to say.

The first man, with odd grey eyes that looked like they could see the undead, slid the envelope wordlessly across the table with a single, bony finger. When the envelope stopped in front of me, he withdrew his skeletal digit and tilted his head to the side, waiting.

I slowly picked up the envelope. It was made of heavy cardstock, and swirling letters that made up my name were written in an elegant hand across it.

I turned the letter over and snapped open a wax seal of the initials EA, wrapped in ivy. Pulling out the letter, I read it quickly, with a strange sort of bubble forming in the pit of my stomach.

Dearest Angus,

Everwood Academy, being of the most prestigious lineage and stout history, welcomes you to its hallowed halls to receive an outstanding education unparalleled in excellence and vigour. Everwood Academy, an exclusive and reclusive school, incomparable in its validity and abundance of opportunity, as well as its fantastical teaching staff and most respectable students, award you this place in response to your unnatural talent, extreme patience, unknowable abilities and stupendous gift, as yet to be determined.

We await your arrival this evening, accompanied by the representatives of Everwood, being the three Mister Smiths, most honourable and worthy in nature and sublime in character.

Kindest and most pleasant of regards,

WRT

I looked up at the Mister Smiths, trying to understand. I wanted to ask a thousand questions, but I could only open my mouth and make some sort of strange spluttering sound. I gave up and returned to the letter, rereading it. I still didn't understand. Was this a scholarship or something? I looked up at the cosplaying elves again. The man with the bony finger finally spoke.

"Good evening, Angus. We're from Everwood Academy. My name is Mister Smith. You have been invited to become a student at our institution."

I didn't know what to expect tonight when I saw these men sitting at my table, but this definitely wasn't it. "But I already have a school," I said dumbly.

Mister Smith exchanged privately humorous glances at his comrades. "I assure you, Everwood Academy is in a different league entirely." Mister Smith smiled a small, tight smile.

"Why *me?* How do you even know about me?" I asked. "I didn't apply for a scholarship or anything."

"We know everything we need to know about you, Angus," one of the other men answered.

"And you are?" I questioned.

"Angus, manners," Mum scolded as she walked back into the room, holding a tea tray.

"I am Mister Smith," he answered.

"I thought he was Mister Smith," I pressed, gesturing to the first speaker.

"We're all Mister Smith," the third man answered. "We are the Smith *brothers*."

Oh. Right. The three Mister Smiths, most honourable and worthy in nature and sublime in character, apparently.

I sized them up again, unsure they fit the bill.

"Of course you are," Mum grinned. "And we are very grateful to have you consider Angus. He's a special boy. I've always said so."

I cringed. I had no memory of Mum ever calling me a *special boy*, thank goodness, but I chose not to use this moment to correct her.

"Indeed," one of the Mister Smiths agreed. "Due to his outstanding performance and stand-out nature, Everwood

Academy is extraordinarily motivated to have Angus join us."

"Oh, really?" Mum was almost blushing. I rolled my eyes. "Well, it is a spectacular school, and Angus would be delighted to attend, of course. After all, your Uncle James went there," she said, nudging me.

I picked up one of the papers in front of me. It was a brochure for the Academy, complete with images of smiling students and an overwhelmingly large building, which, I presumed, was the Academy itself.

It boasted an array of different subjects, including Latin, fencing, horse riding and cooking. Surprisingly, it looked like a school I wouldn't mind attending. Of course, I would miss the daily thronging from Neal, but I was sure I would survive without it somehow. I found myself actually considering it. Could there really be an alternative to the dreary halls of my current school and the uninteresting monotony of dull classes? Were the Smith brothers offering me a chance at an education I could only dream about?

It didn't take me long to decide I wanted to go.

Desperately.

After all, I was supposed to trust these guys. At least, that's what the stranger had said.

The next page of the brochure was a picture of a dorm room. My brows furrowed. "Uh, it's a boarding school?"

"Yes," Mister Smith answered. "Everwood Academy is offered only as a boarding school. We do not accept students who will not agree to live on campus."

My mother's smile began to fade. "Oh. I didn't know there wasn't an option to live at home."

"I assure you, Ms. Finch, that our boarding facilities are above reproach. The students of Everwood Academy are treated to three meals a day, prepared by high-class chefs, and our dorm rooms are outfitted with everything a student could possibly need."

"Right," Mum mumbled. "So, just like that… he wouldn't live at home anymore?"

Another Smith brother added, "No, Ms. Finch, but I must say it is a small sacrifice for such an education. Think of the boy's future."

"O-of course." She tried to smile, and I felt a pang of guilt, even though I hadn't sought out this school or even agreed to go. "All of this sounds quite expensive."

"Everwood Academy has been so impressed with Angus that they have offered to waive the first year's tuition, as well as offer a discount for the subsequent years that I am quite sure you will find more than generous." Mister Smith slid the papers across to Mum in one swift motion.

Mum pressed a hand against her chest. "This is quite a lot to take in."

I sat there in between them, not sure what to say or do. I had long since been a neglected part of this conversation, and I wanted to speak up for myself if only to be heard, but I didn't know what to say. I wanted to go to Everwood, but how could I leave Mum behind? Grandpa and I were all she had. If I left, would she think I was just like my father?

But how could I pass up a chance at studying at somewhere like Everwood? I wanted more out of life than most of my current classmates, who didn't seem to want more than a date for the next weekend. I had always felt like I could be great, if I wasn't such a nobody. Maybe if I went to a place like Everwood, I could be a *somebody*. Was it my responsibility to live for my mother? Was it *hers* to live for *me*? Maybe if I left, she wouldn't have to work so hard. She could step back at work, rest a little. Maybe even take some time off.

"I am afraid we need an answer immediately," Mister Smith said. "We would like to take Angus with us this evening so that he might settle in and begin his education on Monday. Otherwise, there is a risk he will fall behind in the school year. There is already a considerable difference in education quality between Everwood and Angus's current school."

"This evening?" Mum shook her head. "No, absolutely not. That's just not enough notice."

The Mister Smiths looked at each other with sidelong glances, unsure of what to say or do next. I got the impression that they didn't meet resistance all that often. Mum stared back at them defiantly, like an eagle defending her nest. I suddenly had this feeling as if I were standing at a crossroads and my life could go one of two ways. I could hear a loud drumming noise, and it took me a moment to realise it was the sound of my heartbeat as it slammed against my ribcage. I tapped my foot on the ground, releasing pent-up nervous energy. I started to feel hot and strange like my brain was about to burst out of its bony cage.

Trust them.

The words of the stranger pricked through my reverie, like the sound of a symbol amidst an orchestra.

Trust them.

I held up the brochure once more and stared at the imposing, leafy, ivy-covered walls of Everwood Academy.

"We urge you to reconsider," I heard Mister Smith say, but his voice seemed hollow and tinny. "For the sake of your son's future."

"I simply can't send him away tonight. I…I can't." Mum locked her fingers together in her lap, looking down at her hands. I couldn't read her expression. Was it fear? Disappointment?

"Mum," I said, my voice taking on a life of its own, flowing out of me before I knew it. "Mum, it's all right. I'll…I'll go with them."

I watched Mum's eyes widen. "You will?"

"Yeah. Like you said, it's a great opportunity, right? And I can always leave if I don't like it, and there's phone calls, and-"

Mum stood up, and the chair scraped along the linoleum. Time seemed to freeze for a moment as she looked into my eyes, on the verge of tears. "Angus, you won't *live* here anymore. I'll barely ever get to see you."

"That's not true." I turned to the first Mister Smith. "I'm sure Everwood provides times for students to return home to see family, or you can visit the campus, right?"

"Of course," Mister Smith answered. "Many times throughout the year. And Angus will simply have to say the word to get a weekend pass to come home whenever he so desires."

"Well, then, you'd have to come home next weekend. I'll make a roast, and you don't want to miss out on it. I know how much you love my roast."

I really *didn't* love her roast. At all. It tasted like old boots that had been left out in the rain for a week. Even though there was almost never anything worth lying to her about, it was after she had spent hours in the kitchen that I felt justified. So far, to date it was the only lie I ever told that she believed.

"I'll come home," I promised.

"Actually," Mister Smith interjected, "students must stay on campus for the first month for the greatest chance at acclimation. But students are permitted their phones and Angus will be able to call as frequently as you would require."

Mum was not pleased but didn't argue.

She sniffed, and I could tell she was fighting to hold back tears.

"Then you better go upstairs and pack while I sign the paperwork with these gentlemen."

I lifted myself from the table and trudged up the stairs, feeling heavy with the weight I felt I had placed on my mother's shoulders. Grandpa was sitting at the top of the stairs, elbows resting on his knees, his head sunk low into his hands. "I heard everything."

I patted his shoulder. "Then you heard that I have an excellent opportunity in front of me. Education is very important."

"Not as important as family, lad. Never forget that." Grandpa grabbed my wrists tightly, staring deeply into my eyes. "Nothing is more important than family."

"I know," I squeezed his hand. "It's all right."

"No, it's not. This is the same school that took my James. And he was never, ever the same."

"Grandpa, Mum always said that Uncle James was never the same because he got sick. That's why no one ever sees him anymore. He went batty cause he got sick, that's all. Nothing to do with Everwood."

"No, Angus. Your mother was too young to know any better. That's just the story we told her. This Everwood Academy…it *changes* you."

"Nothing's going to change me, Grandpa. It's going to be okay."

He let out a long sigh and then dropped my wrists as if surrendering to the fact he had already lost me. "Off you go to pack, boy."

I headed towards my room, casting a look back at Grandpa, who hadn't moved from his seat on the stairs. Sometimes I worried about him.

a little something to drink

Mum stood by the door with her arms folded over her chest. I felt a little queasy at the sight of her; her eyes were red, and her lips were pursed tightly. I knew that face. The last time she had pulled it was when she had just gotten off the phone with The Man. She refused to let me speak to him, and even though, throughout their entire conversation, Mum was shouting at the top of her lungs, I still wanted to yank the phone out of her hand and speak to him. Just to know what his voice sounded like.

I didn't know who he was, what he looked like or even how they met. It made me feel like a part of me was missing. Sometimes, I wondered why other people's lives seemed to make so much more sense than mine. I always seemed to be out of step, different from everyone else. A person out of time or place. I never really belonged, and I always wondered if this missing piece of me was why. Like there was some whole other life that I should be living. For a while, I was angry at her for not letting me know him. But I knew it wasn't fair. She loved me, and if she wasn't letting my father into our lives, there must have been a good reason.

"You have a mobile phone," Mum said bitterly as I threw my bag over my shoulder, "so use it. Daily."

"I will, Mum," I responded.

"Good. And eat your vegetables. And just because you don't live here anymore," she paused and sniffed back tears, "does *not* mean that your bedtime isn't still 10pm. I think it's perfectly reasonable for a sixteen-year-old to go to bed at ten. It's generous even, so you had better stick to it. I'll know if you don't. Mothers have their ways."

I placed both my hands on her shoulders to stop her from babbling. "Mum. It's okay. I love you, too."

Her lips started to quiver, so I pulled her in tightly for a hug so that I couldn't see her face anymore. I couldn't handle it. Sitting by her feet was Roger. I bent down and scratched him behind the ears, giving a small farewell.

By the time I reached the car, I felt completely wretched. As I placed my hand on the door handle, ready to drop into the backseat, I turned back to the house and waved goodbye to Grandpa George and Mum. They both waved back, Mum weakly, Grandpa George somberly, like he was looking at me for the last time.

As the three Mister Smiths' got into the vehicle and we drove away, I realised I didn't even know where I was going. Where was the campus?

"Excuse me," I started, "where exactly are we going?"

Mister Smith answered, "Not far from here. Just a few hours."

I leaned my head back into the soft leather seats of the stately car. A few hours in the car with these chatty fellows. How the time would fly.

"Would you like a little something to drink?" Mister Smith in the front seat asked.

"Uh, yeah. Thanks." He passed me the drink, and I snapped the seal and drank. It was a sweet drink with a hint of a sour aftertaste.

"It's uh…it's….it…"

My words seemed to falter on my tongue; I couldn't get them from my brain into the air. My mouth tasted like cotton balls. My vision went from darkness to daylight over and over until I understood that my eyelids were heavy, and I could no longer keep them open.

I had just enough time to realise they had drugged me before my eyes closed for good, and my head slumped off to the side.

everwood academy

I wasn't sure where I was, but I felt great. I vaguely remembered feeling bad about something, but I couldn't pinpoint the memory well enough to know why. Oh well. I supposed it didn't matter. My body felt so light, as if my skin had developed the ability to levitate and was trying to drag my sorry muscles and bones up into the air to enjoy a freedom previously known only to birds.

Wait. Was I spinning? Or was it just in my mind? No. Maybe I was falling. I was definitely falling. Fast. I didn't feel so good anymore. I tried to put my hands out in front of me to protect my face, but I couldn't lift them. My limbs weren't floating anymore. They were heavy and rotund, as if I had morphed into an elephant without knowing it.

The ground was fast approaching. I wanted to scream, but I couldn't open my mouth.

That's when the voice hit me, like an ice bullet to the chest. It was loud and clear, exactly as I had heard it on the street.

Everything is about to change.

I sat up straight with a forceful jolt, only to be choked by my seatbelt and thrust back into the seat. I blinked against the cloudiness in my vision. The three Mister Smiths sat unmoving around me. The one that sat beside me regarded me suspiciously with black eyes that wouldn't be out of place on a troll who was considering the best way to cook me.

What had happened became painfully apparent.

"You drugged me!" I slurred, my voice still catching up to my brain.

"For your own protection, Angus," the troll answered coolly.

"Are you kidding me?" I tried to force clarity out of the words, though lethargy fought me. "I want to go home." I looked around, trying to take note of where we were, but I could see nothing but darkness and heavy fog surrounding me.

He chuckled. "I'm afraid we've come too far for that. You must attend your orientation. If you still wish to leave after that, you may return home. We shall take you home the very same way you arrived. Safe and sound."

"Safe and sound and *drugged*." I unclipped my seatbelt, ready to hurl myself out of the car if required. "Where the hell are we, anyway?" I snapped. "I can't see out."

"We are in a safe place. Not far from the Academy now."

"One of you better start giving me answers, or I'm going to jump right out of this car." I grabbed a hold of the handle to drive my threat home.

Whether or not I *actually* had the courage to jump out of a moving vehicle was another thing entirely. I would find out at the same time they did.

"Very well, Angus," the Smith brother behind the wheel responded, a cloak pulled over his head so I couldn't see him. "If you must know, we are currently in Dartmoor. Near enough, anyway."

"Dartmoor? Like…the national park?"

"Yes, indeed."

I blinked stupidly, still groggy. "Why?"

"Because that is where the school is located. We have already passed through the channel and are approaching the Academy now."

"What channel? You can't have a school in a national park. Is this some kind of weird hippie cult thing? I'm not shaving my head."

"Gracious, no. Everwood Academy is not like any other school, Angus. It resides on another plane."

"Do any of you speak English? What does that even mean?" I asked as the car came to a forceful halt. I flew forward in my seat and hit my face on the headrest in front of me.

Moaning, I straightened myself, rubbing my neck. "Guess that's why we wear seatbelts, huh? Should have listened to all those ads."

"I'm afraid we no longer have time for any further questions. We have arrived. Your school representative will be meeting us at the front entrance."

I looked out of the windows but still couldn't see anything but fog. Thick grey fog and an even thicker black night. I couldn't see mountains, or hills, or stars. Just a swirling mist, like we were in a plane flying through a cloud.

This was *insane.* I wanted to go home. Was I about to be murdered? Would I be one of those tragic cases people heard about on the news? Would Mum find my body in a plastic bag or a suitcase or something? Was I going to decay in the sun or be eaten by wild animals?

I felt my eyes sting. I was going to be killed, and my bones would be found a decade later, in Dartmoor National Park, buried somewhere amongst deer droppings and rabbit holes. My family would wonder what happened to me. Poor Mum would never be the same.

Or…perhaps it would be much worse than that. Perhaps they would think that I abandoned them after going to the Academy. They'd talk about me like they talk about Uncle James. A nutter who left the family and never looked back. They wouldn't even know I'd been killed. They would hate me. Mum would never forgive me. That was worse.

Then, when or *if* my bones were ever found, they would realise that I never left them and would feel distraught with guilt for the rest of their lives. "If one of you is going to kill me, at least tell my mother I'm dead," I blurted.

"Get out of the car, Angus," the troll said.

"An anonymous letter. An email. A creepy call from a blocked number. I'm not asking for a face-to-face. Just tell her I died, and I'm sorry."

"Out."

The Mister Smiths stepped out of the car, following their own instruction, and I was left alone in the darkness. It took me a few seconds to deliberate whether or not I would actually get out of the vehicle. But if they had drugged me, I imagined that they wouldn't have too much weight on their conscience if they forcibly dragged me out of the car, so I figured that if I went of my own volition, at the slightest wink of sinister behaviour, I could run as fast and as far as I could. It was my last hope of survival, and hope, I discovered, is what we cling to in our final moments.

I opened the door and got out, my stomach twisting into knots.

For a moment, I was blinded. The fog was so heavy and thick that I couldn't see my hand in front of my face as I waved it around. I reached out to touch the car behind me to steady myself, but I could no longer feel it.

Just as I was about to call out for help or run in whatever direction was *away*, the fog began to lift, and I could start to make out shapes. Stairs, maybe? A tower? Finally, the fog vanished entirely, and I could see that I was standing in front of a warmly lit, grandiose building. Or perhaps the term *castle* would better suit.

For all the cloak-and-dagger behaviour and the illegal drugging of a minor, the Academy looked warm, inviting and even…peaceful. I shivered with relief that there actually *was* an academy after all, and the Mister Smiths weren't going to kill me.

The night around us was bright, a large full moon lighting up my surroundings with a silky silver glow. The building was shaped out of grey stones, stacked to form solid, impenetrable walls that stretched far to my left and right. An aggressively pointed roof hovered over what appeared to be the main section of the Academy, and turrets sprouted up from multiple other points.

Wide stone steps led up to a large wooden double door, with intricate wrought iron braces across it for reinforcement. Enormous lamps, flickering with sentimental firelight, jutted out from the façade, spilling a lovely yellow glow onto the grounds below.

I stepped close to the building, drawn in by some unseen force. This was where I lived now? This was Everwood?

Windows with thick wooden trim were carved into the stone every ten or so feet. I counted twenty windows across and nine windows high in some places. Some of the windows were brightly lit from behind, and others were drowning in darkness.

Above the front entrance doorframe were the words *Everwood Academy* and then *HIC SUNT DRACONES*, which I imagined was something highly intelligent or absurdly ostentatious written in Latin, just like one would see at any other academy.

The grounds around me appeared lush and green, and as my gaze followed the expanse of grass, I looked out across the rolling hillsides lit by the moonlight. A huge lake shone in the silver light, moving and glistening like it was alive.

It was beautiful. Breathtaking even. I couldn't imagine what it looked like in the sunlight. It looked nothing at all like Dartmoor, though.

I turned back to the Academy. It was positively enormous, resembling an ancient fortress that was still in use. I imagined kings and queens having resided here over the years, battles old and new fought around them on every side. I wondered who had walked the halls before me, and who would walk them after me.

I took another step forward, only to trip on my bags. I hadn't noticed they were there. Where were the Mister Smiths? I looked around to find them or the car, but I was completely alone.

The wooden door began to open, letting out a loud, ominous groan. A shadowed figure emerged and descended the stairs slowly, like a wraith. A cold breeze gripped my chest like a hand reaching inside my ribcage and fiddling around to find my heart. I steeled myself.

You can always run, I thought to myself. *If anything happens, just take off. Maybe they won't find you.*

The darkened figure finally stepped into the light, and the face of an elderly man was revealed. He was very tall – enormously so – and half of his face was covered with a greying beard that came to a dramatic point. The other half sported squarish glasses with a thick black frame. He wore olive green linen slacks with suspenders, black shoes shiny enough to reflect the moon, and a long, heavy overcoat over the top of a white button-up shirt.

"Hello, Angus," he said with a smile that cracked his face in half. "It is a pleasure to have you here. Finally! I am the headmaster of this school, your guide, counsellor and constant friend, Sir Walter Robert Thomas, Recipient of the Fifth Order of the Concilium, High Knight of the Vectors, and nine-time winner of the Equitem Cup." He extended a wrinkled hand and gripped hold of mine tightly, shaking it with vigour. His hand swallowed my own, and I felt like a child. "But you can call me Spectre."

"Spectre?" I blurted, confused. Hadn't he just said his name was Walter? "Why Spectre?" His face was so bright it was like it had its own source of light. His wrinkles were deep-set, but he *seemed* younger than he looked. Who was this giant of a man?

"Ah, yes. That. Everyone calls me that." He straightened and looked off into the distance as if confused. Quietly, almost under his breath, he added, "Come to think of it, I have no idea why." He shrugged, his enormous shoulders rising and falling like mountains crashing into the sea. "Come along with me. I'll give you a tour. You must be very curious." He turned and walked away without waiting for my answer. I had to take off after him in a jog, my heavy bag hanging from my shoulder, just to keep up with the wide strides afforded to him by unusually long legs.

"Everwood Academy was founded a very long time ago. It's never been located anywhere other than here, and the people who know about it are few and far between." He slipped through the Academy doors and began, what was to him, a leisurely stroll down a wide hallway with tall ceilings and a long red rug draped over dark wooden floorboards. "The Academy sits on over a thousand hectares of property and is found, only by those who know where it is, within Dartmoor National Park."

"Yeah, I'm still a little fuzzy on that," I said, shaking my head. "Dartmoor is a National Park. They wouldn't let you build an Academy in it."

"They didn't," he answered matter-of-factly.

"Then, how are you here? Illegally?"

"Like I said, it is found by those who know where it is *within* Dartmoor National Park."

I still didn't get it. What was I missing? "That doesn't make any sense."

He sighed heavily, clearly exasperated. "When you were driven here, you drove into Dartmoor National Park, passed through a channel, and are now currently residing in another plane, situated in the same geographical location as Dartmoor National Park, yet outside of it entirely." He huffed out a breath. "Now, where was I? Ah, yes. We offer some of the finest aspects of education available. We currently have two hundred and two, now *three*, students, and-"

"That's not that many," I said without thinking. After the words had slipped from my mouth, I realised how rude I sounded. "Sorry, I just meant that at my old school, there were that many students in my grade, let alone the whole school. I just thought Everwood Academy would be bigger. I didn't mean-"

"Nonsense," Spectre chided, "Say what you think, think what you say. Indeed, it is *not* many students. However, we are a particularly selective academy, and not many students fit our requirements, my boy."

"If I might ask," I probed, "what exactly *are* those requirements? I mean…what is so special about me?"

"Ah," he cooed wistfully. He stopped walking and turned to face me. "This is my favourite part of introducing a new student to this school. You, my dear Angus, are a remarkably exceptional young man indeed."

I scoffed. "Uh, I'm not sure you have the right guy. There's nothing special about me at all. I'm a nobody." My stomach dipped at the concept of being sent home if this was some horrible case of mistaken identity. Now that I was here, I didn't want to leave.

Spectre shook his head gravely. He clasped my shoulders and levelled his face with mine, which required that he bend in the middle. "*Nobodies* are the best kind of *somebodies*, Angus. You should be glad to be a nobody, for that, very assuredly and without any doubt, makes you a somebody. It's the people that are somebodies from the beginning that are nobodies, and it's the somebodies that a nobody like you must look out for, for your sake and for the sake of all the other nobodies."

I blinked. Then I blinked again. "Sorry. What?"

Spectre straightened to his full height and stretched his arms out wide. The tips of his fingers weren't far from the walls on either side of us. "Let me start right in the middle because starting at the beginning is ever so predictable, and I find things that are predictable to be boring, as so many things very often are, and the boring things in life are the dullest, and I don't tolerate dull *things* much better than I tolerate dull *people*. You're not dull, though, are you, Angus?" Spectre bent down again to peer into my eyes, his nose almost touching mine.

I jumped back and tried to regain my composure as quickly as I had lost it. "I don't…*think* so," I answered.

"No, no, indeed. Not dull at all. I can see it right there." He pointed an accusatory finger into my eyeball. "Something very interesting in there, there is." He arched his back and swooped up again, standing tall once more. "*You*, Angus Finch, have history in your blood." This man *spoke* in italics. Every word had its own lilt and rhythm, as if he was singing.

"I have no idea what that means." I felt like I was saying that a lot.

"You'll find out soon enough, I'm sure, and I'm always quite sure, except for when I'm not, but even then, I'm sure that I am not sure, so I'm sure either way, which leads me back to what I said before – I am *always* sure. You have a very great history, which lives and breathes in every heartbeat."

I tried to understand the barrage of words that dribbled out of his mouth like water. "So… I'm here because of my family lineage? I heard my Uncle James went to this school."

His brows furrowed, and he waved me away. "No, no, no. You are here because you are a carrier of something that is *passed down* through your lineage."

"And what would that be?" I asked.

"A very special gift that very few people in this world have. It is a gift that can only be given, not sought after or purchased. Ha, no, no, wait. I shouldn't call it a gift. That means something else entirely here. Let's call it…a genetic disposition. Yes, much better." Spectre turned on his heel and lumbered away.

"You're not making any sense. You do know that, right?" There was something completely bewildering about this giant, peculiar old man standing in front of me. He reminded me of a thin Santa Claus; mysterious, mystical, fabled. Even though he was standing right in front of me, I wondered if he really existed. I wondered if I reached out and touched him, would he disappear?

"All in good time, my boy. All in good time. Things will fall into place, and you'll understand clear as mud." He chuckled. When I didn't respond with anything other than a confused stare, he cleared his throat as if embarrassed by his attempt at a joke. "Hmm. Perhaps we need a more direct approach. Nothing for it, then, eh, old boy? Let's get straight to it. Follow me." With that, Spectre turned back the way we had come, retracing the very steps we had just taken. I followed him back down the hallway until we stood on the front steps at the entrance, where we had first met only moments earlier.

"What are we doing out here?" I asked.

"Do you see these words carved into stone, below Everwood Academy?" he asked.

I looked up to see the Latin phrase I had noticed when I first arrived. "Yeah."

"Read them to me," he instructed.

"I don't speak Latin," I protested.

"I know," he said sadly. "Not many people do anymore. Terribly disappointing. Wonderful language. We owe it a great deal. Go right on ahead and try anyway," he encouraged.

I squinted and studied the words. "Okay, uh, it says hic…sunt…dracones."

Spectre clapped his hands happily. "Very good, Angus. Now, do you know what that means?"

"Something about learning?" I guessed.

Spectre leaned in close. I marveled at the great deal of effort it must have taken to bend himself in half like that. I could see flecks of gold in his otherwise green eyes. "No, my boy. It says…Here be dragons."

here be dragons

The words lingered in the air like the smell of cabbages on a warm day. Spectre was looking at me with such expectation on his wide, joyful face, that I felt sure I was missing something important. "Huh. Is that, like, some kind of metaphor, or something?" I asked.

Spectre almost jumped back. He had a look of utter confusion on his face. "It most certainly is *not* a metaphor. Why in the world would someone go to the effort of carving a metaphor into stone?"

"I don't know," I answered. "It's just that, usually, fancy schools have a catchphrase or something in Latin. Like, be all you can be. To learn is to live. Truth, learning and freedom. Blah, blah, blah. That kind of thing."

Spectre appeared wearied by the world and its stupidity. Or perhaps just by me and mine. "Well, it is not a metaphor, and it is certainly not a catchphrase. It's a warning."

"A warning?" That sounded ominous. "To who?"

"*Whom,*" he corrected.

Ah, so this really was a school. "Sorry, to whom?"

Spectre's face darkened and the glint in his eyes vanished. "It is a warning to anyone who should find this place if they are not expressly invited. The uninvited are the most dangerous kind of people to have at a place you are not expecting them to be. Unwelcome, unknown, unescorted. One never knows what a stranger might carry in their pockets, their hearts, or their brain. Quite a dangerous thing."

"What is?" I asked.

Spectre looked up to the inscription. In a quiet voice that I had to strain to hear, he answered, "Humans."

At this point, I noticed that Spectre had long white hair streaked with black and tied in a tight bun at the back of his head. He was also enormously muscular, which seemed surprising for his age. But it was the tattoo around the back of his neck that drew my eye. It looked like barbed wire, but something told me it was a language I had never seen before.

Suddenly, Spectre spun around with a grin. "But that's not *you*, now, is it? You were invited!"

I laughed. "I would hardly call that an invitation. They drugged me!"

Aghast, he stepped back. "Who drugged you?"

I pointed at the location where the car had been earlier. "The Mister Smiths! They drugged me; knocked me out cold. That's not okay. I thought they were going to kill me."

"Ah, the Smith brothers." Spectre looked up at the sky wistfully. "At it again. I'm afraid they did that for your own protection. The drug was entirely harmless, I assure you."

"That's what *they* said – that it was for my own good."

"See, well, there you go then." He smiled and clasped his hands together over his chest. The wrinkles in his face creased deeply with his grin.

"No, no, not '*there you go then*'. I was drugged! That's illegal!"

"Only a tiny bit, and like I said, it was for your own protection."

Spectre waved his hands wildly at me like he was dispersing my words through the air.

"Protection from what?"

"From entering this place. See, you can't find Everwood Academy unless you know where it is, and the process of getting here can be rather daunting for some, so we just skip that whole process because, quite frankly, it's not the most shocking thing that will be happening to you tonight. We'd rather give you a smoother entrance, you understand."

"That's very comforting," I moaned.

"Isn't it?" he draped a long arm over my shoulders and shook me. "So, what do you think?"

"About what?"

"About all of this!" He gestured to the building, spreading his arms out wide to showcase the Academy in all its glory.

"It's…it's nice. It's great." I hadn't really known what to expect before I got here, and now that I *was* here, I still didn't know what to expect, moment to moment. But I knew for sure I wanted to stay. There was something electric in the air here. Like lightning was about to strike.

Spectre pursed his lips and wrinkled his thick, bushy brows until they met in the centre of his face. "I fear I may have done this wrong. I'm getting old. Obviously, we missed something. You see the words here, yes?" he gestured to the Latin phrase.

I looked from Spectre to the words carved above the doorway, then back to Spectre again. "Yes."

"And you heard what it meant, am I right?"

I squinted. "Yeah, I did."

Spectre clapped his hands together so loudly and suddenly that it sounded like a thunder crack. "Well then! Ha! What do you think?"

"I think…I think…" What did I think? I thought this old man was crazy. "I think that it's a great warning for people in the 13th Century?" My answer sounded more like a question. What did he want from me? Why was I here?

I watched his face darken and his lips sag in disappointment. Clearly, something was going right over my head.

"You don't have anything more to say?" he asked. "Not, wow! Not, I don't believe you! Not, I want my Mum?"

"Why would I say any of those things?" I asked as politely as I could, while growing tired and impatient inside. There had indeed been a portion of the evening where I was thinking, *I want my Mum*, but at that moment, what I was thinking was a little more along the lines of *I want a man in a white coat to come and take this lunatic away.*

"Why would you say those things? Well…because I've just delivered to you the most shocking news of your life, dear boy! That's why!"

I shook my head. "No, all you told me is that this sign is a warning to people who find this place. Then we talked about why the Mister Smiths drugged me. That's it."

"Oh." Spectre tilted his head to the side. "I didn't say anything else?"

I enunciated my next word carefully so as not to provoke the crazy man. "No."

"Ha!" he exploded. "That explains it. I really am getting old, aren't I? Very, very old. Older than you know. I like being old, though. A lot behind me, a lot ahead of me. Lots of memories to keep me company. Let's go!" He bounded up the steps with energy I wouldn't have expected from someone his age and left me – yet again – with no choice but to follow.

"Where are we going now?" I asked.

"To the next spot. I ruined this one with my stodginess and forgetfulness." He hurried down the hallway, taking turns this way and that way, until I was completely lost. "It'll lose its impact if I explain it all there now. Need to go somewhere else. Hurry. Hurry. It'll be starting soon."

"What will?" I asked.

"Why, the night rides, of course. Quickly, quickly."

Spectre halted abruptly before stained-glass doors that opened onto a balcony. The glass depicted images of fire, mountains, and dark skies, each piece of glass vibrant with colour.

I stopped as abruptly as he did, out of breath, hungry, and a little nauseated from the drugs.

Spectre looked like a child on Christmas morning. "As I was saying to you earlier, Angus," he began calmly, "there is a history in your blood, a gift that you have been given…no, no, not a gift. Well, you do also have a gift. Or will do. Or currently do but cannot yet open. Genetic disposition. That's what we settled on. It is going to change your life forever. And that is why you are here. The Latin phrase above our door serves as a warning, yes, but also as a truth, because, my dear Angus, at Everwood Academy… here be dragons."

Spectre flung open the glass doors. His voice was quiet and raspy as he encouraged me forward. "Go on, boy. Take a look."

Tentatively, I stepped out onto the balcony, unsure what I would find. The moon was high in the sky, shining brightly on a massive, cobbled courtyard that ended with a thick line of ancient trees, dark in the silver light, blocking my vision of anything beyond. The crisp, cool air was filled with the sound of students talking and laughing as they mingled in the quad below.

I gripped the banister until my knuckles were white as my eyes raked over the scene in front of me. This couldn't be real. It wasn't possible.

Beside each student was a winged beast, of every size and colour imaginable. Scaled bodies, shimmering in the moonlight, stretched to a point at the tip of a broad, powerful tail, rimmed with sharp spines. Thick horns pointed skyward from their serpentine heads, and round, bright eyes reflected the light of the moon. Wings, double the length of their bodies, furled and unfurled, almost translucent in the light. Thick veins snaked beneath the skin, a pathway stretching to the hooked claws at the end of the jagged wings.

"Dragons." I breathed, my voice barely audible.

Spectre walked up beside me, his frame ghostly in the pale moonlight. "You see, Angus, Everwood Academy is not a normal school, and you are not a normal sixteen-year-old. This is in your blood. You are here to learn how to be a dragon rider. A Vector, we call it."

"What?" I turned around to Spectre, but mere seconds passed before I had to turn back to see if the dragons were still there or if they had vanished back into my imagination. "This… this is crazy."

"Not really," he said calmly. "Dragons are just dinosaurs. Depictions of dragons can be seen throughout history as early as 4500 BC. All those fabled tales of knights fighting dragons – you didn't think they were all made up, did you?" he asked.

"Well," I shrugged. "Yeah. Me and everyone else on the planet."

"Tell me this, my boy. In a world without telephones, the internet, or planes, without widespread exploration or the televised news, how did vastly different cultures, countries and languages all come up with the myth of the dragon at the same time?"

"I've never really thought about it," I admitted.

"That's the problem with today. Nobody stops and thinks, and those that do stop to think spend so much time thinking that they never do any talking, or, worse, they do talk and are told to stop all of their thinking." Spectre proudly surveyed the courtyard below. "Dragons existed in the past, and they exist today, Angus. If you stop a moment and consider it, is there really any other explanation? Carvings of dragons in ancient Mongolia, references to dragons peppered throughout the Old Testament. Ancient Rome, China, India, Europe – dragons are in the history of almost every country and culture. *Why?* How can separate, distinctive cultures, never having touched or connected, have come up with the same legendary creature?"

"I guess they couldn't," I answered.

"The only possible explanation is that they didn't create the myth of the dragon at all. Rather, they simply recorded what they *saw*."

I stared back out at the dragons before me and tried to comprehend what I was seeing, but my mind couldn't reconcile the fiction unfolding before me. But it didn't matter that I couldn't understand; all that mattered was that there they were, standing right in front of me. Dragons. Actual dragons.

I watched as each student climbed atop their respective dragons, settling into leather saddles. A bell rang, resounding like a gong, and suddenly, the wings of each of the creatures spread out to their full extent, and the dragons raised themselves into the air with slow, powerful beats of their wings.

Riders, or Vectors, as Spectre had called them, held tightly as their dragons took off into the night in a colourful cloud of the impossible.

I watched them until they were specks in the distance, mesmerized by the graceful ebb and flow of their wings.

Spectre was right.
Here be dragons.

aglow

"Come now, come, come."

I turned to see Spectre waving me forward. "Where are we going?"

"Somewhere very special." There was mischief in his eye that sparked my curiosity. Where could we possibly be going that was better than this?

I followed the curious old man down the hallway as he tottered along with dramatic speed. Before long, the red carpet turned to stone floors, and the walls, once adorned with artwork, became dark with exposed stone. We seemed to be going further and further downwards. Every few feet were another set of wide, cracking stone steps, which took us deeper into the belly of Everwood until we must have been four or five storeys underground.

Spectre's footsteps never faltered, even when the light grew dimmer and the floors more uneven. I followed him, feeling like I was walking headlong into a dream. If this was a dream, I wanted to stay asleep. Stay here, where the impossible was possible, and I was actually someone. Someone worth being.

We came at last to a large door, as wide as I was tall. It was solid black iron with enormous hinges and a cantankerous-looking lock positioned in its centre. There was a keypad on the left side of the wall. One could be excused for feeling like they were being led into a dungeon to be locked away for all eternity.

Spectre tapped a code into the keypad, and I stepped back as the lock made a loud clanking noise and the hinges unlocked.

He turned to me and stared deeply into my eyes. "This, Angus Finch, is where it all begins. This moment will change your life forever if you let it. If you don't, nothing will ever change, and you'll live a life of breakfasts and suppers and coming home from work for all your days. Your life will be filled with upping and downing and to-ing and froing and you won't even realise what it is that you'll have missed because, to you, you never will have missed it. I want you to pay special attention to everything you see and hear in this room. Every student of Everwood Academy enters this room exactly *once.* Only once, never more. It is the most protected and guarded place in the entire Academy. Behind this door are precious, ancient, hidden things. Are you ready?"

I nodded solemnly, apprehensive. What was I going to find? There was a tightness in my stomach, a wrenching of my chest muscles. Every breath seemed a struggle as anticipation wound its way around my spine.

Finally, the door opened wide, and Spectre gently pushed me inside.

The room was dark and my eyes had to adjust to the dim lighting. It was cooler in the room than it had been outside, and I shivered involuntarily. The air was dank with moisture and the ground was spongey and damp beneath my feet, like it wasn't stone or wood I was standing on but earth. I blinked as my eyes became accustomed to the dull glow emanating from the three or four firelit lamps scattered around the room.

I stepped further into the room and let my eyes scan its entirety. It was like a massive library, with sturdy, old wooden bookcases that reached toward the ceiling. Only it wasn't books on the shelves.

"They're…they're eggs?"

"Yes, they are. They're dragon eggs." Spectre placed a hand on my shoulder. "Each egg you see here is destined for one unique person. One person only. Every dragon waits, dormant, for the touch of their master. However long it may take."

"So, I just reach out and touch-" As I extended my hand towards an egg, Spectre's hand slammed down on top of my own. I recoiled in pain.

"Do not touch any egg but your own," he cautioned. "Ever."

"How do I know which one is mine?" I asked.

"You will walk by each shelf, just as every student of Everwood Academy before you has done. When you reach your egg, it will glow."

"I just walk. It's that simple?" My feet suddenly felt cemented in place. "Do I…do I start now, or?"

Spectre extended a hand, gesturing for me to begin walking. Tentatively, I stepped forward, walking closely beside each table.

As I weaved my way through the room, I realised it was much bigger than I had first thought. It arced around to the left, expanding into a massive hall-like structure that seemed to stretch forever. Wooden beams arched across the ceiling, and lamps were positioned every twenty feet or so. There must have been thousands of eggs.

I paused and stared. "This is gonna take me a while," I said.

I heard a scuttling sound and jumped. "What was that?"

"Just the attendants. Can't leave the eggs alone down here, can we? Someone needs to care for them."

"O…kay," I said slowly.

"Call for me when your egg glows, but do not touch it," Spectre said from his position near the door. He nodded at me. "Take all the time you need, Angus."

I nodded and took another step.

"Oh, and Angus?"

I turned back to face him, my skin feeling prickly and tight. "Yeah?"

"Best not to disturb the attendants if you can help it. Touchy, they are. Don't look them in the eye. Or pose a threat. Or breathe too loud. In fact, try to act like you aren't here."

"What?" I hissed. "How am I supposed to do that?"

"You'll be fine!" Spectre grinned and slapped me hard on the back, pushing me forward another step. "Totally fine."

I understood that he was trying to be reassuring, but there wasn't really much he could do to make the fact that I was walking through a dungeon filled with dragon eggs seem any less weird than it was.

"Right. Just take your time…picking out a dragon egg," I mumbled to myself. "No big deal. Just a *normal* day."

I took wobbly steps on the squishy earth below me, taking it row by row. The air was cold in my lungs as I drew in shaky breaths. The smell of wet earth was strong in my nose. It's funny the difference a day can make. Just this morning, I was in Biology, looking at the root tips of onions. Now, I was wandering ancient halls looking at dragon eggs in a magical academy on a different plane. This couldn't be real. It couldn't be *my* life. My mind wandered back to the family I had left behind, and I thought of Grandpa's warning.

This Everwood Academy…it changes you.

Is this what happened to Uncle James? I had the faintest memory of him standing at the back of the church at my grandmother's funeral. He was a tall, shadowy figure who didn't linger long. He was like a wraith, this cloaked man who flew in and out without a word to anyone. I had only seen him because I couldn't look at the coffin, so I turned around. Even when Grandpa complained to Mum that James didn't bother to attend the funeral, I had never told anyone I saw him because I wasn't sure I actually *did*. He seemed so mythical and out of place that I was sure I must have imagined him. I was only six, after all. Now I was certain it was him.

I looked down at my feet. Was this the very ground Uncle James walked on? Where was he now? I wanted to talk to him more than I ever had before. I had so many questions, questions that I knew Uncle James could answer.

A strange scuttling sound behind me made me spin around. The hairs on the back of my neck prickled and I felt goosebumps rise on my arms. "Anyone there?" I asked into the dark, empty air. When my only answer was silence, I kept walking. I'd only taken three more steps before I heard it again. I turned slowly this time, my eyes raking over my surroundings. There was definitely something there. Was it the attendants that Spectre was talking about? I caught sight of something, just as it rounded the corner of a bookshelf. I was caught between the desire to know what it was and this strange sensation trickling down my spine that told me to walk away. I almost took a step towards where I saw it disappear, but this feeling was so strong that I couldn't do it. It was like an unknown terror had gripped me. I shook my head, trying to clear it, and turned back the way I came.

I jumped back in fear, tripping on my own feet and landing on the ground – *hard*. But a sore behind was the least of my worries. It was standing right in front of me, whatever it was. I wanted to scream, but it was like a cold hand had a grip on my throat and was squeezing the life out of me. I gasped for breath, but it was almost impossible to get any air in. I was being strangled. Slowly my body started to rise off the ground, completely outside my control. I thrashed wildly, but to no avail. My feet dangled in the air, and still the creature sat unmoving before me, one solid hand stretched out in front of it, reaching towards me.

Its body was stout and strong, at least a head shorter than mine. I was reminded of a dwarf from Middle-earth, but that wasn't quite right. Under a forest green hood was a prominent hooked nose. A thick, red beard hung to its belly, and a gold belt wrapped around his waist, but the eyes were all wrong. They were bright blue and huge, like lamps in his head. Too big for his face, they glinted at me menacingly.

I started to feel foggy, my mind befuddled. I couldn't get enough air in. I was going to pass out. *Again*, I thought acidly.

"That's enough Fennick." Spectre appeared beside me, his voice sounding bored. "You'll scare the boy half to death."

I dropped to the ground in a sudden *thump*, my airways clear. I gasped in breaths, spluttering and coughing.

I looked up at the creature that had almost killed me to see him laughing. Actually *laughing.*

I'm sorry… what?

I got shakily to my feet and looked to Spectre as if he had the answers. But he was just rolling his eyes.

The creature finally got a hold of himself. He dropped the hood from his head, revealing sharply pointed ears that popped out from the side of his head like knives. "Ah, boy. Ya shoulda seen yer face."

"What is going on?" I rasped. "That… that *thing* nearly killed me!"

The creature's face was suddenly less jovial. "Eh there boy, there's no need ta be callin' names, now is there? 'Twas just a bi' of 'armless fun."

"Fun? Killing me is fun?"

"I assure you, Angus," Spectre began in a calm voice, "if Fennick had wanted to kill you, you most certainly would already be dead, and what's more you never would have seen, felt or known a thing. Probably would have ended up haunting this place, completely unaware you'd even died, showing up for Mathematics on Monday morning like nothing had happened."

"Wow. That's… comforting," I croaked.

"Fennick is a Pycwyk," Spectre continued. "He is the Head Watcher for the Emporium. A most noble officer, devoting his kind service to Everwood."

When I stared at him blankly, Fennick sighed. He elaborated slowly, using hand signals, as if speaking with a small child or someone hard of hearing. "I watch the eggs, eh? *This* is the 'mporium. Me an' my team," Fennick gestured to the world around him, "make sure tha' no one steals the eggs."

I looked from side to side, and that's when I noticed a dozen or more faces peering out from behind shelves, above shelves and around corners, drawn in by the ruckus.

I tore my eyes from the strange faces and back to Fennick. "Let's not forget to add that you also strangle innocent passers-by. Quite a full service you provide."

Spectre laughed heartily and grabbed my shoulder.

"Golly, Spectre, got yerself a bi' of a pansy, don' ya. Cannae take a joke, this one."

"On the contrary, Fennick," Spectre mused. "Has any other student dared spoken back to the venerable Fennick Son of Fennickson?"

Fennick grumbled something and shrugged before muttering

something about getting back to work.

"I did tell you not to look threatening," Spectre said chidingly.

"Threatening?" I looked down at myself. "What about *this* looks threatening to you? No one in the world has *ever* been threatened by me."

"Ah, see that's the thing, dear boy. We're not in your world anymore. And it's not about this…" Spectre pointed a long finger at my chin and dragged it down to my feet. "It's about what's in *this*." He poked his finger right at my heart. "There's more in there than even I yet know."

Spectre straightened with a grin and waved me on.

"I seriously doubt that," I mumbled to myself as I resumed my stroll through the endless library of eggs that made up the Emporium.

I made it halfway through the massive room before I started to lose hope.

"No eggs are glowing!" I groaned to Spectre.

"Don't worry, Angus."

"Look, maybe you made a mistake. This isn't working. I told you, I'm nobody."

Spectre said nothing. He only smiled and pushed me onwards.

I sighed and kept walking.

Footstep after footstep had me spiralling deeper and deeper into a pit of self-doubt. Each of the eggs remained unlit, rejecting me one by one.

Maybe it was all just a big scam and someone with a video camera would pop out from behind one of these fake eggs, and I would be the next internet loser people loved to laugh at.

Or maybe this was all a dream, and I was actually knocked

unconscious on the sidewalk after smacking into the stranger. Maybe I was in a coma. Could I have hit my head hard enough to have caused some serious, if not permanent, damage? Was I really lying in a hospital bed right now?

As I walked along the final row of eggs, my palms began to sweat. "What do we do if none of the eggs glow?" I asked Spectre, as he walked silently beside me, his footsteps light and quiet on the damp ground.

"I have no idea," he answered. "It's never happened before."

"Oh," I gulped. "Great."

"So, there is no reason to believe it will happen now," he added comfortingly.

There were three shelves left in the row. I walked slowly, cautiously, purposefully past the first, then the second and finally the third.

Not a single egg had glowed.

There was no dragon for me here.

I felt acid roll in my stomach as if I had been punched squarely in the gut. How could the loss of something I didn't even know existed until an hour ago have this much of an effect on me?

I felt heat penetrate my eyes. "I…uh…I guess…I guess that's it."

Spectre looked confused, his brows knitting together like two bushy, very cross caterpillars about to engage in fisticuffs. He mumbled to himself, but I couldn't understand what he was saying. Was he even speaking English?

He held up his hand, and started counting something off on his fingers, then dropped his arms by his side and stared at the wall silently, like he'd run out of battery or something.

"Uh," I croaked, "should I just go? Like…back home?"

Spectre remained silent.

"As long as we can do it without the drugs this time, that is. I guess I'll just get out of your hair." When he still didn't reply, I sighed angrily. "Hello?" I said, tapping his shoulder awkwardly. I just wanted to leave, to force the humiliation to end.

Spectre snapped his head to the side. "No. Not yet. There is one more thing for us to try."

Spectre grabbed my arm and yanked me towards the back of the room. He dragged me faster than my legs could carry me, and I stumbled and tripped, but he didn't let go. He walked with an urgency that scared me, and his giant strides had me running to save myself from the humiliation of eating the dirt.

"Where are we going?" I tried to keep my feet underneath me as he pulled me quickly along the back wall of the Emporium and towards a dark corner. We passed multiple doors with signs that read *No Entrance, Pycwyk's Only, Egg Sorting Room,* and *No Admittance Without Blood Sample.* Finally, Spectre stopped in front of an old, crumbling wooden door that seemed in great need of repair.

Spectre paused with his hand on the bulky iron handle. "I'm not sure what's going to happen if I open this door. I'm not sure if anything will happen at all. But…if it does, I'm not sure what it will be. And that is quite strange since I often know what is going to be, or at least have an idea of the being that's going to be. But you," he laughed, "oh, my dear Angus, *you.* You are quite the puzzle. A conundrum wrapped in an enigma, tied up in a bow and thrown in a box. I have a feeling that things are going to get very interesting. I was right about you. Not dull at all."

I was feeling rejected and embarrassed, and I just wanted him to stop talking. I wanted to leave as quickly as I could and pretend that this never happened. But it appeared that the only way out was through. "Are you going to open the door?"

"Quite. Yes." Spectre shoved against the handle and met resistance. The door was swollen shut with time and decay. He leaned his body against the door and forced his way through. How long had that door been closed? There was no light inside, but there was enough flickering through from the lamp light behind us that I could see a stone bench in the middle of the small room. On it was an oddly shaped ball. It didn't look like the other eggs, which were smooth and pale. It was dark brown, bumpy, and smaller in size.

I stood in the door frame, unwilling to get closer. "Is it an egg?"

"Yes. It is. It is very, very old. Older than I am, and that is saying something."

I stepped a little closer, drawn to it. "Why does it look so different?"

Spectre stayed behind me, unwilling to get any closer. "We have no idea. This egg has been here for centuries. All alone. It is the oldest egg in existence. No one has ever needed to step into this room before this very moment. You are the first. Very soon we will know whether its master has finally come."

"What if it doesn't glow?" I asked, unsure I could handle the weight of another rejection.

"Then you'll begin your walk again. I've never been wrong, Angus. Well…once, with disastrous consequences, but it's extremely unlikely I'm wrong again. Go, go, go. Carefully now, boy. Slowly."

I drew in a deep breath and stepped forward slowly and meekly. With each footstep, it was clear the egg remained unmoved by my presence. I took one last step until my stomach was up against the table. Nothing changed.

"It's no use," I whispered. "There's nothing here for me."

"Just wait," he whispered urgently. "Try again."

I leaned down until my face was just an inch from the egg. Now that I was closer, I could see that the egg's colour was deeper and richer than I had thought. It was a dark brown flooded with streaks of marble-coloured lines, like oil reflecting in the sun.

I could see dust gathered all around the egg, a thin layer spread across its surface, and thick pockets of it covering the small pillow it sat upon. I wondered where it came from and what it must be like to be so alone for so long.

It was beautiful. I watched as my breath blew the dust around, cleansing the egg of the effects of time.

Slowly, pulsating like the beat of a drum, the marble lines began to glow, as if they were being lit from behind. I stepped back in surprise.

"Look!" I shouted. "It's glowing!"

"Touch it," Spectre instructed.

I held out my hand and pressed my fingertips against the egg. It was ice-cold to the touch. It began to crack, and I recoiled. "Did I break it?"

"I don't believe it," Spectre spoke quietly, in an incredulous, almost afraid, voice.

"I'm sorry, I barely touched it. I didn't mean to."

"This egg has been lying dormant for a thousand years. All this time…it's been waiting. It's been waiting for *you*." Spectre looked at me strangely, like I was about to explode or something. He tore his eyes from me and stepped forward, eager for a closer look. His eyes were wide, like a hungry animal seeing its prey after a famine.

There was definite movement underneath the shifting pieces of the shell. Tiny claws protruded through the hard shell until a small scaley face appeared. The sleepy dragon forced the egg apart, breaking its body free. I stared, mesmerised, at the scene unfolding before me.

A baby dragon, no bigger than my hands put together, stumbled around on the ruins of the shell, its eyes still closed. Its body was wet and slimy, covered in fluid from the shell. Its scales flickered green and red, like the lights of a Christmas tree.

Everything began to fade away. My vision darkened, and all I could see was the dragon. My heart rate slowed right down, and air froze in my lungs. The world around me became hollow and avoidable. I felt a curious familiarity with the mythical creature that had come to life before me. Like it shared a part of me, and I a part of it.

I couldn't help myself. It was as if I no longer controlled my body. I reached out my hand and touched its rough skin but was forced back when an electric jolt flickered up through my fingers and into my chest.

"Ah," I exclaimed, my fingers red with pain.

The dragon's droopy eyes began to open, fluttering up and down as it prepared itself for sight. Slowly, its vision came into focus, and it saw me. For a long moment, we stared at each other, unblinking and unmoving, until the dragon toddled forward and pawed at the air, trying to reach me.

"Here, Angus," Spectre said.

I looked back to find him standing behind the door frame, his body out of sight, save for his arm waving a black blanket at me like a flag signalling surrender.

I took the blanket and faced my dragon, who was teetering on the edge of the stone table. Placing the blanket over its back and wrapping it warmly, I lifted the dragon into my arms.

I was surprised by its weight. Though it was small, it weighed at least twenty pounds. Immediately, it curled itself under the blanket, disappearing from view. Before long, I heard the soft purr of a sleeping dragon.

I walked out of the small room and saw Spectre leaning against the wall, with a smug smile on his face.

"See?" he started, "I told you I've never been wrong." He grinned and slapped my back. "Well, except for that one time."

merry

I stared at the ceiling, incapable of sleep.

The fact that, immediately after I had met my pet dragon, they showed me to my new room and informed me it was time for light out was, in my mind, cruel and unusual. How was I supposed to get a wink of sleep when I had a baby dragon fast asleep in the cage at the end of my bed?

I tried to calm my racing mind by familiarising myself with the room from the vantage point of my single bed in the corner.

The floors were polished wood, and the walls were made of stone. A single window was set against the far wall, equipped with thick wooden shutters to block out the light. Two study desks stood at either end of the windowed wall, and beside my bed was a chest of drawers, waiting for me to stuff my clothes into it tomorrow. There was a red flag hanging on the wall with the Everwood crest on it – two gold dragons in mid-flight under an open book with two crossed swords behind it. A wreath of ivy encircled the crest. The words Everwood Academy and HIC SUNT DRACONES were written in a bold, ancient-looking font. Next to it was another flag, but I wasn't sure what it was for. It was dark green, with white accents. In the centre of the flag was a white dragon, mouth open in a snarl, with a vine wrapped around its body. Underneath, it read *Sylva.*

The most interesting addition to the room, however, was the other student, fast asleep in the bed opposite mine. My new roommate, I was told, was named Artie Birtwistle. Not that he told me that himself, as, by the time I was shown to the room, he was fast asleep.

Spectre had turned on the light, placed the cage at the end of my bed, and instructed me to place the dragon inside. I was under strict orders not to open the cage door until the next morning when the wake-up bell rang.

"Aren't we gonna wake this guy up?" I had asked, my voice a whisper, as I indicated to the sleeping figure.

Spectre chuckled. "Heavens, no. That lump of blankets is your new roommate, Artie Birtwistle. He's new, too. And he doesn't wake up for anything but the bell. Not even when a juvenile Oceanic Dragon went wild in the hall just outside his door two days ago. Terrible cacophony. Didn't stir at all. Don't worry. Good as dead, he is, except that, of course, he isn't." Spectre flicked the light out while I was still standing in the middle of the room. "Lights out. It is strictly against the rules for you to turn them back on. We are, after all, an educational institution. So, sleep you must." The door was closed, and I was plunged into thick, inky darkness.

I kicked off my shoes and had to grope for the bed, which I found after stubbing my toe into the solid wooden leg. I flopped onto the bed and was pleasantly surprised to find that it was as soft as a marshmallow. It had taken a while before my eyes adjusted and after they had, I discovered any attempts to think about anything other than the dragon in the room was completely pointless.

I let out a heavy, deep sigh as if the night would never end. My mind raced with thoughts. What would tomorrow be like? What would it feel like to have a pet dragon? Was I actually going to *ride* it one day?

I could hear the baby dragon's soft breaths, in and out, like a rhythm, and I tried to focus on that and push every other thought out of my mind. Eventually, I must have drifted off to sleep because the wake-up bell was like a nuclear alarm. I jolted upright in abject terror with such force that I fell out of bed, tangled in the sheets. I recognised nothing at all, and for a solid minute, I had no idea who I was or where I was.

The shutters to the window were already open, letting in a stream of bright golden sunlight that was, to my sleepy eyes, almost blinding. When I woke up enough to remember I was the newest addition to Everwood Academy, I untangled myself from the covers and stood up.

My first suspicion was that everything that had happened last night was a dream. Upon seeing the cage at the end of my bed, however, my fears were quickly assuaged. Curled in the blanket, still fast asleep, was a green and red dragon.

"Pretty cool, hey?"

The voice startled me. I had forgotten I wasn't alone in here. I turned to see a young guy about my age, with shaggy black hair and thin-rimmed glasses, sitting on the edge of his perfectly made bed.

"Yeah," I agreed. "It's…insane."

"You're taking it all in better than most people do," he encouraged. "She's pretty."

"Sorry?"

"Your dragon," he pointed to the cage. "She's pretty."

"She? How do you know it's a *she*?" I asked.

"The colouring. The males are usually muted colours. I guess so they blend in in the wild. They're often brown or black or a sort of grey colour. The girls are different. The girls have brighter colours, usually metallic. Blues, reds, greens, yellows. That kind of thing."

"Oh," I said pathetically. "I guess I've got a lot to learn."

"Don't worry. Education starts today."

"Isn't it a Saturday?" I asked.

"Yeah, but classes aren't what I mean. This whole place is an education. Apparently, Saturdays and Sundays are usually the days we focus on the dragons in a pretty big way. I wouldn't know. This is my first weekend here. You thought about what you're going to name her?"

I looked over to her and realised I hadn't even thought about naming her. "No, uh, not yet."

"You'll need a name by just after breakfast, when your training starts, so I'd get on that."

"What did you call your dragon?"

"Rose," he answered. "She's not much bigger than your dragon." He gestured to the sleeping dragon at the end of his bed. A bright red dragon lay sleepily on a blanket, feet in the air. I could see where her namesake came from. "I've only been here a few days longer than you have."

"Really? You seem to know a lot."

He laughed. "Comes with the territory, I guess."

"She's beautiful," I said. "Rose, I mean."

"Thanks." He gestured to the dragon at the end of my bed. "I've never seen a two-tone before."

I looked down at my red and green dragon and was once again reminded of Christmas. In an instant, I was taken back to a warm fireplace, presents under a giant tree, tinsel and hot chocolates with marshmallows. I never felt happier than I did at Christmastime.

Mum had always made sure I truly felt the merry in Merry Christmas.

"You know, I think I know what I'm gonna call her," I said.

"Yeah?"

"Yeah. I'm gonna call her Merry. As in, merry and bright."

"Ah. With the red and green. Cool. I like it."

A strange sound, like a high-pitched hissing that was only just audible, hit my ears.

"What is that?" I asked.

At once, both dragons rolled onto their feet and started clawing at their cage doors.

"That's the wake-up bell for the dragons," he answered. "And in about three more seconds…" Another bell, just like the earlier wake-up bell, gonged loudly. "…the breakfast bell will ring." He removed his dragon from its cage, and it scurried up his arm and sat on his shoulder. "Come on, I'll show you to the dining hall."

"I'll just get Merry, then," I said, opening the cage door and lifting her out gently. She seemed perkier than she was last night, and now that the gunk from her head was gone, I could fully appreciate how spectacular she looked. Her sleek body shone with red and green. Her wide head sat on top of a long, strong neck, and her tail stretched out for almost a foot behind her. On top of her back, folded neatly, were two webbed wings.

I realised I hadn't eaten anything since lunch yesterday. My stomach growled in anticipation.

"I'm Artie, by the way," my new roommate said as he outstretched a finger to stroke Merry's neck. "Artie Birtwistle."

"Angus Finch," I replied.

"Well, Angus, welcome to Everwood Academy." He turned and walked out the door.

It took me a few seconds, lingering at the threshold, to be able to follow. As I took my first step into the hallway that morning, I felt like I was crossing over a chasm, saying goodbye to my old life, and walking headlong into a new one.

welcome to everwood academy

I had always thought of myself as a relatively open-minded kind of guy. But being here was hard for me to get my head around. As I followed Artie down the hall, I watched dozens of other students emerge from their rooms. Some were sleepy-eyed and still in their pajamas, while others were jostling about happily, laughing and joking.

To say they all looked normal would be a lie. There was something different about each of them, as if they were in on some epic cosmic joke, while I sat on the outside, bewildered.

I noticed that no one else was carrying a dragon, like Artie and I were.

"Where are everyone else's dragons? Why do we have ours?" I asked.

"It comes down to a problem of size," Artie laughed. "You're allowed to keep your dragon in your room for the first few days. Last night was Rose's last night with me. Now it's down to the stables. They get too big, too loud, too…dragon-y. They're big enough to ride from a few months old. They grow really fast."

I nodded, my stomach flip-flopping at the thought of being thousands of feet in the air on the back of a winged mythical creature. I blinked away an image of falling to my doom.

A shoulder slammed into mine, and I stumbled but managed to keep my footing. Merry slipped on my shoulder, her claws digging into my skin, tearing at my flesh. I felt blood bubble to the surface. I reached up to steady her, and looked around for whoever had hit me.

A tall, black-haired student with dark eyes and resting jerk-face stared down at me.

"You right there?" I asked angrily.

He glared at me and looked down at Merry. An unreadable expression passed across his features, before being replaced by obvious disgust.

"Sorry, Han. We'll get out of your way," Artie said, tugging at my arm and dragging us away.

"Nice guy," I muttered when we were out of earshot.

"That's Han Kang. He's not someone you want to mess with," Artie warned. "*Trust* me."

"How do you know him?" I asked.

"Everyone knows Han. And not in a good way. He's pretty intense. You really don't want to get in his way. Plus, his dragon seems pretty aggressive, so that's a good sign you want to keep your distance."

"What do you mean?"

"You'll go through it all with Spectre, but suffice it to say, dragons and their riders have similar personalities. And that's a pair that *no one* messes with. Come on, breakfast is waiting."

Artie hadn't meant *our* breakfast. He led me outside through the courtyard I had seen last night. The morning sunlight was thick like honey, dappling through the trees and splashing at our feet. To the right of the courtyard, a cobbled path led towards a monstrous collection of stone buildings with wooden beams and massive wooden doors.

"These are the stables," Artie added helpfully. "The dragons sleep and eat in here. Well, when they're not off hunting for game, anyway. I think we're the only two students with dragons this young right now. New students are brought in pretty sporadically. It's actually pretty amazing there were two of us in the same week. Haven't heard of that before."

"Why? How do they decide when it's time for us to come here?"

"I don't know. Spectre just says it's something about timing. Some sort of activation or something. Honestly, who knows what Spectre is ever talking about? He talks so much, it's hard to keep up."

I did my best not to smile, considering Artie had done very little but talk *very much* since I opened my eyes. I wasn't complaining – whatever he knew about this place, I wanted to know, too.

Two Pycwyk's met us about thirty feet from the stables, to take our dragons off our hands. I fought off the urge to run away from them as fast as my legs could carry me. The first Pycwyk had long plaited brown hair, an aggressively pointed beard and bulbous black eyes. The other was blonde, with matted hair hanging loosely around his shoulders. His beard was much shorter, and his eyes were vibrant, venomous green. "Why can't we go in?" I asked them.

"Stables are off limits during feeding times," the brown-haired Pycwyk replied matter-of-factly.

For good reason, I supposed, but I was desperate to get a glimpse in there. I wanted to see the other dragons.

I handed Merry over with reluctance and was informed I wouldn't see her again until this afternoon, when she had finished her first medical assessment.

"Now it's our turn." Artie led me back inside. I took comfort from the fact that he hadn't been here much longer than I had, but he already seemed so at ease. Maybe that's how I would feel soon, too.

The breakfast hall expanded in front of me like the cavernous mouth of a great beast. Long tables sat in five straight lines, stretching the full length of the room. Stone floors muted the sounds of countless footsteps as people made their way to their seats. There was a huge flag of Everwood's crest at the front of the hall, with four other smaller flags beside it. One of them I recognised as the same one Artie had hanging in our room. "What are those?" I asked, pointing to the flags.

Artie followed my finger as we weaved through people. "House flags. Your dragon decides your house for you, depending on what type they are."

"I feel like there should be a manual or something."

"Oh, don't worry," Artie laughed. "There is. I'll be taking you to the bookshop to get your textbooks after breakfast."

"You're in Sylva?" I asked.

"Yeah, I have a forest dragon, so I'm assigned to Sylva. The other houses are Terra, which represents earth; Volare, which represents air; and Oceanus, which obviously represents water. There's a lot to learn. I know, it's overwhelming."

"What type is my dragon?"

"You'll know by the time we get to the bookstore. It's the first thing they test in medical, so that you can get all your stuff."

We took our place in the line, where trays of food were sliding out of slots in the wall. I watched as everyone grabbed a tray and walked to their seats like a wall spitting out food was totally normal. I had to admit, it looked good. Bacon, eggs, sausages, crispy roast potatoes, charred haloumi cheese and soft, fluffy Yorkshire puddings filled each tray. I grabbed mine, my stomach rumbling.

"Where's it come from?" I asked.

"I have no idea," Artie replied. "I'm taking the need-to-know approach to life at Everwood. It's easier that way."

"Fair point."

Trays in hand, we sat down at the end of one of the long rows. Artie greeted the people beside us and introduced me.

"Guys, this is Angus. He's my new roommate. Angus, this is everybody." He started pointing to each person. "This is Nolan, he's our resident computer whizz."

Nolan gave a small wave, to accompany a small smile. He was about my height, with short black hair and chocolate skin. He wore a baggy red sweater and sunglasses on his head.

"That's Kit," Artie continued. "He's fluent in like seven languages."

Kit rolled his eyes at Artie. "He exaggerates. Only four languages. Born in Europe, moved here when I was 12," he answered, like it explained his brilliance away.

Next was Cosette, a short, petite blonde girl with a book in her hands. She barely looked up from the pages as she was introduced. Finally, Artie moved to the last person sitting in our section.

I hadn't noticed her until Artie had called her name to get her attention. She looked up, seemingly dazed from snapping back to reality.

"What?" she asked. "Did I miss something?"

I tried not to stare, but it was a challenge. Her face was stunning. Her porcelain skin was so clear it looked like an ice rink someone could skate on. Her wide eyes were an unexpected bright blue, sparkling vibrantly in the warm light of the dining hall. Her small nose paved the way for plump apricot lips that smiled when she saw me. Hair as dark as midnight was braided down her back.

"I was just introducing Angus to everyone. He's my new roommate. Arrived last night," Artie held his hands out in front of me like as if he was a salesman on one of those late-night shopping channel shows and I was a shiny new brooch.

"Oh, sorry," she started. "Hi, I'm Hana. Welcome to Everwood."

"Hi. Thanks. Yeah… it's kind of…"

"A shock?" Kit guessed.

"Yeah. You could say that. I still feel a bit like I'm dreaming."

"Don't worry," Cosette chimed in. "Reality will hit soon. For all the dragons, ancient halls, and Equitem matches, it's still school. I have trigonometry first up Monday morning."

"I guess it would have been too much to hope for no more math," I conceded. "I kind of feel like I've been dropped in the middle of the ocean and told to swim. I have no idea *what* is going on around here."

"That's where I come in," Artie said. "As your new roommate, it's my job to look after you. It's tradition. After we get your books, I'll take you to your first orientation lesson."

"Which one of you have been here the longest?" I asked.

Everyone pointed to Hana. She shrugged, guilty. "I've been here for three years."

"What's your dragon like?" I asked.

"He's a lot bigger than yours," she laughed, a musical, twinkling sound. "His name is Jeju, after the island I'm from, in Korea."

"You're Korean?"

"Yeah. I've been here most of my life, but Jeju is home."

"What's with the robes?" I asked, just noticing the different-coloured robes that some of the students wore.

"They're flight coats," Hana answered. "You'll get one, too. It'll be the same colour as your house. They're made of some sort of special fabric that stops you getting cold in the air."

The long coats were ankle-length and came in the dark forest green of Sylva, a reddy-plumb colour I guessed was Terra, a deep-sea blue for Oceanus and silver for Volare. The material seemed to shimmer in the sunlight filtering through the high rectangular windows of the hall.

I looked around the room while the others disappeared into conversations that I didn't have the brain space to be a part of. What would Mum think of all this if she knew? I could imagine her freaking out, warning me of the dangers of wild animals and the risk of death from plummeting to the earth from the back of a flying monster. I pulled out my phone and sent her a quick text.

I'm ok, Mum. Don't worry. Don't forget to feed Roger.

I slipped my phone back into my pocket and started to eat.

of books and cats

The bookshop was warm and inviting. A huge fireplace that took up half the wall was crackling comfortingly with tongues of red and orange flames lapping hungrily at birchwood logs. Piles and piles of books were crammed into countless thick bookcases, stacked on round tables, or balanced on top of each other on the floor. Old maps hung on the walls, and soft, thick rugs were layered over the wood floors. Artie and I snaked our way through the maze of books towards a chest-high counter that sported a small handwritten sign that read, *If desk is unattended, do please tell the cat.*

"What does that mean?" I wondered, but before Artie could answer, a large steel grey cat with eyes as yellow as the sun pounced onto the desk. It was more than twice the size of a normal cat, and its ears jabbed towards the roof in pointy triangles. It was almost like a small, silver lion, with a fluffy mane around its distinguished face.

"It's a Maine Coon, I reckon," Artie said. "My mum loves cats. But Dad's allergic, so." He shrugged. The cat sat directly in front of him and stared at him regally. "Excuse me, we're looking for the Book Keeper. Angus is a new student, and he needs his books."

I looked from Artie to the cat, then back to Artie, wondering if this was some sort of joke. The cat turned abruptly and disappeared behind a curtain. We waited for only a moment before there was a loud thud, followed by an *"Oof"* and an *"Oh dear."* Finally, the curtain was flung out of the way, and a short woman with wild hair and positively monstrous glasses appeared. She wore a dressing gown, tied at the middle, and had slippers on her feet.

"Hello, my darlings. Hello!" she greeted us, waving her arms about. "Apologies. I was lost in a very good book. Took three left turns and couldn't find my way out of it again. Never mind. Winslet told me you were here. You must be Angus. The new student in need of books."

"That's right," I said, completely unsure of what to make of the woman in front of me and her cat, who leapt lightly back up onto the table and regarded me the way cats do – like I was entirely beneath her.

"Lovely, lovely. Well, I am the Book Keeper. Two words, not one. Can't do maths, not even a little bit, so definitely not *that* kind of bookkeeper." She popped out from behind her counter and started to weave through the books, grabbing this one and that as she went. "No, no, no, I am the Keeper of the Books. Book Keeper. But you can call me Bookie. Even a well-placed '*Hey you*' is likely to get my attention. Unless I'm reading, of course, and then I'm afraid it's really only Winslet who can get through to me, but that's just because she's so obnoxious. I mean all cats are," she grabbed another book, and another, until she was holding a pile so high it seemed like it would topple right out of her hands, but it never did. "But Winslet is especially obnoxious. I think it's because of the dragon in her. Can't be helped, I suppose."

"Dragon?" I asked. "The dragon in your cat?"

"Or the cat in my dragon. It depends how you look at it."

"That," I said, pointing to Winslet, "is a dragon?"

"Who knows anymore? Is the cat a dragon, is the dragon a cat?" She scoffed. Depends on the day, doesn't it? Now." She stopped in front of me. "Ta-da! Your books!"

She dumped them in my hands, and I nearly dropped them all. "*A Brief History of Dragons, The Dragon Handbook, Everwood Academy: A Complete History Volume 9*, and *Dragons, Dracos and Wyverns, Which is Which,* just to name a few."

"No maths, science, English?" I asked, hopeful.

"Oh, yes. Of course. Look," she reached in and grabbed a book from the middle of the stack, nearly throwing off the delicate balance I had achieved. "*Mathematics in the Life of a Vector*. See?" She jabbed a crooked finger towards the other titles, "*Vector Poetry: a Modern Collection, Essays From The Back of a Dragon, Trigonometry for Dragon Riders: A How-To in Proper Mounts and Dismounts, Latin for Young Riders,* and *The Flame in the Fire: A Comprehensive Guide to the Combustion of Dragon Breath.* Everything you need is right here. You will also have the opportunity to join extra-curricular classes in sword fighting, hand-to-hand combat, and many other fine pursuits." Bookie beamed at me proudly.

"What about his house, Bookie?" Artie asked. "Have you heard which house he's in?"

Bookie spun on the spot and tottered quickly back to her counter. There was a stack of mail sitting in a tray, and she grabbed the bundle and flipped through it quickly. "Boring, boring, terrifying, horrible, worrisome, boring, ah, here we go. Angus Finch." With a glint in her eyes, Bookie opened the letter. She read it to herself, mumbling. Her lips were moving fast, but I couldn't understand anything she was saying. The anticipation was surprisingly painful. What house was I going to be in? And what difference would it make? What kind of dragon did I have?

Bookie looked at me curiously, then quickly folded up the letter and buried it in her pile of mail. "You have been assigned to Sylva," she said quickly, almost dismissively.

"All right!" Artie cheered, slapping my back. "That's my house."

"You'll be needing a flag, a badge and a coat. Wait here."

Bookie popped behind her curtain, and I looked to Artie for confirmation. "Is it just me, or did she seem strange just now?"

"Not sure if you've noticed, but Strange is kind of her middle name."

"I guess."

Bookie returned and dropped everything onto the counter. I balanced the books on a nearby table and took hold of the long, dark green coat. I held it up in front of me, and watched it shimmer slightly in the firelight. A badge with the Sylva crest on it was pinned to the coat.

"Try it on, darling," she urged.

I slipped the coat on and felt its weight against me. The fabric was heavy and warm. I felt a strange sense of belonging wash over me.

"Perfect fit. As usual. I have an eye for these things. Now," Bookie beamed, "get out so I can get back to my book. Ta-ta darlings!"

Bookie vanished again behind her curtain, and Winslet took up her post on the countertop.

"Let's go," Artie said, grabbing some books. "I'll help you carry all this back to our room, then drop you off at orientation."

"Thanks, Winslet," I murmured to the cat before stealing one last glance at the curtain. Bookie had definitely changed when she mentioned my house. I followed Artie out of the room, wondering if I would ever discover why.

seeing double

After dropping my books back to our room, Artie took me to orientation. Orientation at Everwood was an individual affair since they only brought in one new student at a time. Artie clasped my shoulder and sighed, before giving me a look that seemed an awful lot like pity. "Godspeed," he said quietly before leaving to enjoy the rest of his Saturday.

The orientation room was small and dimly lit, with just one seat positioned in the centre. I sat as instructed. Spectre stood before me, his lively frame towering over me. I wondered how long he would continue to stand there, staring at me with his large, inquisitive eyes. I found myself wishing for Merry's company. We had only spent a few hours together, but I already felt a part of me was missing in her absence.

Spectre was unmoving, unspeaking. There was something ghostly and creepy about his presence that was making me feel uncomfortable. He just stared at me with a plastered, awkward smile. Every now and then, his eyes would flicker to the door, then he would look back at me, and his smile would grow even bigger, and more awkward. I decided to distract myself from the discomfort of his closeness by familiarising myself with the room. The carpet was thick and brown, and I could brush the strands this way and that as I moved my feet along the surface. The walls were stone, set against each other in an ensemble devoid of pattern. The chair I sat on creaked when I moved even in the slightest way. The door was heavy and made of wood so old that splinters jutted out of it in different directions.

"I'm sorry," I finally exploded, unable to take the pressure-filled silence any longer. "Am I supposed to be doing something?"

Spectre remained unmoving, smiling at me with gawkish eyes.

"Are you going to say anything? Am I not supposed to be here?" I looked around uncomfortably, wondering whether I should just make a break for the door. "I was told that I was supposed to have orientation."

As I finished speaking, the door opened, and in walked Spectre.

I flew back, jumping out of the chair and knocking it to the ground. I slapped hard against the bookshelf behind me, knocking a collection of books from their home. Looking from the first Spectre to the second, I was officially seeing double.

"Wait...what? I don't understand." Both men wore the same clothes, the same glasses, with hair positioned in the exact same manner. The same crinkles and lines were carved into their faces at precisely the same angles. "What's going on?"

"Ah, Angus," the second Spectre began, looking down at the papers in his hands. "Apologies for being late. Did Spectre keep you company?"

I stared at him blankly. "I'm sorry...What?"

"Spectre." The second Spectre gestured to the first Spectre, who gave a small wave.

I straightened, tugged down the edges of my shirt and then held out a warning hand. "Explain."

The second Spectre grinned. "This, my dear boy, is what we call show and tell. I *show* you, and then you *tell* me what you think."

"What I think about what? This is mad. There are two of you."

"Yes," Spectre declared triumphantly. "Well, two at the moment. Sometimes there's one, sometimes there's more, and sometimes there's none. Like that one time, there was none of us at all. Ghastly experience that was. Anyway, we're getting off track. This is Spectre."

"But…you're Spectre."

"Yes."

"And…and he's you, too?"

"Yes."

I picked the chair up off the ground and sat back in the seat. I spoke in the politest manner I could muster. "If I might be so bold as to say, you're not using your words very well."

Spectre seemed to take a moment to digest my critique before shrugging in some sort of half-hearted agreement. "Fair point. Well, you see, here at Everwood Academy, we all have a gift. And this," he pointed to his doppelganger, "is mine."

"You can, what, clone yourself?" I guessed.

Spectre brightened as if impressed that I had a brain. "No, not at all. But very good try."

"Okay," I pressed, "so you can…?"

"Ghost. I can ghost." As if to prove his point, he brushed through the copy of himself. As he did so, the first Spectre evaporated into smoke and disappeared.

"That's…" I took a moment to find the right words, "fantastic, actually."

Spectre clapped his hands and grinned. "I know! Very handy in a bind, I can tell you. Avoided a few boring meetings this way. I tend to send a ghost on ahead when I know I'm running late. People seem to enjoy his company. Confide in him, even." He paused, and his gaze drifted away. "I wonder if they know that I can hear everything they're saying to my ghosts. Oh dear. That explains a lot about Mrs. Tipney and the large pot of…" Spectre looked back at me, looking slightly surprised, as if he had forgotten I was still in the room. "Angus. Hello. Yes, where were we?"

"Your gift is ghosting," I reminded him.

"Right, yes. Very handy in a bind. Wait, I said that already, didn't I? Ghosting is a very rare gift. I can replicate myself hundreds of times if need be. I can create an army to confuse people as to which one is really me. Or, I can just have company for tea. Whatever the mood calls for, really."

"Do they do anything? I mean, at first, he just kind of stood there…smiling. But then, he waved."

"Oh, yes, yes. They can do everything I can do. They only dissipate when I will them to. Or…you know, they're killed or something."

"Why didn't he talk to me?" I asked. "He just stared at me… and *smiled*." I shivered a little.

"All part of the charm, isn't it?"

"Not really."

"Don't worry, Angus. All in good time. My ghosts have every ability I have, except to further ghost themselves. However, when they split, if I'm in a bit of a hurry, sometimes they take only a fragment of my personality instead of the whole thing. I'm afraid today's Spectre was missing my dazzling wit. Next time I'll be sure to give you a much chattier ghost, if that is your preference."

"I just realised why they call you Spectre," I laughed.

Spectre seemed confused. "I don't get it."

"Never mind. It's incredible," I marvelled. "How did you get this gift? Are you some kind of magic… thing?"

"Magic?" Spectre laughed uproariously. "Heavens no, child. *Magic*." He tasted the word and spat it out. "Magic is only in fairy tales, you silly boy."

"You run a school for dragons, and I'm the one with the problem?"

Spectre seemed to draw no correlation. "Magic isn't real, Angus. What you see before you is not magic, it's genetics. Each and every one of the students here has a genetic code inside their DNA that both connects them to their dragon and gives them a gift."

"I don't have any gift like that," I said, shaking my head. "I mean, I wish I did, but I really don't."

"Tell me something, Angus. When you touched your dragon egg for the first time, did you feel anything?"

"Yeah, a zap. Like an electrical charge."

"Then you definitely have a gift. We just need to find out what it is."

"How?"

Spectre turned from the room. "Follow me."

As he proceeded down the halls, I was struck with the emptiness of them. There was no one around; no students, teachers, dragons. Nothing.

"Where is everyone?" I asked.

"It's Saturday, Angus," he said, as if this explained everything.

"So?"

"So, they are obviously out riding their dragons."

"Right. Still getting used to this."

"Now, there are all sorts of gifts. People who can breathe fire, people who can turn into other animals, people who can breathe underwater. Centuries have proved that there is only one sure way to determine someone's gift."

"And that is?"

"It's just a simple test, really." He waved his hands absently. "Not a big deal."

As we approached a set of double doors, Spectre opened them. He gestured for me to walk into the room first. I stepped inside, expecting to see an exam on a desk in front of me. Instead, there was nothing. Just a huge, dark room.

"What are we doing in here?" I asked, turning back to face Spectre. "When do I sit for the test?"

The floor suddenly started to shake, and a deep, gravelly growl rumbled behind me. My blood turned to ice.

Spectre stared me dead in the eyes. "You don't sit, Angus. You *run*."

blink

I was hit by a bus.

Well, at least that's what it felt like.

I gasped for breath, unsure of what had just happened. I picked myself up from the floor with as much speed as I could muster, acutely aware that the thundering footsteps that had preceded my unexpected flight across the room had started again.

I turned just in time to see a gigantic grey dragon loping towards me.

I had never felt such crippling fear. The dragon was ferocious. Its jagged, sharp teeth glinted in the dim light of the room, dripping with saliva that oozed from its monstrous jaws. The look in its eyes, combined with the blood-curdling growl, told me what I already knew – this dragon was going to kill me.

I didn't have time to stop and think about why Spectre had thrown me into this dragon den to die. All I could do was try to prolong my life as long as possible. If this dragon wanted to eat me, I was going to make it work for its supper.

I dove to my right just as heavy jaws snapped down upon the air I had just been breathing. I was struck at once with the sheer enormity of the beast as it began to change its course to follow me.

The head of the dragon alone was the size of a two-seater lounge chair. Its long neck stretched down towards a thick, scaly body that was the moody colour of a stormy day. How could something so enormous live in the same world as me without anyone knowing about it?

I drew back against the wall as the dragon spotted me, preparing to shoot after me once again. I looked around for something to use as a weapon but found nothing. Switching gears, I looked for an exit, but the door was behind the dragon, so I would have to get past it to leave.

"Let me out!" I shouted as loudly as I could.

There was nothing for it. I had to make it to the door and pray Spectre had not locked me inside. Acid rose in my throat, and my entire body began to tingle. Adrenaline coursed through me, but I couldn't tell if it was helpful or a hindrance.

I ran for the door as the dragon approached but to no avail. I was thrown backwards as its powerful tail struck me square in the stomach, blocking my path.

I slammed into the wall with enough force to make me see stars. I collapsed to the ground as my heart raced faster than it ever had before. The pain was unbearable. A sudden coldness gripped my hands and feet, creeping up my arms and legs, coursing through my veins.

This was it. I was going to die.

Death by dragon.

It was a rather more dramatic death than I was hoping for.

The dragon bared its teeth at me in a show of fury and flapped its enormous, veiny wings. The gust brought forth by its impressive display tousled my hair around my face and made it hard to keep my eyes open against the gale. How did it even *get* in here? If the dragon got in, surely there was another way out of here other than those doors. Maybe I could use it to escape. I looked around, desperation narrowing my focus. I couldn't see anything at all, no way a dragon *that big* made it inside this room, even if the room was enormous. That's when my eyes hit the ceiling. There were huge metal beams connected to a mechanism situated on either side of the ceiling. I would bet money that it raised up the roof, like a bridge to let ships pass.

My stomach sank. That was my last option, my last chance of escape. I couldn't make it to the roof. I had no chance.

"Let me out!" I tried to get up, but my legs wouldn't listen. Screaming for help never worked in the movies, but I was willing to try. "Please!"

"Move, boy." Spectre appeared beside me like a smokey apparition, his face just inches from mine. "Move. Go!"

"I can't!" I croaked as the dragon positioned itself directly in front of me, as if preparing for a run-up.

"If you don't, you're going to die." A second Spectre appeared at my other side, willing me to move. "Do you want to die here?"

"I *am* going to die here!" I shrieked.

"If that is your choice."

The pain in my body was radiating across every inch of my skin. I felt weak with fear and bruised from my unexpected flight across the room. How was I supposed to get out of this? This couldn't be how it ended. Why did he bring me here just to let me die?

Gritting my teeth, I tore my gaze from the dragon to Spectre. There was no way I was going to let this guy see me fail, to die without giving it everything I had. I placed my hands on the ground to give myself a boost and forced my body to do my bidding. I threw myself weakly through the ghost of Spectre and rolled along the floor, closer now to the door than I had been before.

"Go!" Another Spectre ordered, down on the ground beside me. "Get up!"

I heaved in a deep breath, my lungs burning, and rolled out of the way just as the dragon's enormous foot crash-landed beside me in an effort to squash me into jelly.

It roared angrily, a noise that was both loud and deep. The chill in my body had intensified; every inch of me felt like ice.

"Was I wrong about you, Angus?" Spectre asked, as his ghost dissolved and reappeared beside the monster.

"You threw me in here with a dragon!" I shouted back. "I was wrong about *you*!"

"Where is the fight in you?" another ghost asked. "You're lying on the ground. Weak. Pathetic."

"I'm not weak," I said through gritted teeth.

"You're weak!" the ghost confirmed, shouting.

The ice in my veins began to burn. My heart thudded angrily inside me, and my vision began to sharpen. I balled my fists and slammed them down on the ground. "I am not weak!" I shouted, blinking sweat out of my eyes.

In the split second it took me to blink, the world began to topple and shift. Time slowed down, oozing like tar. I watched the dragon freeze and saw the drops of saliva pause in the air as they were flicked from his mouth.

For the longest and shortest moment, I had all the time in the world. I stood to my feet. I looked down at my hands and moved them through the thick air, which was thick like water. They were blurred and unclear, like an accidental smudge in an oil painting. The ghosts of Spectre were frozen where they stood, their faces contorted into a scream, shouting at me to move or die.

What was happening?

The dragon was still as stone, towering over me. I walked up to it, so close I could see each scale as it rippled over his gargantuan lizard body. Saliva droplets hung in the air like rain. I reached out and touched one. It was sticky and thick.

How long would this last? What was happening to me? I had to get out of here. I walked over to the door, pressed my palm against the handle and pushed back the solid door that felt weightless in my hand.

Spectre stood unmoving before me, his face a peculiar mix of anguish and restraint. I closed the door, sealing the monster away. What was happening to me? How did I stop it? I blinked again - a simple, tiny movement I had never given any thought to before. My stomach rolled, and my veins grew cold. Just like that, everything returned to normal.

"Well, well, well..."

I looked up at Spectre, whose face betrayed his sense of surprise. "Unbelievable."

"What just happened?" I asked, somewhat breathless.

"We discovered your gift, Angus," he replied.

"What...I mean...how..." I stuttered, trying to grasp reality. "I don't understand what happened. One second, I was in the room, on the ground, about to be dragon kibble, and the next, everything is frozen. And I just...walked out here."

"Explain to me very carefully what happened, Angus. In as much detail as you can." Spectre's face was grave. He took me by my shoulders, wrapping his large fingers around the tops of my arms.

"I was on the ground. I was scared. I was angry. Angry at you, for saying that I was weak. Your ghosts, they were in there with me."

"Yes, yes, I sent them. I saw everything they saw, I heard

everything they heard. But I saw nothing other than you on the floor one second and gone the next."

"It was…it was like time just stopped. Or, I don't know, maybe it didn't stop, but it just slowed right down. I felt like I had all the time I needed while everything around me was still. I stood up, I walked to the door, I left the room, and then I was here."

Spectre slapped his hands hard against my shoulders. "Oh, my dear boy, this is magnificent. Marvellous. Simply marvellous."

"It is?" I asked. "I mean, what is this? Can I control time?"

"No, no. Better. You can Blink."

"Blink?" My brows furrowed. "Like, blink my eyes? Can't everyone?"

Spectre rolled his eyes at me in a way that made me feel that whatever this gift was, it was wasted on me. "No, not like that. You can Blink in *time*."

"What does that even mean?" I asked.

Spectre sighed, impatient. "When your gift is engaged, you rip open time like a…like a…like a present on Christmas morning. You tear open the space-time continuum and you can move freely about without the constraints of time that is felt by anyone else. Your gift, Angus, is the rarest of them all."

I swallowed hard, thoughts swirling about my mind like a whirlwind. "What…what can I do with it?"

"This test is designed to put you in a life-and-death situation. It forces your gift to the forefront; gives it a jolt to life, like a defibrillator on a heart that's no longer beating. Eventually, once you learn to harness and control your gift, you will be able to go anywhere, anywhere in the world, in the blink of an eye. You'll be able to escape attackers or stop speeding bullets. Angus…this gift is the most powerful and," he added grimly, "the most dangerous, of all. You must not tell anyone. Not a soul. Never a word."

"But I-"

"No, Angus!" Spectre shouted, gripping my shoulders even harder. His eyes were wide with something that looked a little like fear. "You must not tell anyone of your gift. Confide only in me. I will teach you all I know, but you must not share this news with anyone."

"Why?" I asked.

"Spend the day with me, and I will explain. For now, I will just say that there are enemies in this world. Enemies that could spell the end for us all. And should they discover your ability, they will attempt to find you, and use you as a powerful weapon. Angus, you must never let that happen. Do you understand?"

I nodded weakly.

"You have been given an immense burden and an invaluable treasure." Spectre straightened and smiled a small, proud smile. "Angus Finch," he let my name hang in the air like a badge of honour. "Your gift could save us all."

illusion

Spectre seemed happy enough with the progress of the morning. He patted me on the head in a manner that suggested to me that he wasn't entirely confident when it came to affection.

He reached for the door handle to the room I had just fled, and instinctively I threw my hand out to stop him. "What are you doing? That dragon nearly killed me!"

"Oh dear. Best be careful, then." He gave a small hop and pushed open the door.

The brute stood in the centre of the room, teeth bared, blood-red gums pulsing with hunger. He stomped his large feet, and the ground below me trembled.

Spectre turned around to face me, giving me a disapproving look when he noted I was still standing at the threshold, ready to slam the door if the need arose.

"Angus. Let's use some common sense, shall we? This dragon can breathe fire, weighs approximately the same as a Boeing 747, and has teeth that can cut through steel."

"That's exactly why I'm standing here!" I exclaimed.

"Yes. Quite. But, taking all that into account, do you really think that a wooden door is enough to stop him should he wish to leave this room?"

I opened my mouth to speak, but words failed me.

"I can assure you that the weakness of these glorious creatures is most certainly not four-hundred-year-old oak."

"Well," I said, dusting off my trousers for no reason in particular, other than to busy my hands. "I suppose one can't argue with that logic."

"Then step inside," he encouraged.

I have found that there are times in life when you must decide what you are truly going to do. It may be a small decision, such as showing up to a meeting, choosing not to say that harsh word, or, in my case, stepping into a room with a dragon inside, but these seemingly insignificant choices often have remarkable consequences. Like turning left instead of right, and avoiding an accident.

I could tell I was in one of those moments. If I didn't step into this room, Spectre would make up his mind about me being a coward and unworthy of his time, and there would be no changing it. If I did step into the room, I could get eaten alive.

Growing up without a father to be proud of me made the decision quite a simple one.

I stepped into the room.

"Good lad," Spectre said.

The dragon roared loudly, causing spit to fly outwards, drips of it landing on my face. I held my ground, then took another step closer.

"Hold out your hand to him, boy," Spectre instructed. "Reach for him."

I looked to him for clarification, thinking, surely, I had misheard his order, but he simply nodded me forward.

"This is the craziest thing I have ever done," I mumbled, reaching my hand out slowly. I stood just a foot or two from the monster now. He bucked and thrashed his tail, snorting out smoke and gnashing his teeth. My shaking hands were dripping with sweat, but I couldn't back down now.

For some reason, what this quirky old man thought about me was important to me. Important enough that I would risk getting my hand chomped off by a dragon who wasn't feeling very touchy-feely. I couldn't – *wouldn't* – give up. I forced the trembling that started at my shoulders and ended at my fingertips to cease. I took deep and steady breaths and took another step closer.

"There, now," I said to the dragon, "I'm not going to hurt you." I tried not to laugh at the concept of *me* hurting *him*. "Just relax."

The dragon growled a low deep rumble that sounded like an oncoming storm. I grew more determined. "Stop," I demanded. "Stop."

The dragon peered at me, lowering its head until it was at the same level as mine. He stopped moving, and his tail became still. I could still hear the rumble of a growl at the back of his throat, but in one final move, I closed the gap between us and placed my hand directly on the dragon's snout.

I waited for my hand to be bitten clean off. I waited for fire to cascade out of his mouth and sizzle me into ash, not unlike sausages when Grandpa took to barbequing. But nothing happened. The growling had turned almost to a soft purr, and the dragon's eyes were soft.

"Good boy," I said, patting him gently. "Good boy." I turned to Spectre, my hand still on the dragon's face. "I can't believe it."

"Well done, my dear boy. Well done."

"He's just…he's just letting me touch him."

"Yes, he is." Spectre started to laugh. What began as a small chuckle turned into a deep, throaty chortle until he was laughing so loudly I felt an unusual irritation.

"What's so funny?" I asked.

Spectre did his best to compose himself. "I'm sorry, Angus. I'm just…I'm quite stunned."

"Why?"

"Well, no one's ever actually stepped foot back into the room before. Let alone touched the dragon!"

"What?"

"I try this with every new student, but no one ever comes back in." He gave a sly smile.

"Really?" I asked. "I'm the first person to have the guts to come back in?"

"Yes, yes, you are."

"So, you've never tested this before?" I snapped. "He could've eaten me! You had no idea what was going to happen!" I drew my hand back from the dragon, suddenly even more cautious than I was before.

"There's always a first, Angus. Nothing to get worked up about. Besides, look at the way he responded to you. It was like…like you were a shining torch, leading him, controlling him."

I looked back to the dragon. "Really? I did all that?"

Spectre started to laugh again. "No, of course not. This is my dragon, Pilar. I told him what to do the whole time."

"What?" I hissed. "You told him to try to kill me? To smack me so hard with his tail I could see stars?"

"Oh, don't be so dramatic. You were never in any real danger. Pilar knows his boundaries and does not act without my say so."

"So…this was all just a trick?" I asked, my mind whirling.

"I prefer to call it an illusion," he replied. "The test, as I said, is designed to put you in a life-or-death situation that will force your gift to come to the surface. But I couldn't very well actually put you in a life-or-death situation. What kind of headmaster would that make me? Think of the angry letters I'd receive from parents. Ghastly." Spectre looked offended and shook his head. "Honestly, I'm not a monster. We save the life and death situations for when you are fully and properly trained, and not a moment before. If it can be helped, of course."

"You're crazy," I said, looking back at the dragon, who was fixated with something on its tail. "Absolutely bonkers."

"Well, you know what they say in *Alice in Wonderland.*"

"What do they say?" I asked dryly.

Spectre grinned. "All the best people are."

learning curve

The door opened and a man walked in, folders in his bony arms. He was thinly built, like a pencil; his long, languid body came to a graphite point at his dark grey hair.

"Mister Thomas?" the man droned, "I am here to remind you that you are on a tight-" Pilar, Spectre's dragon, shoved his nose into the personal bubble of the lanky man and snorted. I watched as the lips of the man curled slightly in distaste and wondered where he fit in at Everwood. He clearly seemed uncomfortable around the dragon, but not in the sense that he was afraid of him. More like a cat lover surrounded by dogs. He blew away the light smoke that came from the dragon's nostrils with one hand, while holding the heavy stack of files in the other, balancing them precariously on his scrawny forearm.

"You are," he started again, "on a tight schedule. There is a lot for you to get through for Mister Finch, and you asked me to keep you moving."

"Ah, right. Thank you, Cyrus."

I inspected the man named Cyrus with further scrutiny. His face was hollow, and shadows formed in the depths created by the sagging skin between his bones. He stood stooped, like a half-sucked candy cane. His clothes were simple yet elegant: black suit pants, a white button-up shirt, and a suit jacket. His tie was a no-nonsense grey, and his shoes shone so brightly that Pilar's face was reflected in the toes.

He had the overwhelming air of a butler who was bothered that small, irritating things kept getting in the way of his ability to accomplish his tasks.

"Of course, sir," Cyrus responded flatly. "I'll take this opportunity to remind you that your next appointed location is the library. Shall I take Mister Pilar back to his stable?"

"Yes, yes, that'll be fine," he replied absently with a wave of his hand. Spectre had already turned around and was eyeing the back of the room to make his escape. One hand was perched on the back leg of his dragon, stroking the scales with a familiar fondness.

"Come along then, Mister Pilar," Cyrus instructed, giving his back to the dragon as he strode from the room.

"Off you go, boy," Spectre encouraged, patting his leg affectionately.

Spectre remained unmoving after Pilar and Cyrus had left the room. He was staring at a spot on the wall, muttering quietly words I could not understand. I moved to get a better look at his face, and for the first time since I had met him, he looked truly old and frail.

"Are you okay?" I asked.

"What?" he popped, snapping back to the present.

"Are you okay? You seem…distracted."

"Yes, yes, quite fine." He smiled and the appearance of fragility was, in an instant, gone. "Just thinking about you, dear boy. And the remarkable gift you've been given. And your dragon. She's a puzzle, too."

I smiled weakly, unsure what to say.

"Off to the library!" he sang, taking off.

"I'm not going to go get my dragon?" I asked.

"It is a dragon, not a wren. The medical team will be with her for the majority of the day. Not to worry, there will be plenty of time for you two to bond."

I tried not to show my disappointment.

I followed Spectre, lingering a few steps behind. I didn't know what to feel, knowing that it was his thoughts of me and my newfound gift that caused him to age before my eyes. What had he been muttering to himself? Was it just me or did he look almost…afraid? What could possibly have made this seemingly invincible and all-knowing man feel fear?

I wasn't sure that I ever wanted to find out.

One thing was for certain.

I wasn't going to tell a soul about my gift.

"Angus! Are you listening?"

My face slammed into his chest, squashing my nose.

"Sorry," I muttered. I hadn't noticed he had stopped. "I was…daydreaming."

"The time for daydreaming is most certainly not now, Angus," Spectre reprimanded. "I have a lot to go through with you today, and my time is very valuable. You've got the real me, and I've given everyone else a ghost. So, pay attention."

"Sorry," I repeated. "I will. What were you saying?"

"I was saying that Orientation is a time-honoured tradition, of course, but more than that, it is a downright necessity. I'm sure you felt quite befuddled last night as I sent you off to bed with your new dragon. So, imagine if I were to tell you that the fact that dragons exist is not even close to the biggest secret you will learn here at Everwood Academy. And then imagine that I told you absolutely nothing else."

"That would be very confusing." This seemed a pointless conversation. It already was confusing, and he hadn't really told me much else, anyway.

"Yes, it would! Not to mention dangerous. See, Everwood Academy is still a school, no doubt. We have students here as young as twelve, so we cannot very well, in all good conscience, fail them on their education simply because they were born with a genetic abnormality that connects them to a dragon. However, we are also a school of a different sort. Here at Everwood, you will learn basic martial arts." He held his hand out to the right, just as we walked past the open door of a class with students following instructions inside a dojo. "You will also learn languages, history, art. All things a young Vector such as yourself should know."

I recalled the books I'd received from the Book Keeper and wondered if Spectre was aware that most students in the real world didn't study trigonometry from the perspective of getting off and on a dragon.

Spectre continued on down the seemingly endless hallway. I followed, like a blind man following his cane.

"Most importantly, however, you will learn everything inside this room." Spectre stopped, turned to face me abruptly, and leaned back against two double doors.

"What's in there?" I asked.

"In here, Angus, is the library. The library is not only full of all our schooling books but also additional information on dragons, the history of our people, the political structure of our leaders and all the information you need to know about every single gift. Including the very rare and coveted writings on your own gift."

"Why do I need to know about other people's gifts?" I asked.

"If you don't know the extent of another's gifts, how are you supposed to combat them?"

"I didn't know I was supposed to combat them," I responded.

"Angus, it's very important that you realise that the life you used to lead is over, should you choose to continue with us."

"Should I…choose?"

"You always have a choice, Angus. Always," he shrugged, and added, "Except for when you don't."

Spectre opened the door and disappeared inside. I followed him in.

I had always loved books. Reading had been one of the few escapes from the torture that was teenage years in high school. I visited my local library often, but this… this was something else.

The first thing I noticed was the ceiling. It was arched, with a massive, thick beam stretching from one end of the room to the other. It hovered two storeys above my head and was painted with intricate images of dragons and Vectors. A second floor rimmed the room, with wood banisters overlooking the floor below. Rows upon rows of shelves stuffed with thousands of books expanded before me. Each section was clearly indicated with a large sign depicting the nature of the books to be found inside. I read the nearest signs and resisted the urge to run from Spectre and scour through every book I could wrap my fingers around. *Dragon History, Registry of Gifts, Politics, Poetry and Novels, Dragon Lore, Mythology, Interactions with Non-Vectors.*

Long tables, smaller round tables, and soft armchairs were scattered throughout, providing reading nooks or study areas.

Arched windows, like what you would expect to see in a cathedral, were placed around the room in strategic positions to let in the most amount of light. Yet somehow, the entire room felt dark and cozy, despite its enormous size. It felt like winter and hot chocolates, and warm blankets and calm.

A few students lazed on chairs, books in hand, but it was largely devoid of much activity, and almost completely silent, save for the laborious footsteps of the school's headmaster as he weaved his way through the aisles. I took off after him, not wanting to get lost in the maze of the written word. I expected him to stop at any moment, but he continued towards the very back of the library and through a door with a sign posted sternly on its facade.

Admittance Only by Permission from the Headmaster. Signed Form Required.

It was darker in this part of the library than anywhere else. A warm glow from a fireplace was one of the few sources of light. The air felt rich with untold secrets.

The ceiling in here was lower, but still painted like the main part of the library. An army of dragons, whispers of gold clouds, arrows sailing through the air like boats on the water. A falling dragon, blood in the air. Death.

Though the room was still sizeable, it had a heaviness to it that made it feel like the walls were closing in on you. There were three different sections of shelving, forcefully set apart, as if someone was very concerned the books would be returned to the wrong place if the shelves stood any closer.

Portraits of faces I didn't recognise and old maps in frames were scattered around the walls. Thick rugs overlapped each other, covering the floors, worn smooth with years of footsteps pacing from shelf to shelf.

Two chairs sat around a single round wooden table supporting a large pile of parchment paper and pens. Two high-back chairs sat facing the fireplace.

Spectre stopped in front of the first section of books, labelled *Dragon's; Classified.*

"This room is off-limits to all but the most talented students. You and only a handful of others have been inside this room. A gift such as yours requires additional knowledge, knowledge that you cannot be without. These books are very old. Completely irreplaceable. Be very careful."

As a lover of books and knowledge, I wondered just how much information was available at my fingertips. "I will."

"Sit, please."

I sat on the nearest chair. A chill of apprehension ran through me. Was it really only yesterday that I was living my normal life, unaware dragons existed? Was it really just this morning I handed Merry over at the stables? It felt like a month had passed in just twenty-four hours. What would I learn in here? What was this gift I had been given that made me important enough to be in this room?

Spectre reached for the bookshelf and pulled out an enormous, dusty book with thick binding and a leather cover. Embossed on the front were the words:

Hic Sunt Dracones.

I immediately recognised those same words from the inscription above the entrance to Everwood Academy.

Here Be Dragons.

"This book is the oldest book in this library. It contains the basics - an overview of the history of dragons, locations in which there are dragon colonies, and how our system of authority functions and the role it will play in your life. Most importantly, however, it explains exactly what dragons are, which, I presume, you will find quite useful."

"I know what dragons are. I've watched a hundred dragon movies. I mean, it's all based on lore, right?"

"Angus, there are many lessons Hollywood can teach you, but the truth about dragons is not one of them. While certain facts remain true – such as their hard scales, ability to fly, and penchant for breathing fire – these aspects do not fully encompass what makes a dragon."

"Oh," I said dumbly.

"Now, open the book to page 473."

I did as I was told, lifting the cover, and grabbing a chunk of pages. As I let the cover go, it thudded heavily on the table and a puff of dust flew upwards.

"Doesn't everyone else get to know about what makes a dragon?" I asked.

"Of course. Everything an Everwood student needs to know is out there. Lore, facts, genetics, anatomy. But this book also contains a great deal of other information, information about our past, our wars, our *people*, that you will need to know. In here," he gestured to the room, "and in *here*," he poked at the book, "is much more sensitive information that is, shall we say, need to know."

There was something about the way Spectre was talking that made me anxious to hear the answer to the question burning my lips. "Why do I need to know?"

Spectre sat down on the last remaining chair. He folded his arms in front of his chest and looked at me with as much kindness as he could muster. When he spoke, his voice was soft, apologetic. "Because when you have a gift like the ability to Blink, you either become our greatest ally, or our greatest enemy. The only way you can decide which is if you have all the facts you need to make your own decision, regarding what many call the lost faction of our people."

"I'm not going to betray you," I said, shaking my head.

Spectre took off his glasses and folded them neatly in front of him, taking more time and care than was warranted. "It is kind of you to say so, my boy. And I believe you mean it. But sometimes blood overcomes even the clearest and most solid of intentions."

"Blood?" I asked, confused. "You're saying it's in my blood to betray you?"

"No, boy. It's that..." he hesitated. His demeanour quickly brightened. "All in time. Let's not talk of this any further. Onto your training."

I wanted to press, to figure out exactly what he meant by blood, but there was a look in his eyes that made me afraid to do so. I had a feeling it would make him angry if I kept pushing, but there was something else digging at the pit of my stomach that forced me to hold my tongue.

The truth was simple.

Maybe I didn't *want* to know the answer at all.

the new normal

I collapsed onto the bed without much concern for how I landed. A near-death experience, backed up by hours of staring at textbooks, made me feel like I could sleep for a week.

I gripped the pillow tightly and hugged it towards myself, closing my eyes. I could feel sleep taking hold. I allowed myself to drift, only to be disturbed when the door opened, and Artie walked in.

"Hey, roomie," Artie trilled as he dropped his bag by his desk and sat down. "How's day one treating you so far?"

"Oh, great," I mumbled without opening my eyes. "Nearly got eaten by a dragon, learned that everything I know is a lie. Just the usual high school stuff."

Artie laughed. "Yeah, it's pretty unique."

"You can say that again."

"Where's your dragon?" Artie asked.

"She's still with the medical team. I can go get her in an hour." I checked my watch as I spoke. It was three o'clock now, though to me, it felt like midnight.

"What are you doing in the meantime?"

"This," I responded. "Spent the day with Spectre, and then he let me go, so here I am." I waved my hands in the air to gesture to my current place in the time-space continuum.

Artie shook his head, "Uh, uh, this can't happen."

"Why not?" I groaned.

"It's your first day. Come on, get up."

Before I could say no, Artie grabbed both my arms and pulled me off the bed to my feet.

"I'm going to show you around a bit," Artie grinned.

"Haven't I seen it all?" I asked.

Artie laughed. "Uh, I doubt it. This place is massive. Wake up, and let's go."

Reluctantly, I followed my new friend out the door and down the hall. Students wandered up and down the halls, talking, laughing, or reading.

It almost seemed normal.

Except for the giant dragons, roaring outside.

"Don't worry. You'll get used to it really quickly."

"I'm kind of struggling to get my head around it all," I admitted. "I mean…dragons. It's just…weird."

"I know. Crazy, right?" Artie chuckled and slapped me on the back. "But it beats the world out there."

"What about your parents?" I asked.

"What about them?"

"Well, where do they think you are?"

"Here." Artie shrugged.

"Yeah, but don't you feel bad lying to them? I mean, dragons exist, and no one knows."

Artie led us out the doors and into the sunshine. I felt the breeze revitalize me. The sun was warm in the perfect blue sky, and the enormous trees that lingered above me provided the perfect amount of shade. It was dreamlike, almost.

"My parents know all about dragons," Artie replied, stepping out onto the courtyard.

"I thought we weren't supposed to tell anyone."

"We're not, but my parents are Vectors, too."

"What?" I asked, stunned.

"Yeah. It's a bit of a weird situation. Very rarely happens. Most people who are dragon riders have to commit to living their lives sort of in and out of the Academies, the army, or the Concilium. My family are a bit different. My parents are…important."

"In what way?"

"Well, Mum's the, uh, the Commander of the Counter Terrorism Command," Artie said quietly. "Like for the country. Not the dragons."

"Whoa," I responded.

"Yeah. Dad's just a rank below her."

"So…?"

"So, I was raised in London, and my parents would carry on their business, as well as do stuff here, and things for the Concilium. So, when my time came, my parents were all like 'save the world, follow your destiny, harness your powers,'" he waved his hands in the air sarcastically. "Ugh. I just wanted to stay home and play video games."

"So, you've got a bit of pressure on your shoulders, then."

"Yeah. You should see them. I would be certain I was adopted if I wasn't a dragon rider, too. Dad's super buff, and Mum's so smart she makes my brain hurt. But they're good about it, I guess. They know I'm not some kind of superhero or anything. And they know I don't want that. So, we've come to a mutual understanding. They can be Mr. and Mrs. Save-the-world, and I'll be… well, I'm not sure yet, actually."

We were heading down a stony pathway. I tried to take in my surroundings, but it was difficult to believe it was real. Students of the Academy buzzed about everywhere. Outside, where there were no restrictions to size, dragons walked around, their tails swooshing behind them. All different sizes and colours, they wandered around with their riders, free and happy. The place was alive.

"My Mum has no idea about any of this," I said. "She's a nurse back home, and she just thinks I'm at some kind of fancy school. Which is true in a sense, but this is a pretty big secret to keep. I've never been able to lie to her. She always knows."

"Don't lie, then," Artie said. "Just…tell her about all the educational stuff and leave the dragon part out."

As Artie led me down the path, I wondered where he was taking me. The cobbled stones led the way down a slope, thick tufts of green grass sprouting out either side. The scenery was something else. Thick, lush trees dotted the landscape, and beyond them were snow-capped mountains that stabbed jaggedly at the horizon.

We came to a river, the waters of which were so clear, I had to fight the urge to dive right in. Below the water's surface, I could see fish weaving around stones and ducking in and out of the shadows.

"Where in the world are we? Really?"

Artie chuckled. "We're in the National Park, but we're not. We're there, but on top of it, in a way. Overlapping."

I laughed. "That's the worst explanation ever."

"I know," Artie nodded. "I'm not the guy to ask."

"So, where are we going?"

"Just over there."

I allowed my gaze to follow the direction that Artie was pointing. I could see dozens of dragons not far in the distance.

"What's over there?" I asked.

"It's where a lot of us come to race."

"You can't be serious."

"Yeah. We're teenagers, after all. If we can't race our cars, we'll race our dragons." He laughed as we arrived at the mass of people and beasts.

"Is this allowed?" I asked.

"Allowed?" Artie scoffed. "It's encouraged. Equitem is the Academy sport, and racing is the way we practice on our own."

"What's Equitem?" I ask.

"Part obstacle course, part jousting, all chaos. Each of the houses competes against each other throughout the year. Win enough matches, and your house gets the Equitem Cup for that year. Sylva is currently in last place. We need a new Flag Bearer. The Sylva Captain is heartbroken. It's a pretty big deal around here. Good thing the school has a good healer. There's broken bones every match."

"Really?" I watched two riders get on top of their dragons and, upon the signal, launch into the air and take off at ridiculous speed. "It sounds fantastic."

"I know." Artie smiled a toothy grin. "Aren't you glad I brought you here?"

fast and furious

The dragons shot out into the sky with such speed it was almost dizzying. Just a blur of colours and shapes, they were soon only a speck in the distance. The dragons and their Vector's flew to the closest mountain peak and back, which I guessed was about a two-mile round trip. Everyone cheered, drinking cool cider or warm hot chocolate from barrels on a wood table.

"I could get used to this," I said to Artie, taking a deep swig of hot chocolate.

"Pretty awesome, right?"

Nolan and Cosette waved Artie over. Just as I was about to follow, a voice stopped me.

"What do you think?"

I turned around to see Hana standing behind me. Her dragon, shimmering a deep black in the dappled sunlight, was eyeing me suspiciously.

"Hi. It's great." I gestured to her dragon. "He's amazing. Jeju, right?"

"Yeah."

Jeju was big, though nowhere near as large as Pilar. His eyes were crimson, and two ivory horns stretched to a point from the top of his head. Would I ever get used to seeing dragons? Somewhere in the back of my mind, I tried to rationalize it, the way Spectre had. They were just animals. Though their history was shrouded in myth, they weren't that different from elephants or blue whales or Komodo dragons, or any other animal. They were living and breathing, with heartbeats and instincts. But being genetically linked to a dragon was a different story. How did that work? Why me?

"Where's your dragon?"

Hana's voice pulled me out of the reverie I hadn't realised I was lost in. "I can go get her from medical soon. They've had her all day. It must be pretty thorough."

"Yeah, well, veterinary science on mythical beasts is kind of an art."

"When you put it like that," I laughed.

"What do you think of it here?" she asked. "Everwood, I mean."

"I keep expecting to wake up."

"When I first found out about dragons, I was more excited than anything. Kind of like some part of me had always known they existed. Spectre said that was pretty unusual, but then I guess *I* am pretty unusual. I've only been here three years, but I feel like I was never anywhere else. Everwood is home. This plane is the only one I feel comfortable in."

"I'm not really sure how this whole other plane thing works," I admitted.

"It's pretty simple, really. It's all explained by quantum mechanics and superposition."

I stared at her blankly.

Noting the expression on my face, she continued, "The fact that one photon can exist in two different states at once."

"No, no, I know what it means. I just didn't think…"

"That a girl could know about quantum mechanics?"

I paused, surprised by her comment. "No," I clarified, "I just didn't think it had been proven. I thought it was all still theoretical."

"Oh," Hana smiled sheepishly. "Sorry. You'd be surprised how little people expect of you when you're a girl. It's always a surprise to people when they realise—"

"That you're super smart?" I finished.

"Well, that's not how I was going to put it, but… yeah." Hana laughed.

"It's not a surprise to me," I said, venturing out a hand to touch her dragon. Jeju pressed the side of his face into my palm.

I could tell Hana was looking at me, but I didn't want to meet her eyes. I kept my focus on the dragon, suddenly nervous, though surprisingly *not* because I was petting another dragon as if it was a labrador. It struck me how the most dangerous creatures at Everwood Academy weren't necessarily the dragons.

People could hurt you much worse.

"All right, all right, that's enough everyone!"

I turned to see Spectre approaching us with his hands raised to quiet the crowd. His enormous dragon lumbered along behind him.

A tall man with a grumpy demeanour was walking beside him. He looked a little like the Mister Smiths; he wore a black linen cloak, boots, and a white shirt.

Artie came up beside me.

"I thought you said this was allowed," I whispered to Artie.

"I thought it was," he whispered back, shrugging his shoulders.

Artie's voice was a whisper. "That's Professor Cullen. He's the house head for Sylva. Everyone says he's the reason we're losing in Equitem – he's too hard on the players. The Flag Bearer quit after he broke both legs in practice."

"Everybody stop!" Spectre said, as the sea of students parted to allow him through. He paused and looked around, his face stern.

I waited, uncertain of the punishment for dragon racing. Every eye was on Spectre and his dragon; every mouth was tightly shut.

"I cannot believe you have all been so rebellious and discourteous that on a perfectly fine Saturday afternoon, you are here racing your dragons!" Spectre boomed. Confused faces looked to each other for comfort. "Without me!" Spectre added, a smile suddenly stretching across his face. "Now, who is brave enough to race me?"

I laughed as the crowd erupted in cheers. Wooden mugs crashed together, spilling liquid, as everyone toasted to Spectre. Students started to chant his name as he jumped on top of his dragon and went to the starting line, where a queue of students who wanted to race him was quickly growing.

"I've heard no one is faster than Spectre," Artie said as we pushed our way forward for a better view. "His dragon is insane."

Han Kang was the first to race. I could already feel an intense dislike growing in the pit of my stomach. If he didn't seem so standoffish, he likely would have had every girl in this school hanging off his arm. He was good looking, that much was obvious. He was also much better built than anyone else here, like he had a few extra years on us all.

"Ready to lose, Han?" Spectre asked.

"Don't cry too hard when I win, old man," he responded.

"Old man?" Spectre repeated. "More like ancient."

The two took off into the air, and even though Artie said Spectre was fast, I was still surprised at how quickly Pilar was flying. I would have expected that such an enormous, heavy dragon would have been slower than Han's smaller, nimbler one. But I was wrong.

Each swoosh of his wings propelled him forward with such speed

I couldn't imagine how Spectre was hanging on. Though I could tell Han's dragon was fast, it was no match for Pilar.

He was already at the mountain peak, while Han was only halfway there. I watched the dragon loop around, taking the corner widely, then gracefully begin the return journey.

There was a part of me that was getting used to seeing a dragon in the air, like there was nothing more normal. Seeing Spectre glide towards me, I suddenly felt as though I had been here forever, and I had never known a world without dragons ever existed. It's funny how quickly you could forget the past and embrace the future.

Spectre and his dragon flew above the finish line, then landed softly near me. "What do you think, my boy?" he asked, looking down at me from the back of Pilar.

"I think this is the greatest place on earth," I replied.

Spectre smiled. "That's what I wanted to hear. Now," he turned, addressing the crowd. "Who's next?"

confrontation

I arrived at the medical bay ten minutes after four. My skin was prickling with excitement at the thought of collecting my dragon. *My dragon.* A spark of excitement ran down my spine.

I was instructed to sit and wait, so I dutifully took a perch on the end of a wooden pew. The waiting room was cool, the scent of herbs and earth and spice strong in the air. There was a reception desk in the very centre of the room, with various flyers, pamphlets and other informative materials. Sitting on a squeaky chair was a narrow-faced woman with glasses in the shape of a crescent moon and a beehive where her hair should be.

Every few minutes she would glance up at me as if to assure herself I was causing no trouble. Every time her eyes met mine, I would smile gingerly, concerned that, at any minute, she would kick me out.

After what seemed an age, the veterinary nurse finally walked out with Merry's cage in her hands.

"Well?" I asked, jumping up out of the seat on which I had impatiently waited.

"She's doing very well. She's a little smaller than we normally see, but I was informed about the unique nature of this case, so, really, we have nothing to compare it to."

"Unique nature? What does that mean?"

"Her egg. It's thousands of years old. There's no way of telling exactly how long she sat waiting for you."

I swallowed hard, unsure what to say next. What a strange feeling – to have someone wait a hundred lifetimes or more just for you.

"Has someone informed you about her status?" the nurse asked.

"No. I don't know what that means."

"Well, dragons come in four types – water types, earth types, air and forest."

"Right. The houses."

"Yes. Usually, a non-invasive preliminary test informs us as to which classification a dragon belongs, but in Merry's case, the test was non-conclusive."

"What do you mean?" I asked. "I was assigned to Sylva. Doesn't that mean she's a forest type?"

"No. After discussing her case with the headmaster, he decided to assign you to the same house as your roommate. But Merry doesn't seem to have a type."

My brows crumpled. "What does that mean?"

"We're not sure yet. As I mentioned, her case is entirely unique. There is no record of another like her. I'm afraid in this case it's a watch-and-see. However, rest assured she appears to be the picture of health."

The nurse handed her cage over to me. "She'll need plenty of rest, and don't let her miss any mealtimes."

"What do I feed her?" I asked.

"*You* don't feed her anything. Just bring her to the feeding area when the bell tolls, like everyone else. Just like you did this morning."

"Right. Sorry. I'm new here."

The nurse had already turned and walked away.

I looked down at Merry in my hands. She looked up at me with familiar, hopeful eyes. Just like that, I was given a dragon and sent on my way. No training. No special license. Nothing. Just me and my dragon.

I walked out of the medical bay in somewhat of a daze. I made my way down the halls without registering much of what was going on around me.

When I found myself outside, I chose the nearest grassy clearing to sit and gather my thoughts. I let Merry out of her cage, and she crawled out, rolling around in the grass like a puppy. The metallic red and green hues glistened, begging to be touched. I ran my hand down the length of her spine, all the way to the tip of her tail. Was it just me, or was she bigger than she was yesterday?

I took the opportunity to investigate her further. She had rows of small sharp teeth trapped inside her snake-like jaw. Her eyes were clear and bright, white on the outside, with two different coloured pupils – one red, one green. They were soft eyes, almond shaped. There was something delicate and feminine about her face that I couldn't pinpoint. Was it the way her jaw narrowed towards her nose? Was it the roundness of her face?

Merry rolled over onto her back. Her belly was a light shade of red, and she had four short legs with talons. She was no bigger than a terrier, but I suspected that wouldn't last long.

Did it matter that she didn't have a type? Was there something wrong? I wondered what made her so different, why her egg was separate from all the others and why she had waited so long for me. I hoped I was worth the wait.

What was I doing here? How was any of this suddenly my reality?

I felt dizzy. I lay back on the grass and stared up at the sky. Merry clambered onto my chest and wrapped herself in her wings, like a blanket. The sky was a slick icy blue, the kind I rarely saw back at home. Not a single cloud hovered overhead. The wind was the perfect temperature as it caressed my skin, and the tree leaves that danced overhead were a new shade of green. It didn't seem like Autumn.

Maybe I really was in a different plane. Why not? It was the least confusing thing that I had to face so far.

"What are you doing out here?" a male voice asked. I sat up and saw Han Kang standing above me. I hadn't noticed his approach. What was he, a ninja?

"Nothing," I answered.

"Spectre sent me to find you," Han said coldly.

"What for?"

"You have a call. Apparently, that makes me your secretary."

"I'm sorry," I said, standing to my feet. Merry dropped down beside me. "Did I *do* something to you?"

"Excuse me?"

"I don't even know you, and you act like we're enemies."

Han let out a short bark of a laugh. "I couldn't care less about you."

"Good to know." I picked up Merry's empty cage and brushed past him, smacking into his shoulder the same way that he had done to me.

The universal symbol for, *it's on.*

Han didn't say a word. I kept walking, Merry trotting along beside me. Anxiety was building in my chest. It wasn't like me to do something like that. I was the suffer-in-silence type. Get beat up, don't do anything about it, go to class type. What was I doing picking a fight with Han Kang? I had already been told he wasn't the kind of guy I should cross. But after going face to face with a dragon, I didn't want a *human* to push me around ever again. Even if I did feel like my stomach was trying to burst out of my mouth.

I held my breath, wondering what he was going to do. I was relieved to hear that moments later, his quiet footsteps rustled the grass behind me, slowly and melodically. He wasn't chasing me down.

The phone was attached to the wall in a quiet hallway few people seemed to tread down.

"Your mother would like to speak to you," Spectre said, gesturing for me to take the phone. He silently reminded me to tell no one about the dragon currently tugging at my shoelaces.

"Why didn't she just call my phone?" I asked, as I lifted the phone to my ear. "Hi, Mum?"

"Angus," a hoarse voice shot through the phone and down my ear.

I looked up to Spectre in alarm. That voice did not belong to my mother.

"Who is this?" I asked.

Spectre stepped closer, towering over me. "What's going on, Angus?"

"Angus, listen to me," the voice said quickly. Why did it sound so familiar? "I need you to be ready. Nothing is what you think it is."

"Ready for what? Who are you?" I asked.

Indifferent to my question, he continued. "You can't trust anyone. Not even Spectre."

I looked over to Spectre, who was standing close to me, head bent in concern.

"*Especially* not him," the voice continued. "Be ready, Angus."

The line went dead.

I placed the phone back on the receiver, not sure what just happened.

"What was that?" Spectre asked.

"I don't know. But it wasn't my mother." I walked away from the phone as if it had a disease I could catch.

"What did they say?"

"I'm not sure," I answered. "It didn't make any sense."

You can't trust anyone. Not even Spectre.

The voice repeated in my ear, like a whisper from a ghost. Spectre's inquisitive eyes peered into my soul.

Especially not him.

"I don't know. Maybe it was for someone else," I shrugged, starting to walk away.

"It was nothing you're concerned about?" he pressed.

I shook my head. "No. It's fine. It was nothing."

Spectre let me walk away, but I could feel his eyes on my back. I kept my pace as slow and steady as I could, so I wouldn't looked rushed or afraid. Merry strode along beside me, looking up at me curiously.

I wasn't sure why I lied to Spectre, but I reasoned with myself that maybe I just wasn't ready to share. I wanted some time to digest what just happened.

I made my way to my room and slipped inside. I had the place to myself, so I afforded myself the luxury of sitting down on the end of my bed and replaying the phone call in my head, over and over.

Who was that man? There was something about his voice that seemed familiar, but I couldn't place it. It was like trying to extract information from a dream, a week later. Then it hit me.

The stranger in the street.

Was I imagining it, or was the voice the same?

A chill ran down my spine.

The stranger had been right – they *were* coming for me. The Smith brothers. Everything had changed, just like he said it would. Did that mean he was right this time too? What was coming? What did any of it have to do with me?

I lay back on the bed and stared at the ceiling, trying not to listen to the question going around and around in my mind. If the stranger was right about me coming to Everwood…

…did that mean he was right that I couldn't trust Spectre?

school for thought

The weeks that followed were as normal as they could be, given that I was at a dragon academy in an alternate realty, or parallel world, or whatever. I settled into the rhythm of classes, training, and taking care of Merry.

The first day or two after the call from the stranger had had me on edge, but when nothing happened, I found the memory of it drifting to the back of my mind. Spectre had done nothing to warrant my distrust, and I was happy here. Happier than I ever could have imagined. Artie and I had become fast friends, and I sat with him, Hana, Cosette, Kit and Nolan every lunch and dinner. It felt like I had been here forever. More than that, I felt like my life had always been leading me here. To this place. To Everwood.

I had private classes with Spectre every week where he gave me a crash course in everything *dragon.* When I asked why, he told me that my gift made me different, and that meant taking certain precautions.

My classes had been long and informative. Page 396 of what had to be the largest book in human history had a copy of a hand drawn illustration of a typical male dragon. It looked just like the dozens of male dragons I had seen, only now I could see some of the finer details, sketched out in a diagram.

The tail of a dragon was long, usually reaching 5 meters for a fully grown male. It was partially prehensile, which was a term, I learned, used to describe a tail that could be used to grasp things and suspend the creature it belonged to from branches or the like. For a dragon, this meant that they had a considerable amount of flexibility in their tails.

The tail stretched up to two hind legs, thick and scaled. Along the top of their backs ran large spikes, which were, in fact, bones, offering the vague resemblance of a stegosaurus. I remembered visiting the Natural History Museum when I was young. The intimidating spikes on the back of the stegosaurus had ensured it would remain my favourite dinosaur, and the illustration adorning all future pairs of pajamas, until I was nine.

Ten.

Fine. I still had them.

A dragon's neck was normally at least two meters long, stretching to an enormous flat, diamond shaped head, over a metre in width and the same in length. Between two and four long bones jutted out of the back of the head, further protecting the scalp.

Artie had been correct when he spoke of the colours. The duller, more earthy tones were typically attributed to a male dragon, while the more vibrant colours were indicative of the females.

This, I pondered, was the polar opposite to the majority of nature, where it was normal for the males to be more vibrant in order to attract the females.

When I asked Spectre about why it was different with dragons, he simply said that the females are white diamonds and the males are black diamonds. They both shine, just differently.

"What about Merry?" I asked. "She is two-toned. Red and green.

I don't see anything about that in here."

"You won't find anything about Merry's colouring in there, that's why."

"Why not?"

"Because, Merry is what we call a Glitch."

"That doesn't sound very nice," I said, offended and suddenly protective. "She's not a Glitch. She's fine."

"Glitch is not a bad word, Angus. As you know, she doesn't fit into Sylva or Terra or Oceanus or Volare. She's different. Glitches have their very own book, which I will show you later. Glitches are the most unique, rare, and sought after of all dragons. You must keep a very keen eye on her outside of these walls."

I wanted to read the book of Glitches first, but Spectre said I had to learn to crawl before I could walk. I tried not to take it as an insult and continued to learn.

Dragons had two rows of teeth on the top and bottom of their mouths. These teeth were very large and very sharp, as were the claws on their front and back legs.

As for their diet, dragons could be either carnivorous or herbivorous, and, as far as scholars could tell, this choice was purely individual, suggesting that dragons are less colonised in thought and less bound to their history than expected.

Countless other things culminated in one school of thought – dragons were just as intelligent as humans. If not more so.

Perhaps the most fascinating part of the dragon was the wings. Stretching six meters on either side, they created a grotesquely frightening image. The wing of a dragon was veiny and thin on the underside and armored with scales on the other. Two pointed pones, claw like and sharp as daggers, were situated at the very front tip of the wing.

All this information regarding the appearance of a dragon failed to be as shocking as what the dragon was capable of.

Spectre was right – they could fly and breathe fire, but the similarities with Hollywood ended there. Dragons could hold their breath for up to an hour, and were excellent and speedy swimmers, but unless they were water-types they didn't take to the water unless absolutely necessary. This ability meant that they could swim through the Thames from one side of London to the other without being noticed.

Apparently, they frequently did.

But most dragons still flew more often than they swam, since they were unable to be detected by radar. This made flying from country to country as easier task, so long as they stayed out of the eyesight of other people. They could fly extremely long distances with ease; the longest recorded flight without landing was two thousand miles.

When they did need to land, dropping down onto the surface of the water and floating like a duck was sufficient, a visual I found both comedic and endearing. Water types would often swim, since they were faster in the water.

In addition to their stamina, dragons were also experts at camouflage and could see in infrared.

Classes with Spectre were my favourite, but I couldn't tell anyone about them. No one was supposed to know I was different. So I had to make excuses every time I disappeared to go and see him.

Outside my private lessons, I quickly found that History was the most enjoyable class. Professor Vida was a small, round woman with a kind face and a lilting voice. Everything she taught seemed to come alive. Learning that Everwood Academy was founded by the last in the line of the first-ever Vector, all the way back in 1286, was surreal. How could this place be so old?

Vector Poetry with Professor Gravelle was Artie's most hated class, but I loved it. Professor Gravelle seemed perpetually cross and slightly bored, but when he read aloud long poems of epic battles between dragons and men that happened hundreds of years ago, his voice took on a haunting cadence that gave me chills. Of course, he was famous for giving out the most homework, but since I liked to write, I didn't mind. I spent a lot of time in the library working on my homework, but when I could escape unseen, I went to the quiet, lonely room marked *No Admittance* and read as much as I could.

Latin was a slog, but it was mandatory for every Everwood student all the way until graduation. But most of my other classes were interesting.

As we took our seats in Professor Cullen's Politics class on Friday afternoon, I wondered what was in store for us today. Two days ago, he taught us about ancient execution styles for traitors, and three students ran out of class and puked in the hall. Professor Cullen seemed to find that very satisfying.

"Quiet," he ordered, and the room was immediately silent. "Today, we are going to work on our essays. Three thousand words on whether you believe it is right that dragons are concealed from the public."

The class groaned like they were one entity. Except for me and Han. I shared almost every class with the guy, and had so far managed to avoid any more run-ins with him. He sat at the back, brooding like some dark, poisonous cloud. I could feel his eyes boring into the back of my neck. At least Hana was in this class as well, though focusing on the teacher and not the way her hair fell past her face as she leaned over her desk was difficult.

"Now, now, this is a gift," Professor Cullen drawled. "I'm giving you an entire lesson to get a head start on your essay, worth sixty per cent of your grade. I could always get back to executions. There was much more to say, but I ran out of time."

There was a cacophony of rustling papers as everyone started flipping through their textbooks and opening their notebooks.

"Didn't think so," he smirked.

Professor Cullen started to pace the room, so I followed the rest of the class and pulled out my textbook and started to scribble thoughts down in my notebook. The last thing I needed was to get on the wrong side of Professor Sullen, as Artie called him. Last week he gave a girl detention, but instead of writing lines or scrubbing off the boards, she had to clean out the muck from the dragon stables. Every single one of them. I shuddered at the thought.

I just had to make it through the day, and I would be home free. Literally. I had been at the Academy for long enough that I could spend this weekend at home. I had learned the reason we weren't allowed to visit home for the first month was a simple one – we couldn't leave our dragons any earlier. The connection was too fragile.

I didn't want to go, and for that, I felt guilty. But how was I supposed to leave Merry behind? She was huge now. Bigger than a hatchback. I was told dragons grew fast, but this was insane. I had no idea just how big she would end up being.

I tried to focus on the notebook in front of me as Professor Cullen drew nearer to my desk.

Mum had already sent me a dozen messages in preparation for my return this weekend. She was cooking her roast, and she had washed my sheets and tidied my room, and Grandpa had even washed the dog. I kept reminding her that I wasn't a guest, and my room could be left alone, but I knew this past month had been hard on her. I'd had plenty of things to occupy me, but it wasn't the same for her. There was a gaping hole in her life where I used to be. I was trying to be considerate of that but leaving Merry behind for two entire days had me nervous.

"Is anyone supposed to be able to actually *read* your handwriting, Mister Birtwistle?" Professor Cullen leaned over Artie's desk. "Or is this the ancient language of chicken scratch? I'm afraid I'm not familiar with it. Perhaps you'd be kind enough to teach it to me on your lunch breaks so I can decipher your essay when the time comes to submit it."

"Sorry, Professor," Artie mumbled.

Professor Cullen straightened and I could see his face snap towards me out of the corner of my eye. I shifted in my seat and kept writing as he approached me. He stopped at my desk. I kept my focus on my book, scrawling what I hoped was an intelligent sentence about the dangers modern day society posed on dragon-kind. Professor Cullen suddenly cleared his throat. I looked up at him, racking my brain for anything I had done wrong.

Please don't let him make me clean the dragon stables, I prayed silently.

"Is there something wrong, Professor?" I asked quietly.

"Finch." He elongated my name, chewing on it. "I have decided you will replace Magdelene Aisling as Flag Bearer for Sylva's Equitem team."

I blinked. A full thirty seconds passed, and I still hadn't spoken.

"Did you wake up without the ability to speak English, Angus? Should I try Latin? *Potesne me intelligere?*"

"Sorry, Professor Cullen," I said when I could finally connect my brain to my mouth. "Me? I have never flown a dragon. I don't even know the rules."

"Believe me, Angus, you were not my first choice, but needs must. Everyone else lacks the stomach for such a role. We need a

Flag Bearer, and you are the right size, and quick on your feet. I have watched you and your dragon. You will do fine. Find me Monday morning."

My mouth popped open to speak, but Professor Cullen walked away. This was *not* good. I couldn't play sports. The only time I ran was to run *away*. I had never flown a dragon, and I didn't even know the rules to this game. I spent the rest of the class trying not to hyperventilate.

When class finally ended and everyone filed out into the hall, I approached Professor Cullen slowly, like I was walking to the gallows. Me? On the Equitem team? Didn't Artie say their last Flag Bearer quit after breaking both of their legs?

"Professor Cullen?" I squeaked.

Professor Cullen looked up from his desk. "Finch?"

"I was wondering if I could talk to you about this whole Flag Bearer thing. See, I don't think I'm the right choice. I don't know the game at all. I'm afraid I'd only let the team down. I've never really played sports before."

"I'm afraid it is out of both of our hands. You are the new Flag Bearer, whether we like it or not," he replied flatly.

"What do you mean?"

"The headmaster seems to think you are the perfect fit for the role. My complaints were as unheeded as yours are now, I'm afraid."

"Spectre is making me be Flag Bearer? Like…as a joke?"

"A cosmic one, it seems." Professor Cullen picked up his books and headed for the door. "Sylva has lost the Equitem Cup for the last seventeen years. That is going to change. Monday morning, Finch. The Equitem field. I will train you myself."

I followed him out the door, dragging my feet. If a talented player who knew what in the world Equitem even *was* broke both their legs, then I was going to break my entire body.

"So, Flag Bearer." Hana was waiting for me just outside the door. "Quite the responsibility."

"I think I might die," I replied.

"The school healer is pretty good. I'm sure you'll be okay."

"That's very comforting."

"I think you'll like it. The Flag Bearer is an important role."

"Then why doesn't anyone else want it?"

"Well," Hana shrugged, "it's also the most dangerous. But don't worry. You'll be fine. Sylva needs someone to drag them from the bottom. Everyone's afraid to be the person that makes or breaks the team."

"Lucky me." I needed a change of subject before I puked. "Big plans for the weekend?"

"Oh, yeah. Huge."

"Really?" I asked.

"No," she laughed. "Same as usual. Not like I can go anywhere for the weekend."

"Yeah, I guess. Where are your parents?" I asked.

She was silent, and I immediately regretted asking.

"Sorry, I didn't mean…"

"It's fine. It's just that I don't know who my parents are," she said quietly.

"I'm sorry," I said quietly.

As we walked slowly down the hall, I wanted to say something, anything, that would make it better. But there was nothing I could say that would make it better, and no one knew that better than me.

"I've never met my father," I said, almost without thinking.

"Really?"

"Yeah, he left before I was born. He and my mother were never married or anything. I guess it was just one of those boy-meets-girl things, you know? But then, surprise – a kid. Wasn't what he had in mind."

"What's your mother like?" Hana asked. Her big blue eyes searched my face, and I had trouble concentrating.

"Uh, she's great. She's a nurse. She works too hard, and worries too much, but that's pretty standard for a single mum, I guess. I'm going home this weekend."

"You must be looking forward to it."

"Not really, actually. I don't really want to leave Merry. I'm not really sure how to slip back into normal life."

"I'll look out for her. Don't worry."

I smiled. "Thank you. That would be great."

"Angus!" Spectre's voice cut through the crowd. I turned to see him usher me towards him.

"I guess I gotta go," I said reluctantly. "I think I have to kill the headmaster."

Hana laughed. "Sure, yeah. I'll see you when you get back."

I lingered, not wanting to go, but the moment grew more awkward as Spectre waited impatiently for me. I chuckled and nodded. "Okay, bye."

As I headed towards Spectre, I couldn't help but notice how being a Vector with a miraculous gift was really getting in the way of being a teenager.

"You called?" I said unenthusiastically.

"Why the long face?" he asked.

"I'm plotting how best to kill you, and get away with it."

"Ah. Very tricky. Difficult to avoid the Demeres."

"What are those?"

"Truth-seeing judges. Tiny eyes, hooded faces, claw fingers."

Spectre shuddered. "Now, what have I done to warrant my immanent demise?"

"You volunteered me as Flag Bearer!"

He beamed. "Lucky little ducky! That was my position, too."

"Lucky?" I scoffed. "There are tortoises that have better athletic prowess than I do!"

"Pish-posh," Spectre said, waving his hand away and heading down the hallway. I followed him.

"But-"

"It's going to be fantastic. Sylva needs a leg up, and you're going to be brilliant."

"You can't be sure of that!"

"I told you Angus, I'm always sure."

I groaned. "But-"

"What's done is done, dear boy." Spectre stopped and faced me. He looked down at me from on high. "Can you not trust that though *you* don't know the game of Equitem, I do. And I think that you are the right person for the role. *I* believe in you. Isn't that enough?"

Words died on my tongue.

His eyes were earnest, his face sincere.

He believed in me.

And it *was* enough. Now, instead of being sickeningly terrified of being the Flag Bearer, I wanted more than anything to prove I could do it.

"Okay. I'll do it."

"Excellent. Now, come with me. We have something much more exciting to do."

baby steps

I was going to learn to fly.

Spectre had led me outside and I had followed dutifully, as I was getting quite used to doing. Merry was already there, waiting for me.

I ran my hands over her rough scales, and she pushed her cheek into my hand.

"She's big enough?" I asked.

"She certainly is. It's time for you to learn to fly, Angus," Spectre announced.

"Really?" I asked, childish excitement bubbling out of me. I had been waiting for this day impatiently, but Merry hadn't been ready. "Wicked."

Pilar lumbered up beside Spectre and with a movement that should have been impossible for a man his age, Spectre alighted atop Pilar and waited for me to do the same.

"What, like here? *Now?* In the middle of the courtyard?" I looked around, suddenly very aware that there were countless other students wandering around, relishing their Friday afternoon.

Spectre just stared back at me expectantly.

"I guess so," I said quietly. I approached Merry, not sure how to climb up onto her back. "No reins, or saddle?"

"It's not a horse, Angus," Spectre chided.

"Right. Of course. It's just a magical flying beast with a thirty foot wingspan." I petted Merry's head soothingly before stepping up onto her knee and crawling, in the most awkward and cumbersome way possible, until I was lying on her back, like a moron. I scrambled myself into a sitting position and looked for something to hang on to. Surely, I would get better at this.

Spectre was kind enough not to laugh.

I tried to focus. I ran my hands along her neck, and my fingers gripped into a divot in her neck. I felt along the other side of her neck and found a matching indent. "What are these, grips?" I asked.

"Something like that," Spectre advised. "Hold on."

Pilar alighted into the air with surprising agility. He seemed weightless, his enormous wings gently rising and falling, sending gusts of wind out across the courtyard.

As he lifted further into the air, Merry looked up at him and cocked her head to the side. I could tell she wanted to follow. "Let's go," I encouraged. "Slowly. Come on."

I realised she wasn't listening to me when she bolted off into the air with incredible speed. I held on as tightly as I could, but I was going to fall. I screamed in what I hoped was a manly, not-completely-embarrassing way.

Pilar squawked, and suddenly she slowed down and straightened up. Breathless, I took the opportunity to get a better grip. Pilar had come in beside us, and he was making strange clicking sounds, jerking his head in different directions. Merry responded in kind.

"What are they doing?" I called to Spectre.

"Communicating," he called back. "She's been flying a lot, as you know, but never with a Vector. He's teaching her how to fly with you on her back."

I watched their interaction with new fascination as Pilar talked and Merry listened.

"Angus!" Spectre shouted. "Look around! You're flying."

I had been so enthralled by them, that I almost missed it. The view before me was expansive; hills, and mountains and forests stretched out over the landscape like a crumpled bed sheet. We were high – high enough that my stomach flip-flopped when I looked down. The Academy was far below us, the turrets of its castle-like structure reaching up like fingers trying to pluck us out of the air.

I was dreaming. I had to be dreaming.

And if this was a dream, I hoped I stayed asleep forever.

a step out of time

My farewell to Merry had been brief, since the Smith brothers were waiting for me. I hurried down the steps with my weekend bag in hand, and paused a moment when I saw Mister Smith standing beside the back door of the car. "No drinks this time, right?"

Mister Smith just opened the door without a word.

I slipped inside, throwing my bag across the seat. The other Mister Smith was in the driver's seat.

"Only two of you today?" I asked. "Where's the other one?"

"Do you require three escorts home, Mister Finch?" Mister Smith asked. "Is there something to be concerned about?"

"Only if you're late. My mum isn't exactly patient."

The other Mister Smith slipped into the front passenger side, and we were moving before the door closed. We drove past the front entrance, and around the looped driveway and over the long bridge that lead towards an ever expanding view of rolling hills and snow-capped mountains. Everything looked pretty normal, so far.

But that didn't last long. As we passed over the bridge, I noticed tall, front gates that I'd never seen before. I guessed I was still unconscious at this point last time. Mister Smith pulled up in front of the gate and parked the car.

"Out," he instructed. The other Mister Smith followed.

"What are we doing?" I asked, quickly stepping out of the car. The Mister Smiths were just standing at the gate, staring out across the grounds. As I came up beside them, I realised they they were actually staring at themselves in a huge mirror as big as a dragon.

"What is this?" I asked, reaching out to touch my reflection. Spectre appeared beside me, like a puff of smoke.

"I have something for you, my boy," he said, opening his hand to me.

I looked down. Sitting on top of his palm was an old, tarnished looking pocket watch. "What is this?" I asked.

"This is your way home," he replied. "Every student is given one of these when they choose to embrace the life of a Vector. It is what connects you to this place."

"How?" I asked.

"A very long time ago, before I was even born - and that's saying something - an old inventor created these. They say he was the first Vector to ever Blink. He built these pocket watches as a portal to this Academy, to keep it safe."

"What about the other Academies?"

"They each have their own pocket watches, created for their Academy by this one incredible inventor."

"What was his name?" I asked.

"Nobody knows," Spectre shrugged.

"So, what do I do?" I asked.

"As you already know, this Academy exists on another plane. That is made possible by us existing just a step out of time."

"This sounds like something out of *Doctor Who*." I looked at the mirror and regarded my reflection curiously. Something seemed off about it.

"These pocket watches are called Dragon Dials. They allow you to slip between a crack. A crack in a reflection, made possible by a slip in time."

"That's…"

"Genius?" he concluded.

"Impossible, actually. Impossible is what I was going to say."

"Well, why don't you find out?"

"What do I do?"

"Open it, and press the dial."

I turned the old pocket watch around in my hands, inspecting it from every angle. It was brass, in need of a polish. There was some sort of intricate pattern on it, like leaves or filigree or something. I popped it open. The crystal was smooth and clear. There was no face, just the brass mechanisms ticking away, safe behind the crystal. A single second hand ticked along slowly; something didn't seem right. It was like it was slightly longer than a second.

I pressed the dial and waited for something to happen, but nothing did.

"What now?" I asked.

"The pocket watch creates a split in time, which is only accessible by a reflection."

"Why a reflection?"

"The mirror reflects your world in reverse. A very real world, just a step out of time. The pocket watch puts *you* a step out of time, as well, matching the world you wish to enter, creating compatibility. Watch."

The Mister Smith's stepped into the mirror and disappeared inside it. I stared, mouth agape, unsure what I had just seen.

"Where did they go?" I asked.

"Follow them and find out," he instructed. "They will accompany you home today, and collect you Sunday. After that, you will do it alone."

I stepped up to the mirror slowly and lifted my hand to touch the glass. Instead of my fingers hitting cool glass, they fell straight through, disappearing somewhere behind it.

"What the…" I mumbled to myself.

"See you when you return, Angus," Spectre said with a smile.

With one last look at Spectre, I lifted my foot and took a step into the mirror. When my leg disappeared, the rest of my body followed.

My body was cold, and everything was dark, until light filled my vision. I blinked against the brightness and when my eyes adjusted, I found I was standing outside of my house, right in front of a window. My reflection stared back at me. I looked down at my hands and saw the pocket watch. The second hand was frozen in time. I slipped it into my pocket.

The Mister Smith's stood like sentinels next to my front steps.

"Am I ever going to get used to this?" I asked.

Their silence wasn't exactly encouraging. I rolled my eyes and walked past them to my front door. "See you on Sunday, gents."

home

It felt strange to finally be home. Mum almost broke my spine with the bone-crushing hug she gave me when I walked in the door.

Grandpa was wary at first, as if I was going to come back a completely unrecognizable person who didn't love him anymore. I hugged him tightly, and he seemed to relax a little.

"You could stand to call a bit more," Mum said as I opened the fridge to rummage through whatever I could find in there.

"Sorry, Mum," I said, guilty. "It's been pretty busy. I have a lot of homework."

"What's it like?" she asked.

"It's…" I searched for the right word. "It's fantastic, actually. It's nothing like I thought it was going to be. But it's great."

"And are you making friends?"

"Yeah. My roommate is pretty cool," I shrugged.

"Is that all I get?" she pressed.

"What else do you want to know?" I asked pulling out a container of leftovers. I snapped open then lid and started chomping down food like I hadn't eaten in a millennium.

"Are they not feeding you?" she asked.

"I just missed your cooking," I said, laughing through a mouthful of pasta.

"Yeah, right." She flicked on the kettle and pulled out three mugs. "It's good to have you home." Her voice was quiet, almost drowned out by the bubbling kettle.

I couldn't really imagine what it was like to have your only son disappear for a month, to a brand-new school, with barely a word from him. But from the look on her face, I could tell it mustn't have felt good. She seemed upset and relieved all at once.

I put down the container and wrapped my arms around her again. "Love you, Mum."

I spent the evening with them, watching Mum's favourite shows, and telling them everything I could about Everwood. Grandpa seemed uncomfortable with the conversation, but Mum wanted to know every last detail, right down to the colour of paint on my classroom walls.

By the time she let me leave the room without following, it was late. I fell into bed, surprised at how unusual I felt being at home. It was like I was a different person now. Even though I had only been gone a month, I felt a little out of place and kind of uncomfortable, as if I was shoving my feet into shoes that didn't quite fit anymore.

I guess that's what people always talk about when they say you can't go home. Once you've left, you're changed, and the people you left behind haven't changed in the same ways. They've changed in different ways, and what used to be like puzzle pieces fitting together now don't fit quite as well. Maybe you couldn't ever go back.

I kicked my shoes off and let them flop on the floor. Roger was curled at the end of my bed, and it provided a small comfort, since Merry was far away. I closed my eyes and remembered the view from high up in the sky. Was there a better feeling than that? I wasn't so sure.

My phone buzzed silently in my pocket, and I dragged it up to my face with a heavy hand. When I saw who had texted me, I dropped the phone on my face, then scrambled to sit up properly, almost falling off the bed in the process. I stared at my phone for an entire minute, just relishing the feeling of her name popping up on my screen. *Hana.* She had reached out to me. She wanted to talk to me. Whatever she was doing right now, my name had popped into her mind, and she had texted me.

I shook myself free of my teen dream moment and opened the message. There was a picture of Merry, curled up next to Jeju, Hana's dragon. They seemed content together.

She's happy. Don't worry. I'm taking good care of her. Focus on your mum. I'm sure she misses you.

While I was delighted she had messaged me, it, obviously, presented an entirely new issue. What would I say in response? Should I even reply? I checked the time. It was 10:30. I had to think of something quickly.

I typed four or five different responses but kept erasing them.

I finally settled for the bravest of all actions. I called her. Despite it being incredibly unfashionable to actually speak to people these days, I did it.

Mostly because I accidentally hit the call button and didn't want her to have a missed call appear on her screen.

"Hello?" she answered.

"Hi," I said, a little too loudly. "Hello."

"Hello," she said again, breathing a laugh.

"How… how's it going?"

"Good," she answered. "How is it at home?"

"Weird, actually," I answered honestly. "Feels kind of different."

"It was like that for me when I first went back to Korea."

"Why did you leave?" I asked.

"Spectre came and found us there. He heard about our gifts, and he offered us a place at Everwood. The Academy in Korea is amazing, but Spectre has experience with Han's particular ability. We were young when our gifts manifested. The youngest Spectre has ever seen. So we've been here most of our lives."

"Any idea why he hates me so much?" I asked.

"He doesn't hate you, he's just… quiet."

"Yeah, well, he quietly hates my guts."

"Han is okay," she said gently. "He's just focused."

"Focused? He seems a little aggressive. Artie said his dragon's aggressive too."

"Jia isn't aggressive. She's just…"

"Focused?" I interrupted jokingly.

Hana gave a small laugh. "Yeah."

"Jia? That's his dragon? Interesting name."

"It means beautiful in Korean."

"He's Korean, too?"

"Yeah," she smiled a small knowing smile. "He's my brother."

"Wait, what?" I felt like a deflated balloon left over after a children's party.

Hana laughed. "If he finds out you're on the phone to me, he'll hate you even more."

"I guess he doesn't approve, then, hey?"

"Of what?" Hana asked.

Things were suddenly quiet and tense. I was internally kicking myself for saying something so offhand. Approve of what? There was nothing to approve. I hadn't even told her I liked her, and I was acting like as if we had some sort of special thing going on.

"Of… of us being… you know… friends," I stuttered.

"Oh," Hana's voice sounded strange. "Probably not."

"We're being rebels then, right? We can be…"

"Friends?" she finished.

Had I just accidentally friend-zoned myself? "Yeah."

"Sure," she replied.

This was going badly.

"It's late," Hana said. "I should go."

"Right," I said, deflated. "Of course.

"Okay."

How was I letting this happen? I just basically told her I only wanted to be friends. What was wrong with me?

"Wait!"

The word slipped out of my mouth, before I realised I said it.

"What is it?" she asked.

"Um, what I said before about being friends…"

"Yeah?"

"I guess your brother would hate it even more if we were… more than friends." I needed to find a very large hole and bury myself in it.

Hana was silent.

How did I keep making it worse? I shot up out of bed, feeling like a right moron. I slapped my palm against my head and waited breathlessly for her to respond. I opened my curtains. Maybe there was a sniper on the neighbour's roof ready to put me out of my misery.

"He's my brother," she answered, "not my father. He doesn't have to like everything I do."

My hand fell down to my side. I stared at the wall opposite me, my mouth hanging open. I realised much too late she needed a response. "Right," I answered dumbly. "Cool. Yeah."

"Goodnight, Angus," she said.

"Night," I answered. I hung up the phone and raked my hands through my hair like a maniac. Flinging my arms out to the side, I fell into my bed, grateful I had accidentally pressed the call button.

surprise visit

I didn't get out of bed until 10am, and frankly I was surprised Mum hadn't barged in and woken me up to go shopping with her or bake cookies, or do something equally as suffocating.

I hoped she would be calmer today, less panicked about time passing and me living somewhere else now.

When I thudded down the stairs, sleep still beckoning me back to bed, I saw a pancake breakfast waiting on the table and decided she was probably not going to be more relaxed today.

"There you are," she huffed. "You sleep like the dead."

"Well, I'm a growing boy," I answered sardonically.

"A little more every day," she said wistfully.

I tried not to roll my eyes. "What's all this?'

"I just thought you might like a nice big breakfast." She shrugged. "What? Don't act like I've never done this before."

"You know I've gone to school in the country, not been adopted out, right? Or shipped off to war?"

"Shut up," she snipped.

I walked over and kissed her cheek before I sat at the table to devour my weight in pancakes. Anything less would be an insult.

"Have you seen James yet?"

I turned around to see Grandpa walk in. He was looking older today, like life had been zapped out of him while he slept.

"Like Uncle James?" I shook my head. "No. Why would I?"

"I told you. He went to that school you're at." He dragged the chair out from under the table. It scraped along the floor. He sat down slowly, uncomfortably.

"Sorry, Grandpa," I shook my head. "I haven't seen him. Have you heard from him lately?"

"Of course not," he said, with a wave of his hand.

"Have you called him?" I asked.

"I gave up calling him years ago," he grumbled.

Guilt pierced my stomach. I hoped that would never be my story.

The day passed restlessly. It was hard to spend a normal weekend at home when I knew a dragon was waiting for me back at Everwood. With last night's conversation with Hana, I was quietly hopeful that maybe, just maybe, I hadn't completely munted my chances with her.

I felt like there were ants in my veins, so I offered to pick up Indian food from the local restaurant for dinner. I could use the walk.

It was cool and crisp, and the air was clear. I walked slowly, not in any hurry to be back inside the walls of my house. I didn't like that I was so eager to leave. Maybe I was becoming just like Uncle James. Would I abandon Mum and Grandpa, too?

I shook my head free of the thought. No. I couldn't ever do something like that. Mum had sacrificed everything to raise me. I wouldn't turn my back on her the way James had done.

"Angus."

The voice behind me caught me off guard. I stopped and turned to see who had called me, but there was no one there.

Had I imagined it?

I turned back around slowly, but the voice called again.

"Okay," I said to myself. "I'm going crazy. Excellent."

The voice was eerily familiar. Why did I recognise it? I looked around, but there was no one around. I kept walking, faster now.

"Angus! Listen to me!"

I stopped dead in my tracks. I realised where I knew the voice from. The phone call at the Academy. That same voice told me that I couldn't trust Spectre.

"Who are you?" I said into the air.

"Angus!" The voice shouted, eager and forceful.

To my right there was an alley. I ran into it and pressed myself up against the wall. What was happening to me?

I leaned my head back and tried to calm down. I closed my eyes.

"Angus." The voice was quieter now. Softer.

I opened my eyes. A man stood in front of me, dressed all in black. He was tall and solid. His dark hair was cropped short, and his eyes were dark brown, like mine.

"Who are you?" I asked.

"That's a complicated question," he answered.

"How do you know who I am?"

"I've always known who you are. But that's not why I'm here."

"What do you want?"

"To talk," he answered simply.

"About what?" I looked to my left and right, trying to find the best direction to run. He took a step closer, towering over me. I straightened. "Who are you? Tell me."

"You know who I am," he replied.

My breath quickened in my lungs. I had to get out of here. I lifted my hands and shoved against his chest, only… I didn't. My hands fell straight through him as if he was a ghost. I fell forward, the momentum sending me to the ground. I scrambled back from him. "What the hell are you?"

"Think, Angus. Think," he spat.

Who was he? What did he want with me? I tried to make it all make sense in my mind. He was the same voice that had called me at the Academy. That meant he knew about Everwood, about the dragons.

Spectre hadn't mentioned him.

"I don't know. I don't know who you are."

He shook his head and took another step closer to me. His face was dark and sombre. The words he said would change my life forever.

All of time and space came to a sudden halt. My breath was loud in my ears.

"Angus," he said, his voice shaking. "I'm your father."

who's your daddy?

After taking approximately thirty seconds to process this tidbit of information, I responded with an emotion that surprised even me.

Anger.

Blood boiling, muscle cramping, skin splitting *anger*.

I got to my feet in one swift motion, all fear dissipating.

"Excuse me?" I hissed.

"I'm your father, Angus."

"Nice of you to show up after all these years."

"Angus-"

"No. No, save it. I have spent years of my life wondering what I would say to you if you ever showed up. Now that you're here, all I want to say is one thing."

"What's that?" he asked.

I set my jaw into a hard line, fury raging through my body. My blood was rushing through my body so fast I could hear it like waves crashing against the shore. "Get away from me."

My father took a step back, as if I had physically assaulted him.

"Did you really think you could just show up after all these years and expect a hug? You *abandoned* me. You abandoned *my mother*."

"Angus, you have to understand."

"No, actually, I don't." I scoffed and started to walk away. I had imagined meeting my father hundreds of times, but I never, in all of my wildest scenarios, imagined I'd respond like this. But the anger was so real, so raw and deep, that I couldn't bring myself to say anything else.

I wanted to ask him questions. I wanted to know who he was, and what he was doing, and why he had waited so long to come into my life. But the words couldn't make it from my mind to my mouth. All that bubbled out of me was rage.

"I know you're angry," he called after me. "But this is more important than that."

I spun around and stomped back towards him. "More important? More important? How can you say that? My entire life, I've wanted to know who you are. Why you left us. There's been a gaping hole where you should have been! Now you appear out of nowhere and think that whatever you've got going on is more important than that?" I shook my head in disgust. "I'm leaving."

I turned around to leave, only to come face to face with my father once again. I jumped back. How had he done that? I paused, remembering that just moments ago I had fallen straight through his body. The fact that he was my father had overshadowed that tiny detail until now.

"How are you doing that?" I asked. "What are you?"

"I'm not really here," he said, almost reluctantly, like he was embarrassed.

"You can ghost," I said, without thinking.

"Yes."

"So, you couldn't be bothered sending the original to see your son for the first time? I get a copy?"

"Please just listen to me, Angus. Things are coming for you."

"You called me at the Academy, didn't you?"

He nodded. "And I warned you they were coming. On the street that day."

I froze. My mind drifted back to that day on the street, when I bumped into a stranger who told me they were coming for me that night. I knew the voice was the same as the one who called me, but the reality hit me harder than I expected. It was my father. He found me on the street that day. If I hadn't been so dizzy from knocking my head, I would have seen him. My father. For the first time.

"Look, Angus, I never meant for you to get caught in the middle of this. I know…" he groaned, and rubbed his face, frustrated. "I know none of this makes sense, and I know you want answers. But I can't give them all to you. Not now. Not here."

"Then why did you come?" I asked.

"I need you to be prepared." His voice was low. He leaned in close. "You have no idea what is coming."

"And you do?" I asked.

"Angus, this is serious. It's dangerous. Your life is in danger, your entire world is in danger. Your mother, your grandfather. Everything you've ever known and loved. You don't know what's at stake."

"So, tell me."

"I wish I could, Angus."

"You know what that sounds like? It sounds like control, and manipulation. And lies. You don't care about me. You never have."

"That's not true, Angus. I…" he hesitated, his mouth caught between his head and his heart. "I love you. You're my son. I... I love you. I always have."

I wanted to be tougher than I was, but his words made me pause. I couldn't respond. What was I supposed to say? I had wanted to hear those words for my entire life.

"You don't know the whole story, kid. I know it seems like it's black and white, but maybe it's not. Maybe there's more to it. You can't trust what Spectre tells you."

That was enough to make me pull away. "Don't."

"Angus, just please. Don't tell anyone about your gift."

My stomach dropped. How did he know I could Blink? Who was my father *really*?

"I have to go. Don't tell anyone you saw me. Just please try to trust me, okay? Trust me on this one thing. Get ready, kid. It's coming."

And with that, he was gone.

secrets

I was relieved to arrive back at the Academy. I had said goodbye to a teary Mum and a stiff-upper-lip grandfather at lunch time on Sunday and arrived back at the Academy within the Blink of an eye. I was going to like this kind of travel.

My first stop was to see Merry. I marched across the courtyard, still shaken and angry from seeing my father and pretending for the rest of the weekend like I hadn't. Following the snaking path that led to the stables, I stomped each step like I was squashing my father's face with every footfall.

Merry's stable was the closest since she was smaller than the more developed dragons. She must have heard me coming, because she was waiting for me at the gate, her long tail flailing in the air.

It was funny how complete I suddenly felt. Like a missing piece of me had slotted back into place. She stretched her head towards me and pressed her head against mine. I lingered there, listening to her gentle breathing, and tried to forget the encounter that had plagued me.

I hadn't dared mention to Mum that I had seen him. I didn't want to tell anyone. I was struggling to process what had happened and right now, all I wanted to do was forget about it.

"How was your visit home?"

I turned around to see Hana standing there, with Jeju beside her.

"It was great," I lied.

"Then why do you look like that?" she asked.

"Like what?" I asked.

"Like someone just ran over your dog."

I scoffed a laugh and opened Merry's gate. "Just tired, I guess. Thanks for watching out for her." I opened the gate and Merry lumbered out of her stable.

"She was pretty low maintenance." Hana smiled, and I was struck dumb.

What was it about this girl that tangled me up so much?

"We…uh…we were…" I needed to get my head examined. It was just a smile. Everyone had one. "We were just gonna get some fresh air. You want to join?"

"Sure," she shrugged.

Just as we were about to leave, Spectre appeared beside us.

"Angus, how marvelous to see you have returned," he said happily.

Why did he always show up at the worst possible time?

"Yep, I'm back. We were just going to go-"

"Was your time at home pleasant?" he asked, interrupting.

"Yeah, it was fine."

"I'll meet you out there," Hana said, leading Jeju out of the stables.

I sighed, hoping Spectre hadn't just ruined my afternoon with Hana.

"Angus," Spectre said, oblivious to my internal teenage angst.

"What is it?" I asked.

"Is there anything you need to tell me?"

"About what?" I asked, my face growing hot.

"About your time at home?" Spectre's inquisitive eyes held my stare. I had to look away.

"No," I said. "Everything was fine."

Spectre smiled a small, tight small. Did he look… sad? "Very well. Hana is waiting. I won't keep you any longer."

He vanished into smoke, just as my father had done.

I felt guilt eat at the base of my spine. I didn't know why I didn't tell Spectre about meeting my father. Spectre had been good to me. He had cared about me, and spent countless hours teaching me, helping me to understand this new world I was a part of.

Maybe part of me was worried that if I told him, he wouldn't trust me anymore. My father could ghost, and he knew about the Academy. That must mean he was a Vector, too, but something told me he wasn't someone Spectre would like me talking to.

If there was bad blood between my father and Everwood, or worse, between my father and Spectre, I didn't want to get caught in the middle, or have Spectre think I wasn't someone he could rely on.

I didn't think I could handle it if Spectre abandoned me, too.

equitem

Monday morning brought a dread with it that had me hesitate getting out of bed. Meeting Professor Cullen on the Equitem field was something I had managed to forget about until last night when I was trying to sleep.

Now that I could fly Merry, there was no reason I couldn't join the Equitem team as their Flag Bearer.

It was drizzling and cold, with dark heavy clouds that looked as grumpy as I felt. My feet bore my weight reluctantly all the way to the field. I could see Professor Cullen standing in the middle of the field with two dragons and I moaned. I had hoped that failing to bring Merry today would guarantee this would be a purely theoretical meeting. But Cullen had beaten me to that, and Merry stood proudly beside him. His gigantic blue dragon was waiting on his other side.

I began my slow descent down the stairs towards the field, which had been dug deep into the earth, with stadium seating all around it, so that it was essentially two storeys underground. It was no ordinary field, either. It was about the size of a typical football field, but instead of being plain grass, there were trees, ditches, mounds of dirt, poles, and sludges of watery mud.

I had only heard a few things about Equitem so far, and none of them made me think I would be a natural. The first match was next week, with Terra playing Oceanus.

"Good morning, Angus," Cullen droned, already sounding bored.

"Good morning, Professor."

"You'll be pleased to note I took the liberty of collecting Merry from her stable."

"I can see that."

"I wouldn't want you to have forgotten her. I know how difficult it is for teenagers to function before noon on a Monday."

"Appreciate it."

"Mount your dragon."

"Whoa," I held up my hands defensively. "Aren't we going to go over the rules? I don't know how to play."

"The best way to learn is to do, Finch."

"Great," I sighed. I approached Merry and rubbed her snout before I crawled up onto her back. I was slightly less embarrassing than the first time I had tried, but since I was in front of the formidable Professor Cullen, it was mortifying anyway.

"What a privilege to witness such athleticism," he purred.

"I'm still getting the hang of it. Your dragon is pretty." Changing the subject seemed like the safest way to hide how red my face was going.

"This is Sonnet," Professor Cullen said, introducing his dragon. "She will bite your face off if you touch her."

"Good to know," I murmured.

"Oh, relax, Finch. Teachers have a sense of humor, too."

I breathed out the breath I didn't realise I was holding.

She was pretty, though. A beautiful metallic blue, that flickered in the sunlight like every scale was alive. There was a leather sheath strapped around her, and I wondered what it was for.

"Let's go."

He took off into the air with shocking speed. Merry soon followed. We hovered above the field, level with the top row of seats.

"You will begin flying lessons now that Merry is large enough to bear your weight. They'll be starting this week. Use them as a practice. In addition, you will have practice with the team three times a week."

"Okay."

"Equitem is the oldest game for our kind. Academies have been playing it since the first Academy opened its doors. Every two years is the Equitemis. A battle between the top teams from *all* dragon academies. Sylva has won the Equitemis three times." He paused. "Two hundred years ago."

"Oh."

"As you can imagine, our recent slump is an embarrassment to the name of Sylva. I want to win, Angus. And you're going to help me."

There was something so fierce in his eyes, something so much like longing that I couldn't help it. I wanted to win, too.

"I'll do what I can, Professor."

"I know you will," Cullen replied. "Equitem is part jousting, part obstacle course and part capture the flag. I am sure you are familiar with all of these from your previous life."

"Yeah. Sure."

"There are seven members on each team. The Flag Bearers are responsible for using these…" Cullen reached down and pulled a long, thick wooden pole with a hook at the end from the sheath strapped to his dragon.

"This is your lance. It is with this that you, Angus, will take the flag from your opposing Flag Bearer. Once you do, you must return to your base through a series of obstacles. The other team's Flag Bearer will be chasing you down. It's not over until your team manages to hang the flag back at your team's base."

"What does everyone else do?" I ask.

"While the Flag Bearers battle, the rest of the team must compete for points, first with a race to those mountains…" he pointed to a snow-covered mountain in the distance, "… then back to the obstacle course where they will defend you. There are five tokens for them to collect along this journey, each worth 100 points. If a token is missed on the first attempt to collect it, the token is void. Their job is to help you fend off the other team and so you can safely make it through the obstacle course and back to your base, where you will end the game."

"First to hang the flag wins?" I ask.

"Not necessarily. Hanging the flag ends the game and grants the Flag Bearer 300 points. If you have missed your previous tokens, and the others have not, they still stand a chance at winning."

"Where is the flag? How do I get it off them?" I ask.

The way Cullen smiled at me had me wishing I never asked. "You are the Flag *Bearer*, Finch. Where do you think it is? Let's practice. Follow me."

It turns out, the flag is clipped to my back, like a cape. I would literally have to *wear* the flag that a staff wielding jock was going to try to rip off me from a hundred feet in the air on the back of a dragon.

Cool.

This was fine.

I wouldn't die.

Probably.

The Oceanus Flag Bearer collided with the Terra's, and she fell off the back of her dragon, plummeting towards the ground fifty feet below her.

No.

This was not fine.

I was definitely going to die.

This was Equitem? No. What had I gotten myself into?

The Flag Bearer's orange dragon dropped like a bowling ball to catch her. I held my breath until it caught her and carried her back up

I sat in the stands watching Terra verse Oceanus, reflecting on my training sessions, first with Cullen, and then with the rest of the team. I was getting better, but it had only been a week and there was definitely no way I was ready to be flung off the back of my dragon.

I was sitting with the rest of my team, and they were cheering wildly, like ancient Romans in the Coliseum. The Captain of the team was Orson Bickerstaff. He was a burly eighteen-year-old with shaved hair and a dragon double the size of Merry. Then there was Varian Grantham, Thiago Haywood, Odette Sweetenham, Beatrix Nettle and Hopper Finkley. I was glad to know I wasn't the only new member to the team. Professor Cullen had hand-picked each of them for this year, except Beatrix and Hopper, who were both seasoned players.

Artie and Hana came and sat beside me. Artie had a big box of popcorn and a wooden mug of hot chocolate.

"Are you sure you can do this, without, you know, dying?" he asked through a mouthful.

"I guess we'll find out."

Hana handed me an extra mug of hot chocolate. "Spectre wouldn't have picked you if he didn't believe you could do it. And Professor Cullen seems almost happy lately. He let a girl out of detention in Politics yesterday. She was even crying, and that usually makes him double the punishment."

"You think he's happy because of *me*?" I asked, unable to believe that I was anything other than a constant disappointment to him.

"He's happy with this year's team. I know he is. I heard him talking to Spectre in the hall."

That filled me with a little encouragement. I looked back to the game to see a one of the players collide with a tree.

"I'm going to be sick."

in-flight entertainment

Once you got the hang of it, flying wasn't so hard.

Flying through a natural airborne obstacle course, on the other hand, was. This was going to be good training for Equitem, but my stomach was heaving all the same. This wasn't a course I was familiar with. I pushed the fear down deep into my stomach. Flying classes were getting harder and harder. Today's flying class was basically a practice Equitem match.

Our class had been separated into teams, most noticeably me and Artie versus Han and Hana. Cosette and Kit had teamed up against Nolan who was lucky enough to be partnered with Odette, from my Equitem team. The team that made it through the course the fastest would be declared the winner. Though the focus of the game was on speed, agility was also a huge factor. We had been talked through the path that would act as our course, and as I stood beside Merry at the starting line, I tried to picture it in my mind, visualising every turn, every obstacle.

We had to start on the ground, then fly straight into the forest ahead of us. As Sylva all our dragons were supposed to have an affinity for the forest; be better at camouflage, faster at weaving in and out of branches, more adept at balancing. But Merry wasn't

Sylva, not really. She didn't fit into any of the types. Inside the forest we would be faced with giant trees, rocky crags, and cavernous caves. At each point of the course, there was as flag we had to retrieve. Two teams would fly at a time.

The rules were simple – complete every section of the course, do not use your gifts, and do not lose your partner.

Spectre was in charge of our flying class today. He asked if we were ready and we each nodded in turn.

"Hana, Han. Step up. Artie, Angus. You, too." He waited as we took our starting positions beside our dragons. "Begin!"

I threw myself on top of Merry, and we took off without delay. Artie was right behind me on his larger dragon. Hana and Han were already a fraction ahead. We sped into the forest. Our first task was to throw ourselves into the mess of trees and weave in and out, around, up and down. At the top of the large oak tree in the centre of the forest was a flag. There was only one flag, so the competition was fierce. We sped through, weaving in and out of the trees, throwing bunches of leaves this way and that.

I felt exhilarated. All the fear and nerves dissipated the second Merry took into the sky. I had only been flying a short time, but it was like I was born for it.

I could feel Merry's muscles tense and release as her body effortlessly glided through the air, ducking and weaving away from the countless things that obstructed her path. It seemed as though she reacted to every thought I had, responding swiftly, as we flew together through the dense air of the forest.

The first flag sat somewhere inside an enormous tree that stood taller than any of the others surrounding it.

Han and Hana had the lead, but that didn't guarantee them the flag. They still had to find it. Though Artie's dragon was slightly larger than mine, ours were both smaller than Han and Hana's. That meant we had the advantage. It would be easier for us to get closer to the branches, search deeper into the tree for the flag.

"You take the lower half!" I yelled back to Artie. "I'll take the top."

Together we spiraled up and down the tree. Han and Hana had had a similar idea – Hana went up, and Han went down.

I tried not to be distracted, though I found my eyes flicking over to her constantly. She looked so calm and confident on top of her dragon, as she flew higher and higher. I struggled to keep speed with her on my younger, smaller dragon. I decided to use my advantage and flew Merry closer to the tree. Branches whipped past my face; a thin tree branch sliced my cheek open, and I felt the hot blood rise to the surface. Gravity tried to pull me down but I tightened my legs around her and sunk my hands into the grips on the back of her neck until my knuckles were white.

I saw a flicker of yellow up ahead, as the flag waved in the wind. Hana didn't seem to have spotted it yet. "There it is, Merry," I encouraged. I felt her push harder, looping in amongst the branches. I held my hand out as she whipped past. My fingers wrapped around the fabric, and I pulled it close to me.

Without warning, Merry arched her back and led with her head as she brought us into a freefall, tucking her wings in to her side. We fell with astonishing speed towards the ground that grew ever closer. I let go of any fear and doubt as she extended her wings, moments before we would have hit the ground, and lifted us in line with Artie. My breakfast was threatening to explode out of my mouth, but it was worth it.

"Artie! I've got it! I've got the flag. Let's go!"

I could feel Han's eyes on my back as we sped ahead to the next section. The forest gave way to rocky crags that were overgrown with moss. The flag was in here somewhere, but where?

Han sped ahead of me. The gust of wind from his dragon's wings nearly knocked me off Merry. Startled, she arched her wings and slowed us down. Quickly recovering, she darted forwards, but Han was already circling around a small red flag tucked into the rocks below.

"One more!" Artie shouted as he came up beside me.

"It's ours!" I shouted and we looped around to head back through the other side of the forest. Hana appeared beside me. I looked over in time to see her unleash a killer smile, then speed ahead, leaving me in her dust.

There was no way we were going to beat them. Our dragons were smaller and slower than Hana and Han's. We would need to fly through the tight mess of tress, to stand a chance, while, I was sure, they would fly above the canopy for speed.

I watched to see if I was right. Hana and Han both rose higher, heading towards the tops of the trees, where the branches were further apart, and they could move about more freely.

"Artie!" I called, "Follow me!"

Merry nosedived towards the ground below, leaving my stomach behind. The air tried to rip my skin from my bones, but I held on with everything I had. I couldn't remember why I had been so nervous just moments ago, when my feet were still on the ground. There was nothing better than being on the back of my dragon.

When we reached the lower branches of the trees, Merry pulled up and started to dodge and weave through the trees. I turned around to see Artie was right behind me. Looking up, I could see that Han and Hana were further back, high up in the thinning branches.

It was working. We were ahead.

But we were heading for an enormous cave, with stalactites, thick and sharp, hanging from the ceiling. We'd be plunged into almost complete darkness. It was here we would have to rely on our dragon's eyesight and their keen senses. I would be blinded. This was new for me. In the training sessions I'd had with the team, I'd never gone through a cave and been plunged into darkness before. I wasn't sure now was the best time to test out how it would go, but I could not – *would not* – let Han beat me.

The cave was just ahead. I could see its wide-open mouth, hungry for something to devour. My hearted picked up speed. This was insane.

"We're going in there?" Artie called.

"Yep," I shouted back.

"Are you freaking out or is it just me?" Artie added.

"I'm freaking out," I conceded.

"Okay good," he shouted over the sound of the wind. "Just checking."

"Whatever you do, keep your head down!"

We burst out of the forest and flew directly into the cave. We were still ahead of Han and Hana. It wasn't long before the light vanished, and we were engulfed in darkness. It was cold in the cave, oppressively so. The sound of Merry's wings beating was louder than ever in my ears. She swept from side to side, and I kept my head low against the back of her neck. I knew she must have been dodging stalactites, and all I could do was keep down and trust her.

I pressed my face against her rough skin. I could hear her breathing. It was quiet and rhythmic; she was in control, calm.

"Artie!" I called, to make sure he was still with me.

"I'm here!" came his reply.

"You good?"

"I think I'm having a heart attack! Tell my parents I love them."

"Tell them yourself," I laughed.

"Faster, Merry," I encouraged. She tipped to the side, and I held on to stop from falling. My eyes had adjusted to the darkness just enough to see she slid between two enormous stalactites. They were mere shadows to my eyes. I could see the end of the cave, just a pinpoint in the distance. Merry dove to the floor, spreading her wings out across the bottom of the cave floor. I looked down to see dim light bouncing off a river snaking through the cave.

Uh oh.

"Merry," I said warily.

She tipped to the side and one wing sliced into the water. *What was she doing?* I held on tightly, but her wing was almost completely swallowed by the water. My leg dipped into the frigid river. "Merry!"

Slowly straightening, she let out a low rumble, as if she was trying to tell me something. Fear prickled the back of my neck.

Without further warning, she plummeted straight into the water. I had just enough time to suck in as deep a breath as I could before I was immersed in the cold water of the cave river.

There was complete darkness underwater. I was grateful for that. I wasn't sure I wanted to see anything under here. I had never been a good swimmer. When I was a child, I'd fallen into a river and almost drowned. I remembered seeing stones and fish and slithering eels. Plants tickled my face as they danced with the ebb and flow of the water. I was wearing boots and a thick jacket, and I had plummeted to the bottom in moments. I didn't remember feeling afraid. I guess I didn't realise that I could die if I went without oxygen for long enough. I felt like I was in another world, watching it all unfold. The next thing I knew, my mother was right beside me.

She grabbed hold of me and dragged me up to the surface. When we were back on solid land, she was a shivering, shaking mess. She yelled at me, screaming something about how I could have died. I could still perfectly recall her blue lips, and the deep black shadows under her eyes as if all life had nearly been completely drained from her. That's when I started to feel afraid. I guess that's how it works sometimes. Our parents' fears often become our own.

I wrapped my arms around her as tightly as I could. Was it just me, or were we going faster?

She was slicing through the water so fast that I could feel my hands slipping. My lungs were burning. I needed air. I gripped onto her as hard as I could, my fingernails digging into her scales. The water rushed over me with aggressive force, and I started to feel light-headed.

Suddenly, I was floating in the water, my body sliding backwards, spinning wildly in the bubbles and turbulence left in Merry's wake. My hands had given way, and I'd lost my grip on her. She sped off ahead, without me.

Breathe. I needed to breathe. I couldn't quite figure out which way was up. It was totally dark. I felt terror grip at my chest and my head started to throb. I was going to drown. I was actually going to drown.

I flailed my arms madly, trying to swim to the surface, but I wasn't sure if I was going up or down. It was pitch black.

I heard a loud noise. A deep, throaty roar that echoed through the cave and reverberated into the water. A dragon's cry.

My eyes started to roll back in my head. My movements slowed. Any second now, I was going to pass out. My heartbeat settled in my chest, and everything became quite and calm. I was suspended in the water, which suddenly felt warm, embracing me.

I was tired. I wanted to go to sleep. My limbs felt heavy, and I felt myself drifting into oblivion.

Without warning, thick claws gripped my floating arms. I was being pulled through the water, until ice cold air stung my face. Air. I could breathe.

I gasped for a breath, the icy air bringing back my senses. The claws released me, and I fell to the ground, thudding against mud at the mouth of the cave. Sunlight blinded my eyes. I heaved in deep breaths, my chest burning with each gasp.

I looked around, expecting to see Merry. Instead, I saw Han. He was staring at me, sitting on top of his enormous dragon.

"Thanks," I rasped. "You saved my life."

Han held my stare, then, without another word, he flew away. I watched him disappear as I sat there, soaking wet and shivering. How had he seen me? I was out of the cave – Merry had taken us a long way under water. The wide river kept going for another hundred feet or so before it disappeared out of sight. Had Artie seen me go under? I doubted it. It was near total darkness when she plummeted into the water and she did it without a sound.

I was freezing. I stood up on shaky legs and slipped in the mud and fell. I slammed down and landed solidly on my elbow. I cried out in pain. At least there was no one here to see me.

"Are you okay?"

My stomach dropped. *Of course.*

I felt the gust of wind from Hana's dragon as it hovered in place. I looked up and saw her staring down at me with concern.

"Oh, yeah," I answered, waving my hand. "Totally fine. Just felt like a refreshing swim."

Hana laughed. "Need a ride?"

I considered saying no, but I knew the walk back would be long and I wasn't sure I had it in me. I scrambled to my feet. "As long as there's room enough for two."

helping hand

When we landed back at the start, I saw Artie waiting anxiously beside his dragon, and Han holding the flag.

Spectre seemed relieved when we finally crossed the finish line. I jumped off Hana's dragon as quickly as I could. I looked around for Merry, feeling angrier than I had expected. How could she have done that to me?

Artie ran up to me. "What happened? You were there one second, and then gone. Rose was freaking out. She cried so loud I thought my ears were gonna burst. Next thing I know, Han arrives. I tried to stay, but his dragon nearly bit Rose's face off and she flew away."

"Merry went under water, and I lost my grip."

"Are you okay?"

"Yeah. Fine. Where is she?"

I saw her curled up under the shade of a leafy tree. When she saw me, she got up and walked towards me, like a puppy excited to see its person.

"What was that?" I reprimanded. "You nearly killed me."

Spectre approached us and pressed a hand against Merry's head. "You need to learn to speak to your dragon, to understand her."

"What does that even mean?" I asked.

"As time passes and you become more familiar with each other, you will grow more and more connected. Unfortunately, at the moment, the connection is very weak. You have moments of clarity, but it can falter easily."

"How am I supposed to fix that?" I asked.

"Don't worry. You have plenty of time."

"It didn't feel like it today. I nearly died!"

Spectre looked over his shoulder to where Han was standing with his dragon. "You'll notice I paired you with two riders who are much more developed. Han's dragon is quite phenomenal. You should be very grateful that she heard Rose and saved you."

Spectre walked away and called for the next group to step up and take their places.

I made my way over to Han. I *was* grateful. If it hadn't been for him, I would have drowned. I felt foolish and angry and embarrassed.

"Thank you," I said, my voice hoarse and raspy.

"Don't thank me. She's the one that stopped," he replied, nodding to his dragon.

Why was he making this so difficult? "I'm grateful. Really."

When Han didn't respond with anything other than one of his famous death-glares, I took it as my cue to leave. I turned around and started to walk away.

"You shouldn't be here," he said coldly.

I paused. Artie was just in front of me, sitting by his dragon. He looked up, his eyes wide with concern. I turned around and tilted my head to the side.

"Excuse me?"

"You heard what I said," Han replied.

"You know, ever since I got here, you've had it in for me. What is your *problem*?" There was a time not so long ago that I suffered in silence as the school punching bag, but I wasn't about to let that infest my new life. I was different. This place was different. And my dragon alone was proof that I belonged here. I wasn't going to let go of that.

"You're the problem," he answered calmly.

"And why exactly is that?" I asked.

"You walk in here like you own the place. You're nothing here. You're no one."

I wanted to fight back, to tell him that I did matter. That my gift was the rarest of them all, but I couldn't. I promised Spectre I wouldn't say a word. "Do you see that dragon over there?" I asked, pointing towards Merry. "She's mine. No one else's. Living, breathing proof that this is where I belong. So, if you don't like that, keep your head down and stay out of my way, because I'm tired of staying out of yours."

Han stepped up to me, getting close – too close. He was taller than me. Stronger, too. I had no doubt he could beat me to a pulp, but it was nothing I hadn't experienced before. I refused to back down. If I backed down here, it would never end. Han would win and would forever think of me as beneath him. "I see the way you look at my sister," he snarled. He looked over my shoulder, and my eyes followed his. Hana was standing close, her large, inquisitive eyes concerned.

I looked back to Han, my stomach in knots. "So, that's what this is really about?"

"It's about you, not belonging here. You thinking you can take what doesn't belong to you. You think I'm stupid? I know that Spectre treats you differently."

"I don't know what you're talking about," I responded.

"I know there's something going on. I can feel it. You want to know what *my* gift is?" Han grimaced, his face inching closer to mine.

I waited in silence for him to speak. What *was* his gift? We weren't allowed to parade our gifts around, so I didn't know what it was. From what I had seen, Han kept to himself. He was quiet and aloof, and when he walked down the hall, people gave him space. He sat alone to eat, usually with a book in his hand.

I opened my mouth to speak, but something stopped me. There was a cold hand of fear gripping the base of my neck. I started to shake. Ice crept through my blood and rose up my back, slipping into my brain like fingers digging into every nerve of my body. My heart pounded in my chest. I was terrified, but I didn't know of what. I dropped to my knees, unable to hold myself up any longer.

"Han!" I heard Hana shout, but her voice sounded muffled and far away.

Terror gripped my throat, clenching it shut until I couldn't voice my horror. I was deathly afraid, but I didn't know of what. I clutched at my chest. I wanted to run as far away as I could. I didn't want to be here anymore.

"Han!" Hana shouted again. "Stop!"

"Han, don't be a jerk!" It was Artie this time.

The fear began to subside, only to give way to the undeniable truth that I was alone. I was a failure. There was nothing about me that was worth anything. I had always been afraid that I was going to stay a nobody forever, and I had never felt more certainty that my fears were right. I could pretend all I liked, but dragon or no dragon, Academy or no Academy, I was still the same Angus. A failure, a loser, a nobody.

"Enough!" The voice was loud, and it pierced my clouded thoughts. The emotional vice grip released me. My head was clear again, but I was breathless. What had just happened?

Spectre approached us, his heavy footsteps causing the ground to shudder beneath me. "Your gifts are not the things of playground disputes!" he snapped. "Han, I expected better of you. Return to your room immediately."

I looked up at Han, trying to understand what had just happened.

"You're not the only one who is different," he snarled. Slowly, he walked away, leaving me gasping for breath.

The feeling was gone but the memory remained. Han had made me feel like a failure, like something he stepped in. I wanted to throw up. I turned around and saw a dozen pairs of eyes on me. Spectre looked down at me sadly.

"My dear boy," he began, but I didn't let him finish.

I pushed myself off the ground and stormed away. I needed to be anywhere but here.

volare vs sylva

I spent the rest of the week avoiding everyone, except Artie who was pretty unavoidable, seeing as how we shared most of our classes and a dorm room.

I'd seen Hana in the hallways a few times, but I always did an about-turn and hurried away, or pretended I didn't see her. Almost drowning and then having the brother of the girl you like shrink you to the size of a pea in front of everyone while your soul is chipped away and every ounce of self-confidence is shredded, is about as humiliating as it can get. There was no coming back from that.

My sour mood started to lift by the following Friday when my match against Volare was looming large. In two hours, I'd be playing in my first Equitem match.

But that was two entire hours away, and I had three more pages of my essay to write for Cullen, and a dismount diagram to do up for Trig.

The library was my favorite place in the Academy, especially in the last few days when hiding from everyone had been my biggest goal. I sat at a far table, tucked in behind two bookshelves, completely out of sight.

Dragons and Modern-Day Machines, Humans and Dragons: A Tragic Alliance, and *Human Warfare Against the Animal Kingdom* were all open on the table, and I was busy scribbling out every thought I could think about why I didn't think the rest of mankind should know about dragons. A shadow fell over the desk, and I looked up, expecting to see the librarian scowling at me since I was supposed to return these books (and finish my essay) yesterday so I could prepare for the match. But it was Hana.

"Hi," I said quietly, before turning back to my books. If I looked busy, maybe she would walk away.

"Hey. Haven't seen you around much."

"I've been busy."

"I can see that."

Silence fell between us, and I did my best to keep writing, to focus on the textbooks, to block her out.

"I'm sorry about my brother," she whispered.

Please, no. The last thing I wanted was to have this conversation. There was nothing more mortifying. I got it – I was weak, I was pathetic – I really didn't need her pity.

"Not your problem," I replied coldly.

"Han is… he means well, he's just got a lot of pressure on him, and I-"

"I really, *really* don't want to have this conversation," I said, looking up from my books. "I don't need you to apologise for him, and I don't need you sitting there feeling sorry for me, okay? I just need to write my essay."

Hana looked stricken, like I'd bitten her. I flinched. I hadn't meant to snap, I just…

"You know, if you spent less time feeling sorry for yourself, and more time around the people who care about you, you might know that Han has done that before, and that there is *no one* in this entire Academy who can stand up to him, except Spectre. You'd know that no one thinks badly of you, and we all just want to make you feel better. Feel seen. But your pride is so wounded that you won't even look at us. I didn't think you were like that. I thought you were different. But I guess you don't care about me enough to risk another encounter with the big, bad wolf." She scoffed angrily. "Sorry to have bothered." She stood up to leave, but my hand flew out and grabbed her wrist.

"I'm sorry," I said quietly. "I shouldn't have said that. You're right. I'm just… embarrassed, I guess. I feel like I was stripped bare in front of everyone. I thought you wouldn't want to know me after you'd seen that. I'm sorry."

Hana's face softened, and she slowly sat back down. I relaxed my grip on her wrist, but moved my hand to gently touch her fingertips instead.

"No one looks down on you because you're new here, Angus," she said softly. "It's only been a few months. No one expects you to be able to defend yourself from him, or have your bond with Merry perfectly solidified. The only one who is putting any pressure on you is yourself. The rest of us, we just like you for you. Not because you're the Flag Bearer for Sylva, or because of your gift. I don't even know what it is. We… *I*… like you for *you*."

Her hands trembled in mine. Had she just said what I thought she said?

She liked me?

I leaned in close. She did, too. "I… I like you, too." My voice was barely more than a whisper. Our faces were just inches away now. Her eyes were even prettier this close. I reached a hand up to touch her face, and she leaned into my palm. My skin tingled and my stomach flip-flopped. This was it… I was going to kiss her.

"Dude, you did *not* say that to Cullen!" Artie's voice shattered the moment. We separated quickly, as Artie and Kit came around from beside the bookshelf and headed to my table.

"I told them I was coming to find you," Hana said, biting her lip.

"Kit says he told Cullen he was gonna do an extra two thousand words of the essay," Artie said, laughing, dragging a chair back and sitting at the table beside me.

Trying not to show my disappointment, I sat back in the chair and scoffed. "Why would you *do* that?"

Kit raked his hands through his hair like a man torn apart. "He was just looming over me, staring at me like I was a bug to be stepped on. You know what he's like! I felt like I had to defend myself. It just came out."

Hana laughed. "You're such a baby. Professor Cullen isn't that bad. I kinda like him."

"You would."

"What's that supposed to mean?" Hana gasped in mock horror.

"You're the teacher's pet in every class! Cullen held up your paper last year as an example of what we should all be doing."

"I can't help it that I'm brilliant, Kit."

"What's he like in Equitem?" Artie asked.

"He's fine," I answered. "Tough, but good. You should have joined the team. Your flying last week was brilliant."

"No thanks. I value my life. You're forgetting why the last *three* Flag Bearers quit."

The blood drained from my face. "The last three? I didn't know *three* quit! I thought it was only the last one."

"Probably because I didn't mention it. Speaking of, it's almost game time."

"You guys gonna be there?" I asked, but I was looking at Hana.

"Wouldn't miss it," she answered.

"Of course," Artie replied, but I wasn't listening.

The crowds were cheering loudly enough that I couldn't hear my own breathing, despite the fact that I was almost hyperventilating.

We stood on the field, huddled around Cullen. We were all wearing our forest green flight coats, and our dragons were huffing steam above our heads.

Cullen was looking sombre, dressed in his own green flight coat that matched ours, save for the teacher's crest sewn into the chest. "We have trained for this. We have prepared. We will win."

His words were simple, but they were all we needed.

Orson had us put our hands in the centre. "This is it!" he roared. "Sylva on three. One, two, three!"

"Sylva!" we all shouted. As we broke apart, each heading to our own stations, Cullen called me back. "Their Flag Bearer is faster than you, but she doesn't have Merry's agility. I've never seen another dragon like her. I heard about what happened in Spectre's flying class. Travelling in the water like that. A true Sylva wouldn't voluntarily make that choice. I spoke to Spectre and he told me the truth. That she isn't Sylva. That she isn't any of them."

I started to protest, but Professor Cullen held up a hand to silence me.

"This is a *good* thing, Angus. I've done some research. If I am right, she can do it *all*. Equally at home in the sky, as a forest, as the water, or the ground. You will save this team, Finch. I know you haven't been Flag Bearer for long, but…" he paused, and a painful expression passed his face, like what he wanted to say was physically uncomfortable. "I believe in you."

I stood there, unsure what to say. Cullen cleared his throat and walked off the field.

I sighed. Well, now I *definitely* had to win.

The horn blew, and both teams flew into the air without a second's delay. The nerves were gone now. All that was left was desperation. Desperation to *win*. The rest of my team took off, and I was left to fight for the flag strapped to the back of Volare's Flag Bearer, Hadleigh Gifford. She was lithe, and small, with grey eyes and short blonde hair that was cut in a severe straight line at her chin. She was crouched animalistically on the back of her brown dragon.

She eyed me with sadistic pleasure as I hovered thirty feet away from her. "Mmm, look. Fresh meat," she called. "And I'm a carnivore."

She flew towards me with shocking speed, and Merry dropped twenty feet like a bullet and tore forward, ripping through the air below Hadleigh. My flag whipped through the wind behind me, crackling in the breeze created by Merry's disarming speed.

The field was set up to create a load of obstacles we had to make it through, as well as perfect places to dodge or hide. Trees, tall poles, a muddy ravine, boulders, and netting created chaotic hurdles we had to make it through unscathed. I quickly looked to my left. The team had reached the mountain and were about to turn around.

I had to get the flag. *Now.*

"Come on, Merry," I encouraged.

She zig-zagged between the trees. Where was Hadleigh? My head whipped from side to side, frantically trying to locate her. Her enormous brown dragon appeared from above, slotting in behind us.

"Faster, Merry!"

"I've got you now, Finch!" Hadleigh laughed.

I turned around to see her lance outstretched, ready to rip the flag off my back.

A thought from me was all it took, and Merry followed. We were perfectly in sync. I could feel her twisting through my veins, like a ribbon. I took hold of my lance, as Merry arched her back and the wind caught her wings. Suddenly we were upside down above Hadleigh, narrowly avoiding her lance as she threw it forward with a final burst.

I stretched out my lance and hooked it around Hadleigh's flag as Merry flipped to right herself.

It happened so quickly. The crowds were completely silent, as Merry slowed, and abruptly changed directions. I looked down at my hands.

I had Hadleigh's flag.

The roar of the crowds erupted, as they realized what happened. I quickly attached it to my back, atop my own flag.

"Get back here, Finch!" Hadleigh bellowed, outraged I'd managed to get the flag off her.

It wasn't over yet. I still had to make it through the course and hang the flag back at our base – a large flat platform on the far right side of the field. At any moment, Hadleigh could take the flag from me and the tables would turn.

The rest of my team was almost here. I just had to hold her off until they arrived, then I'd have reinforcements. "Go, Merry!" Merry ducked below the branches of a tree, as Hadleigh gained on us. Her dragon was fast, but Merry was nimble. She executed a perfect pinhead turn around a pole, and suddenly we were going in the opposite direction. I heard Hadleigh's dragon roar as he turned.

But Hadleigh was Volare. The air was where her dragon excelled.

He was on us again in moments, and his speed was astonishing. He looped around us, taunting us, and then he was gone.

I looked around, my head scanning the world around me as it whipped past. *Where is he*?

Hadleigh's dragon came up from underneath Merry and slammed his head into her stomach. Merry jerked violently to the side and I was thrown off her back. My hand's refused to let go, as I dangled in the air, fifty feet above the ground. I heard the crowd howl in indignation, but while it was a dirty move, it wasn't illegal. She was allowed to throw me off my dragon if she could.

"Merry!" I screamed, but our connection was gone, and I was reminded how much further we still had to go before our bond was strong enough. Two huge black dragons hovered in the air with their riders, two Professors. They were about thirty feet either side of me. Referees. I knew they were there for our protection, for situations just like these. There was no way anyone without a perfected bond would be allowed to play without them. But I didn't think I would need them, and certainly not on my first match.

My knuckles were white as I gripped harder and harder. My arms burned like fire as my muscles tore as I pulled myself back into a seated position.

Gasping for breath, I tried to find Hadleigh again. This time she was above me. She had a wild glint in her eye. Merry tipped her left wing, and the air pushed us back, but Hadleigh was quick to respond.

Merry tried to dodge as Hadleigh drew nearer and nearer. Her dragon's mouth was open, heading straight for Merry's tail. I watched in horror as the jaws hovered over Merry.

Suddenly, Odette and her dragon slammed into Hadleigh's and she was pushed back, just as his jaws slammed shut.

We had to get away from here and go through the course. Merry and I had done this a hundred times in practice. We could do this.

She soared towards the muddy ravine, and I braced myself for the cold and wet. We hit it *hard*. She skidded through the water, and I was soaked instantly. Hadleigh's team was defending her against my own team, and she was breaking through. Merry zoomed through the water and took off again at the other side of the ravine, up and out into the mass of trees. Hadleigh wasn't far behind. Her dragon, muddied and wet, was slowed by the ravine, but he would be on us again in moments. We had to dodge between all the trees, and Merry was making quick work of it. Branches whipped past my face and slapped against my arms, but I barely noticed.

I was focused on what was next – the poles. They had sounded easy when Cullen explained them to me, but they were anything but. "Your dragon must fly to the top of the hundred-foot poles, then down towards the ground. She must stop as low as she can, then turn around and do it all over again. There are three poles. You are familiar with roller coasters, in your world, are you not?" Cullen had smirked. "This is much worse."

He had been right. This was our weakest obstacle in practice, and I had no reason to presume it would be any different today. Her size was the problem. She wasn't as big as the other, older dragons, and couldn't keep up with their speed.

"Come on, Merry!" I encouraged. We had to keep our lead. As Volare, this is where Hadleigh could gain ground.

Merry approached the poles and pointed her nose skyward. Her wings beat quickly, as she pushed herself higher and higher. Gravity pulled down on me, and it was everything I had to hold on. Out of the corner of my eyes, I saw the referees appear on either side of me. Clearly, there was concern I was going to plummet to my death.

Fair.

We were almost at the top of the first pole. I looked back and tried to keep my lunch in my stomach. Hadleigh was approaching the poles.

Merry rounded the top of the first pole and dropped like a stone towards the ground. I screamed. I couldn't help it. The ground was rushing up to meet me so fast and my natural reaction was abject terror. But I pushed past it, beyond it, and reached for something stronger.

Willpower.

Merry's tucked in wings had us falling fast, and when she whipped them out again, the air caught us, and I slammed my face against the back of her neck so hard I saw stars. I felt blood bubble on my lip, but there was no time to wipe it away. She was climbing again. Hadleigh was at the top of the first pole, just about to drop. We soared past him, and I could hear the rattle of Merry's breath as she went beyond her own strength and found something new.

She reached the top of the second pole, as Hadleigh was a quarter of the way up it. She dropped again, and sick rose up in my throat. I swallowed it back down, and lay flat against her, my face pressed firmly against her neck, so I wasn't smacked again.

One more.

Merry started to rise again, and I saw Hadleigh was right behind us. I could feel her dragon's breath, hot and sticky, on my back.

"Orson!" I screamed for Sylva's Captain. I needed defense now. I turned around. Hadleigh's eyes were wide and wild as she extended her lance towards my flag, and her own.

A sunset-orange dragon flickered into my vision, and Orson reached out a hand to swat away her lance as his dragon nipped at Hadleigh's dragon's front leg.

"Go! Go, Finch!" he shouted.

Merry, spurred on with adrenaline, rounded the top of the pole and fell towards the earth. As we reached the bottom, she spread her wings and soared low along the ground. Next was the net – this was *all* me. I had to time it perfectly, or I'd lose our lead.

Ahead of us was a net stretched out like a spider web between two posts. Merry had to fly under it, and I had to crawl up it, then scuttle along a rope hung taut between two trees and meet her on the other side. Then it was straight back to our base to hang the flag.

I stretched my hands up, as Merry flew towards the net. My hands gripped it tightly, the rope cutting into my fingers, despite the leather gloves I wore. My body kept going and I was flung forward, but still I held fast. I swayed like a pendulum, as I fought to regain composure. Then I started to climb.

I pulled myself up, up, up and my torn arms were on fire. I raked in icy breaths, my lungs aching. I felt Hadleigh collide with the net and I knew I had to go faster. I could see my team battling against Hadleigh's, as both teams tried to delay the enemy Flag Bearer. I had to hand it to my team – they were doing a brilliant job. Volare hadn't been able to get close to me. Orson was calling out instructions, leading the team like we were fighting for our lives.

I hauled myself onto the top of the net, even as it shook wildly with Hadleigh's rise. I grabbed hold of the rope that stretched twenty feet ahead of me and looped my legs around it, until I hung like a sloth. As fast as I could, darted along the rope. Hadleigh was right behind me.

Merry was waiting at the end of the rope for me. She roared, encouraging me along. I felt the rope starting to sway and shake, as Hadleigh started to yank on it, and swing side to side. The crowd jeered, and my hand slipped. I could hear cheering from the rest of the Volare team. There was no way I was going to give them the satisfaction of watching me fall. I reached the end of the rope and hung straight. I let go, dropping lighting onto Merry's back as she waited below.

She took off with startling speed, heading for our base. Hadleigh screamed in frustration as she mounted her dragon and took off after me. It was a straight line to the base, but Merry couldn't beat Hadleigh in a drag race. There was no point darting into the trees, or going anywhere else – Hadleigh would just stake out our base and wait for us. All we could do was keep going, as fast as we could, and hope our team would help us.

I turned to look behind me, and I saw Hadleigh just a few feet behind.

"Defense!" I shouted. "Defense!"

My team descended on me quickly, three hovering around base, and the other three flying next to Hadleigh, snapping at him, and ramming into him.

"Hurry, Finch! We've got this! We got the tokens. Hang the flag and we win!" Orson yelled, then rammed his dragon directly into Hadleigh's dragon's ribs. He was thrown off course, and Hadleigh was knocked off. Her dragon immediately stopped, and folded in his wings. He plummeted after her, and caught her in his talons. Orson had slowed them down.

I just hoped it would be enough.

Merry closed the final gap between us and the base and I jumped off her back. Ripping off the flag, I hung it as quickly as I could and the crowd exploded into cheers.

We won.

Breathless, I looked around at my team as they yelled and screamed and applauded. Volare were furious, never expecting to lose Sylva. I looked to the stands and saw Professor Cullen. He was watching me closely. He wasn't clapping, or cheering, but there was a small smile on his face. He nodded once, just a small movement, but it was all I needed. I grinned, then looked for Hana and Artie in the crowds. I saw them on the bottom row in the Sylva section, pressed up against the barricade. They were waving and cheering.

How had I won this game? Me? Somehow, I had managed to beat an experienced team, at this impossible game I never even wanted to play.

Merry nudged me with her head and I turned around and hugged her tightly. "Well done, girl. Well done."

She tipped her head from side to side then sauntered off to lie in the shade, satisfied she had done a good job.

I dropped down onto the platform and laughed as I tried to steady my breathing. I did it. We won.

Maybe there was more to me than I knew.

history lessons

After winning Equitem, Sylva celebrated in the hall over a huge feast. Every team got to participate, but no one was having a better time than Sylva. Hot steaming roasts, mashed potatoes, boats of gravy, and jugs of apple cider were passed around. I didn't get a chance to talk to Hana alone again, and the next morning I had a private lesson with Spectre first up.

"Perhaps, however," Spectre chimed, "the very greatest thing about dragons is their unique connection with their rider. It remains included in and unaffected by its rider's gift."

"I'm sorry, what?" I asked. I hadn't realized I'd zoned out.

"Where *is* your head this morning, Angus?" Spectre chided. "If I didn't know better, and I do, I'd say your head was clean off your shoulders."

"I'm just tired from the game yesterday." *And* everyone else was either sleeping in or flying their dragons, since it was a Saturday, but I was cooped up in the private room in the library instead. Despite the two warnings from my father, and the pressure Spectre was putting on me to learn more and *be* more because of my gift, nothing bad had happened, and no one knew about my gift, and everything was fine. I wasn't sure why I had to be singled out like this anymore.

"Sorry, what did you say?"

"I *said* that dragons remain included in and unaffected by their rider's gifts."

"Meaning?"

"Meaning that, when you Blink, your dragon won't freeze in time like everything else appears to. Rather, he will be able to accompany you as you move through time."

"She," I corrected.

"She. My apologies," he responded, suitably chastised.

"That's…useful," I murmured.

"Very," Spectre agreed. "Now, move to page 904."

The next hour was spent searching through one giant, dusty book after another. A growing feeling started to blossom in my stomach. I couldn't concentrate. I wanted to know more about my gift. Ever since that day with Spectre's dragon, Pilar, we had barely spoken about it. I know Spectre wanted to do things slowly, and ease me into life at Everwood, but everyone else was doing well in the Gifts class, and I wasn't even allowed to attend. Everyone was under the impression that I didn't even have one yet.

I hadn't been able to Blink at all since that day. I didn't even know how I had done it *then*, so there was no chance of me trying to replicate it. Even if I wanted to, I wasn't allowed to let anyone know about my gift, so practicing was out of the question. If I still couldn't talk to anyone about it, then it must be a big deal. What did it mean that there were people out there who would seek to use me as a weapon? Spectre hadn't said much more about it. Surely, I had been here long enough now that I deserved to know more about myself… and the people who posed a threat.

Who were these people? How could they use me? What would they do to me to force me to help them? Would they hurt my mother? Would they go after Grandpa George? Was there even a real threat, if no one would talk to me about it? Nothing had happened so far, and I'd been at Everwood for months.

I scraped my fingernails along the table, trying to control the ever-growing concern at the base of my spine, until I could hold my silence no longer.

"I need to know," I spluttered.

Spectre looked confused at my sudden outburst. "Know what?"

"Who else is out there?" I closed the book in front of me and leaned forward over the table. "Who wants to use me against you? Why? How?"

My father's unexpected visit affected me more than I wanted it to. I had done everything I could to push it out of my mind, but when it was quiet, or I was alone, it replayed in my mind on a loop. He had said people were coming. What was that supposed to mean? And why did I have to be a part of any of it?

Spectre was silent for long enough that I started to grow angry.

"You said you would tell me." I squeezed my fingers into a fist, then shoved my chair back and stood to my feet. "This is *my* life. I have a right to know."

"I agree. It is your life. But you must understand the gravity of the situation. There are few people in the Academy who know what I could tell you."

"I think I should make the list, don't you?" I took a deep breath and steadied myself. "I'm supposed to have this all-powerful gift, but I don't even know how to use it. I'll keep it to myself," I assured him.

"That's just the thing – I'm not sure you'll be able to. It is not a fairy tale that we're living in, Angus. This is real life. But there are many similarities to the tales of old, I suppose. There are great beasts and noble heroes, and, of course, evil men who wish to do harm."

"Yeah, I get it. I know – the world is full of bad guys. But if this directly impacts me, I need to know about them. These *specific* bad guys."

His hesitation lasted only a few moments. When he began to speak, I sat down and took in every word.

"There are two factions of our people - those who are led by our governing leadership, and those who are not. Dragons are in every country, and every country has a council of seven people. Seven authorities. One of those seven takes the role of that country's leader, much like Britain has a Prime Minister. Though, instead of governing laws like whether or not crossing the road other than at a set of traffic lights is a crime, our governing body makes laws around life with dragons. These laws are for the safety of the dragons, and the safety of their riders. Each leader from each country makes up what we call the Concilium. The Concilium meet many times a year, and though they function more or less as a democracy, they are led by the Ascensor."

I nodded, following along, as Spectre got up and started pacing the room. The fireplace flickered quietly behind him, and his long shadow stretched across the floor. The air grew thick and heavy. His footfalls fell silently on the wooden floor, as if he wasn't even there.

His voice became hurried and quiet. "The Ascensor is the supreme leader of our people. He has been in power for two hundred years. He has seen us through many dark times. Of course, there has always been dissension among our people, and there always will be, much like there is between people in the world you are most familiar with. But in the last years, things have grown much worse. A leader has emerged from within those who wish to challenge the Concilium. His name is Grayne."

"Grayne?" I questioned.

"Yes, Grayne."

I crinkled my eyebrows together, unsatisfied.

"I'm sorry," Spectre sighed, "is something wrong?"

"Well, it's just that Grayne is just so unthreatening. I mean... he's supposed the be this ultimate villain in the world of dragons, wreaking chaos, making everyone afraid and his name is Grayne. That's the name of a pastry chef, not a tyrant."

"What were you expecting?"

"I don't know. Something more...medieval, I guess. Grayne. It's just so...Grayne."

"Stop saying Grayne."

"Sorry."

"Can we move on?" Spectre snapped. "This isn't a joke, Angus. I told you this wasn't a fairy tale. Dragon's existing is no more obscure or bizarre than lizards, or dogs, or cats, or toucans existing. It's an animal. But people are the worst kind of animals – and I am trying to help you."

I drew a line over my lips, then pretended to throw away the key that locked my mouth shut.

"Thank you." Spectre exhaled. "As I was saying, Grayne has started a rebellion that has stirred the anarchists into a frenzy, to the point where they are actually posing a viable threat. I never said we were afraid, by the way. They are simply a threat that needs to be neutralized. However, your ability to Blink is extremely rare, powerful and very much sought after. If news of your gift were to reach the rebellion, they would undoubtedly find you, take you, and force you to help them in their quest."

"Which is?"

"As far as we can tell, their quest is to overthrow the Concilium.

But this is not something you will have to deal with for a very long time. You are safe here. I have kept the knowledge of your gift a closely guarded secret, so no one knows."

There was a burning curiosity inside of me, desperate to know more about these rebels. I wanted to know who they were, why they felt as though they were in the right. There had to be more to it than one man's desire to overthrow the powers that be. If that was all there was, the Rebels would never have amassed enough followers to be a threat.

Spectre hurried through an explanation, but I could tell that every word was one he didn't want to share. He didn't want me to be a part of this.

But it wasn't his choice.

There were thousands of Dragon Riders, or Vectors as they were called around here, in every Colonium. So, for there to be any sort of significant threat, the Rebels had to have either the numbers or the abilities to concern the Concilium.

Since Spectre had spies within the Rebels, he knew which. Though their numbers were no more than a few hundred, it was their top four leaders that were the reason Spectre was preparing me to fight back.

Grayne, their leader, had the most powerful ability. He, like Spectre, could Ghost. Second to Blinking, Ghosting was the most powerful gift. Second in command was Jun-Ha, then his twin sister, Ji-Ha. Grayne had recruited them from within the South Korean Colonium. Jun-Ha's was capable of erupting into flames and Ji-Ha could read minds. The fourth in command was a man named Kael, and he sounded *awesome*. In a dangerous, evil villain kind of way, of course. Kael had a form of teleportation mixed with telekinesis. His gift was called Shifting.

"But why?" I asked.

"Why what?" Spectre responded.

"Why bother? Why do all this? It all seems a little…medieval. You said that they want to overthrow the Concilium. But why?"

Spectre took that moment to stop pacing and sit down in front of me. He clasped his hands together on the table. "Grayne was once a member of the Concilium. When time came for the last Ascensor to step down, he believed that he was next in line. But the Concilium chose someone else – our current Ascensor, Heinrich – and Grayne couldn't handle it. He started keeping secrets, and thinking that the Concilium had ulterior motives. He spread dissention, and a few people followed. From there, his rebellion has grown. I believe he wishes to overthrow the Concilium, and place his own people in charge, sitting himself at the head of the table as the Ascensor."

"And that would be very bad," I guessed.

"Oh, yes, my boy," Spectre nodded gravely. "If Grayne places himself in charge, he will undoubtedly harm everyone who does not wish to follow him as leader. He will stop recruiting new Vectors, leaving an endless line of people without their dragons, living a life that was not intended for them. He will do damage beyond what you can imagine, Angus. Only the strongest of men dare go against him. It will take an army to see him fall."

I stared at him blanky, all the blood draining from my face.

"But as I said, you will not have to deal with any of this for a long time." Spectre smiled to reassure me. "You are here at Everwood to train to be a Vector. I take that responsibility seriously. You are safe here, Angus. I am sure we will have taken care of it long before it ever becomes an issue for you."

"So…I'm not really in any danger?"

I thought back to what my father had said. I wanted Spectre's words to erase everything, but they were still there, lingering like shadows.

Spectre stopped pacing and looked at me with an expression resembling sympathy. His face was dark and shadowed, but there was a small, kind smile on his lips. "Undoubtedly not *yet*, Angus," he said in the resigned tone of someone who knew the burden they were placing on another. "I am quite certain that –"

Spectre was cut off by a rumble that shook the ground, followed immediately by an immense crashing noise.

We stared at each other for a moment. A woman screamed.

Spectre fled the room. I took off after him, following the growing sounds of chaos. Students filled the halls, peering out windows, while others shouted and called for help. I ran as fast as I could behind Spectre, as he flew through the corridors. Suddenly, we were at the front steps of Everwood.

I came to a dead halt; in front of me, at the very bottom of the steps, was a crumpled dragon, wounded and battered. Its rider lay moaning on the ground, a bloody gash bubbling in his chest. Spectre dropped to the rider's side, removed the scarf around his neck and pressed it tightly against the wound. The dragon breathed in and out so slowly that with the release of every breath, I wondered if it would be its last.

An ear-shattering screech caused the gathering throngs to look around. Two more dragons were in the air, clawing at each other, while thick swirls of orange and red flames shot through the sky.

I stared in disbelief at the tumbleweed of time unfolding before my eyes. I squinted against the sun to see that each dragon bore a rider.

I drew my eyes from the scene in the sky to the one before me. Spectre was leaning in close to the man on the ground, his ear beside his mouth.

"Go!" I heard a familiar voice shout. It was Cyrus, who I had already dubbed the Butler. There seemed nothing meek or weak framed about him now, as he marched down the stairs, shouting into his earpiece. "Go, go, go!"

Before I could wonder at whom he was yelling, five more dragons appeared out of nowhere, speeding like bullets towards the dragons in the air. One by one each dragon began a synchronized assault, singling out one of the dragons and launching attacks left and right.

"Attend to the dragon!" Cyrus shouted, as four men in black coats forced their way down the stairs, one of them knocking me so hard I nearly fell to the ground. "Students, go! Move! Clear the way!"

I jumped off the stairs, onto the ground below, as the men each took a different side of the dragon. They scanned over it, keen eyes missing nothing, attending to each of its many wounds.

A deafening cry drew my attention back up to the sky, where I watched as a rider fell at least a hundred feet to the ground. The thud was as ominous as it was final.

"The dragon!" Cyrus shouted into his earpiece.

The six dragons rolled in a flurry around the riderless beast and began to slowly descend. When they landed, softly on the ground, the dragon was subdued, releasing pitiful moans and shrieks at the loss of its rider.

"No!" Spectre shouted, his voice calling me back to the injured rider. Spectre was holding the wounded man off the ground by his shirt. "No!" He shook his body, which remained limp and unresponsive, before releasing him and allowing the body to rest in a crumpled heap on the ground.

Sick rose up in my throat. A large pool of sticky crimson blood surrounded the body, and I knew with hideous certainty that he was dead. Spectre stood up from the body and turned. He scanned the faces of the crowd until his eyes fell upon mine.

He walked, one solemn step at a time, towards me. His white shirt was covered in red blood, his hands were stained, and his knees were drenched. He looked like a casualty of war.

I wanted to run away, but I kept my feet planted, my knees locked together so they wouldn't buckle beneath me. As an enormous stretcher appeared and the wounded dragon was placed upon it and taken inside, Spectre held out his hand to give me something.

I opened my palm. "I'm sorry, Angus," he said softly. "I'm so sorry."

I stared down at my hand, upon which a crumpled, blood-stained piece of paper took residence. With trembling fingers, I uncrunched the paper. Two words were etched onto the parchment with confident accuracy.

As I read the words, my heart began to pound in my chest, faster and faster, until I felt like it might give up from sheer exhaustion. My father's face flashed in front of my eyes. I looked back up to Spectre, my eyes barely able to register his face, as all I could see were two words flashing before my eyes.

Don't Blink.

fast forward

Later, when I would look back on the events of that day, I would know it was a turning point – it was the moment that everything changed forever. But while I was living the chaos, I couldn't think clearly.

"What is happening?" I asked as the clamour grew around me. 'What does this mean?" I held up the blood-stained paper in my hand.

"Nothing, nothing," Spectre responded, wrapping my fingers back over the paper and looking around, as if to make sure no one saw.

"Don't lie to me!" I shouted. "What is going on? Who are these people?"

Spectre looked behind him as authorities of Everwood began ushering everyone inside. "It's…complicated."

"Explain!" I yelled. "There is a dead body lying right in front of me, so just…please! Explain."

"These two men," Spectre said quietly, "are rebels. And that note," he gestured to the paper in my hand, "is a declaration of war."

"What?" I breathed. "I thought you said that none of this was happening now. That there wasn't any immediate threat. That no one knew!"

"I did say that. That's what I thought...I must have missed something. Someone must have alerted the rebels that you're here...that you can Blink."

"How?" I asked. "That's not possible. I only just found out myself! No one knows. No one but you."

A sinking feeling hit my stomach.

My father.

My father knew I could Blink and I never told Spectre.

What was I supposed to do? I couldn't tell Spectre about meeting my father, not after this. He'd never trust me again. It had been too long.

"There are three very rare types of gifts, Angus. Ghosting and Blinking are two of them. These gifts affect a very, very small percentage of dragon riders. What makes them easy to track, however, is the fact that they are hereditary."

"As in, passed down the family line?" I asked.

"Yes."

"You mean James?"

"Not necessarily, no. There are others in your family line who are dragon riders."

"Who?" I asked.

"Your grandfather, for one."

"Grandpa?" I started shaking my head. "No, no, no, you've got your facts messed up somewhere. My Grandpa is not a dragon rider! He never even leaves the house. I'm not even sure he's sane."

"I assure you, Angus, dragon riding is in his DNA. But...he doesn't remember that."

"What do you mean?"

"You are not a prisoner here, Angus. You are free to leave any time you like. But returning to life as you know it and turning your back on what is in your blood, well, dear boy, it comes at a price. The price is that you forget."

"What do you mean?"

"To leave, and not return, you must take a pill that ensures you forget everything you have learned. We cannot watch everyone, Angus, and the information you learn here is too important, and too dangerous in the wrong hands, to be kept idle in the back of someone's mind while they return to life before Everwood. Your grandfather chose to leave. So, he had to forget."

I tried to respond but no words escaped my mouth.

"Angus, I meant it when I said you were important. There are others, too, in your family. Somewhere along the line, someone could Blink. Someone knew you were coming, Angus. Someone who knew that Blinking was in your blood."

"So…you put me in that test even though you knew I could Blink?"

"No. I didn't know you could Blink."

I shook my head, confused. "Let's get back to the dead bodies. Can we discuss that? Cause it's way more than I signed on for."

"Those men were rebels. They were coming to take you, Angus. We stopped them, but there will be more."

"I saw him whispering in your ear. What did he say?"

Spectre drew in a laboured breath. "He said that they knew about you. That more of them would follow in the weeks to come. That an army, bigger than we could imagine, is coming our way. He told me war is coming."

I swallowed hard. My stomach was in knots. The smell of blood was in the air, hanging like a jacket on an old coat rack. I wanted to run away, to feel the cold breeze on my face as I pushed my legs harder than they had ever gone before. I wanted to be at home, to hide in the safety of my room. But there was no safety anymore. Even if I went home, they would find me there. The only way out was through.

I wasn't sure that I was prepared for whatever was coming my way. But what other choice did I have?

I looked up to Spectre, and steeled my resolve. "What do I do?"

Spectre straightened, and suddenly he seemed taller than he ever had. "You start training. In fast forward."

"Okay," I said, nodding. "Let's get started."

"I'm glad to hear you say that, boy. I'll arrange everything." He turned to walk away, but paused, slowly spinning to face me. There was something strange in his expression, and not for the first time, I couldn't read it.

"What is it?" I asked.

His lips spread into a small, waifish line. "Nothing. It's just...you remind me so much of him."

I tilted my head to the side. "Who? My grandpa?"

He shook his head, as if hurrying the thought away. "No, never mind." His eyes grew hard, his voice cold. "Don't worry Angus. I won't make any more mistakes."

"What are you talking about?"

Without another word, Spectre took off and, yet again, left me in a confused daze. Once again it was down to me to chase him down the halls.

lost

I walked behind Spectre, who scurried ahead of me. I had trouble keeping up. It was as if there was a fog around my head that I couldn't quite see through. My hands were like ice, my head, pounding. Vaguely, I took in the faces of students I passed. They all looked the same; fear mixed with curiosity, sprinkled with a little anxiety. Rides for the day had been cancelled and everyone was ordered to return to their rooms, but it seemed few people were listening to instructions.

I could hear a voice calling behind me, but it wasn't until someone yanked on the back of my shirt that I realised it was me that they were calling.

"Angus, you okay? I've been shouting out for you." Artie stood in front of me, looking frazzled and a little sweaty.

"Yeah. Sorry. I was just…I didn't hear you."

"Did you hear what happened?" he asked.

"Yeah, I did. I…I saw it, actually."

Artie's eyes grew wide. "Tell me what happened."

Spectre had stopped and was eyeing me impatiently. "Meet me in the study," he ordered, then briskly walked away.

I blew out a deep breath and looked back to Artie. "It

was…awful, actually. I don't know what other people are saying, but it was like a nightmare. Two people died, right in front of my eyes. Died…like as in…dead." The word hung stiff in the air and a sour taste filled my mouth.

Artie's face grew pale.

"There were dragons fighting in the air. It all happened really quickly, but from what I could tell there were two attackers and then another few that were defending the school. I don't know who they were."

"They would have been the Initium."

"Another group of people I don't know about?" I queried.

"There's a small group of, I don't know, I guess you would call them defenders? They're not students. Or, I guess, they were, but they graduated. They're kind of like our own small military. There's only a few of them."

"Oh. Guess that explains it."

"So, they killed the attackers?" Artie asked.

"Yeah. I guess so. One of them…uh," I swallowed hard to chase back bile. "One of them fell from his dragon and the, uh, the fall killed him." I remembered the thud as he landed. I could imagine the crunch of bones, the squelch as organs were crushed and penetrated. "The other guy…I don't know what happened to him, really, but he was just a few feet away from me. He…I guess he bled out."

My stomach rolled. I felt dizzy.

"That's insane. I can't believe you saw it all. I wonder what's gonna happen now." Artie said quietly. "Where are you going? We're supposed to be in our rooms, but no one is really listening. Me and the others are gonna meet up outside and talk everything over. Cosette's pretty freaked out apparently. Coming?"

"No, I can't. Spectre needs me. Probably wants to tell me not to talk about everything I saw." I force a laugh.

"Okay. Well, if you change your mind, come and find us." Artie slapped my shoulder, and I walked away.

The journey to the study may as well have been a thousand miles. My legs felt like sacks full of stones and my lungs felt half drowned as if I was trying to breath underwater. I had heard about people dying from my Mum. Being a nurse, she was around death and sickness and pain all the time. She tried to hide it from me, but I always knew when she lost a patient. There would be something different about her…something sad. She would do the exact same thing every time it happened; she would walk in the house, come up to my room, sit on the end of my bed and say only one thing - "Love you, bud."

Then, she'd get up, head into the bathroom, and close the door behind her. A few seconds later I'd hear the bath running, and she wouldn't come out for at least an hour.

This was usually the time that Grandpa George would tell me about the time that she lost her first patient and how much her reaction had scared him. He'd tried hard to get her to quit, but she refused. He'd finish off his story by saying how proud of her he was, and how he wishes he could do more for her.

I felt sick. I stretched out my hand and ran my fingers along the wall for support. There was something about the cool touch of the stone that brought me back down to earth. I dismissed the nauseating memories just in time to hear a painful shriek. I looked over and saw the doors of Medical. The shriek sounded again.

My feet started drawing me towards the doors before I knew what was happening. It was like I wasn't in control of my own body.

I pushed open the doors to find that the reception desk was

empty. The shriek was bloodcurdling. It sent a shiver down my spine. I followed the sound, my body taking over.

At the end of the hall were double doors, with a glass hole chiseled out in the centre. I approached the glass, the painful sounds growing louder and louder.

My eyes grew wide with horror as I focused on what was behind the double doors. A dragon lay, tied down, on an enormous bench. It was on its side, revealing a large open gash. I could see its bones, and muscles and sinews through the gaping hole.

It moaned loudly as half a dozen veterinarians hovered over it, swabbing, stitching, wiping, and cleaning. The only part of it that could move was its head; the rest of its body was tied down.

Why don't you just anesthetize it? I thought to myself. Surely the dragon didn't need to be awake for the procedure. The pitiful groans were enough to make my hands shake.

I wasn't sure how long I stood there watching it. Time seemed to stand still. I wished there was something I could do, but I could only stand there, dumbly. The dragon's rider was dead, and it was not far behind, by the look of things.

Then, without warning, the dragon snapped its head up and its eyes met mine.

There was such pleading and horror in its eyes that my face grew hot, and my own eyes began to sting. Wide and round, and wet with moisture, his eyes bore into mine, as if he was seeing right into the depths of my being.

Before I knew what I was doing, I flung open the doors and rushed towards the table.

"What are you doing?" I shouted at the shocked faces of the veterinarians who now stood staring at me. "Put him to sleep! Why is he awake? You don't need to operate on him while he's conscious!"

"Nurse, get him out of here!" one of the men in medical masks shouted.

The dragon's brown eyes were imploring me, begging me.

As soon as I closed my eyes to blink, a normal, natural movement I gave no thought to, it happened again. The world froze; the veterinarians paused, scalpels mid-air. The nurse who had been rushing towards me was still as a statue, her arm extended towards mine. The world was smudged, like a rippled reflection in a still pool of water.

I had somehow Blinked again. I looked down at the unmoving dragon, with glassy, unseeing eyes. I lost control of myself. My hand moved towards the dragon's face of its own accord. My fingers gently traced the brown scales leading from his nose to his horns. His skin was cold to the touch, rough and jagged. He felt different to Merry, who was warm and soft.

Suddenly, with my hand still pressed against his face, the dragon's eye shifted. Then his head moved. I pulled back, surprised. I looked about me and everyone else was still frozen, but the dragon was no longer still. He closed his eyes, then opened them again, his pupils growing large. He let out a quiet moan and suddenly I was struck with the knowledge that if the dragon was no longer affected by my ability to Blink, that meant that his wounds weren't either. I had to get the medical crew operating again, before he bled out in front of me.

I Blinked.

Time restarted with a jolt. The nurses hand grabbed mine and she dragged me from the room. The veterinarians started working again. All the while, the dragon kept his eyes on me, aware of the secret we shared.

"What do you think you're doing?" the nurse shouted at me. "You can't just walk in while they're in surgery!"

"I'm sorry," I spluttered. "I don't know what I was thinking."

"Get out of here. Now," she ordered.

"You can't do this! That dragon is in pain."

"It's an enemy dragon."

"Since when are animals our enemies?" I was being dragged through the waiting room with surprising force. "Why aren't you anesthetizing him?" I shouted. "He shouldn't be awake for that procedure."

"You're a vet, are you?" she snapped.

"No, but I am the son of a nurse, and you pick up a few things. It's not fair what you're doing."

"Look, kid," the nurse said, huffing out a breath, "that dragon is an enemy dragon. We don't need to waste our limited provisions. We have our own kind to take care of."

"That's ridiculous!" I shouted. "It's just an animal. The rider might have been your enemy, but that dragon in there is not. And he is in pain. You have to do something about it."

"I don't decide these things, now get out of here."

The nurse shoved me out and into the hall. She slammed the door in my face and walked away.

I turned and ran down the hall.

There was no way I could allow this to happen. I had to do something.

There was a pain in my chest, a twisting in my stomach. I heaved in breaths, feeling a strange and agonising sensation rupture through me.

I ran through the library, only vaguely aware of the people around me. I slipped through the door and into the dark, warm study.

Spectre looked up at me, without the hint of surprise on his face, and tilted his head to the side. I was breathless, clutching at my chest, sure I was having a heart attack. He was reclined slightly, his chair twisted out to the right so he could cross his left leg over his right. A pipe, with a thin fragrant trail of smoke, was perched in his hand. His face was creased with concern, and grief.

"They won't put it to sleep," I gasped.

"What is wrong with you? You seem in pain." Spectre replied calmly.

"The dragon! The one that was hurt. They're doing surgery, but he's awake. They won't put him to sleep. He's in pain. It's completely unethical!"

"Did they say why?" he asked.

"Because he's an enemy dragon and they don't want to waste provisions."

"Well, that much is true," he conceded.

"How can an animal be an enemy?" I asked. "The rider, sure, but the dragon? It's just a big... I don't know, a big lizard."

"No, Angus. A dragon is much more than that. A dragon and its Vector are linked. The purpose of the rider becomes the purpose of the dragon. A dragon is only good when its rider is good."

I dropped down on the highbacked leather chair beside me, unusually wearied and worn. Sweat dripped down my face. My breathing was uneven and fast.

"You've had a very trying day, Angus. Perhaps you should retire to your room for a rest, and we'll deal with everything tomorrow."

"No," I said, shaking my head. "This isn't right. There's something special about that dragon. Even when I Blinked, it was like...it was unaffected."

Spectre straightened in his chair. "I beg your pardon?"

"I can't breathe," I gasped. "My chest…" I gripped at my shirt.

"Did you say you Blinked again?"

I nodded weakly.

"You Blinked and the dragon was unaffected?" he clarified.

"Yeah," I wheezed. "Something's wrong with me. I… I've got this pain in my chest. I feel like I'm dying."

"That's because you are."

"What?" I shrieked.

"Explain what you mean very precisely, my boy, without missing a dot or a comma. If you do, I shall know, and knowing can be a very dangerous thing, particularly when you don't tell me what it is that I need to know to undo the danger that knowing could do."

I tried to disentangle his words in my mind but gave up. "I burst into the room while they were doing surgery. I didn't mean to…I just kind of, *did*. And I got so upset that it just happened, I just Blinked. At first, everyone was frozen. Even the dragon. I just felt so bad for him; he was looking at me. He was in pain. So, I touched him and-"

"You touched the dragon?" Spectre asked.

"Yeah," I answered. "Can we call for the Healer or something?"

"While you were Blinking?"

"Yeah. When I touched him, his eye moved, then he blinked. He was unfrozen, but I figured that meant that his wounds would start bleeding, so I Blinked again to get everyone else unfrozen too." I threw myself back in the chair as pain splintered through my chest. I groaned in agony. "Something's wrong!"

"What did I tell you!" Spectre said, popping out of his chair like a meercat out of its hole. "I told you never to touch another person's dragon while you are Blinking!"

"What? No, you didn't!"

"Yes, I am certain that that is something I would have told you during our lesson earlier today. It was on my lesson plan."

"Well, I don't know if you remember, but out lessons were interrupted. You never told me that."

"I didn't?" he sat back down.

"No. Look, you just said I'm dying; can we focus on that?"

Spectre was silent. He tapped his pipe on his lip over and over, lost in some other world.

"Please!" I said loudly, to snap him free of his reverie.

Spectre jumped, as if he had forgotten I was there. "Yes, yes. Quite."

I watched as he picked up the phone and dialed. "Yes, hello. You have a dragon in theatre at the moment. It is to be given the same accord as a dragon of Everwood Academy. Place it under anesthesia immediately. Is that quite understood? Spare no medical supplies." He hung up the phone and I was left dumbstruck.

I stood there, open mouthed. "That's it?" I asked. "What about me?"

Spectre just stared at me blankly.

My chest heaved up and down and I felt dizzy. What was happening to me? I started to feel cold. Why wasn't Spectre helping me? Was I going to die right here?

Suddenly the world started to tip on its axis. I stretched out my hands to stop myself from falling over. My jaw felt heavy and unhinged, my skin like it was floating off my bones.

"What is happening?" I slurred.

Just when I thought I was about to black out, it stopped. The pain vanished, the dizziness dissipated. My breathing returned to normal. I felt completely fine.

"What the hell just happened to me?" I asked Spectre, who eyed me curiously.

"Bother. It is as I suspected," he said, as if only to himself. Without warning, he split apart from himself, and there were two of him.

"Does this mean what I think it means?" his ghost asked.

"I daresay it does," the original replied. "This is of grave concern."

"It's also quite excellent," the ghost said gleefully.

"For *us*, not necessarily for him. You would do well to remember that, and keep your enthusiasm to yourself."

"Of course," the ghost responded, suitably chastised. A glimmer of mischief sparked in his eye. "Although, it is very noteworthy that the first Shadowing in 400 years is happening *here*. At Everwood."

"You are right, of course."

"I usually am."

"Can't argue with that."

"Of course, we can't share this information just yet," the ghost said regretfully.

"No, no. Not yet. Must wait, must wait."

"Or… must we?" the ghost asked.

"Whatever do you mean?"

"Well, knowledge of the boy has obviously already made its way to the Rebellion. Isn't now the time to alert the Concilium of our greatest weapon?"

"He is not a *weapon*!" Spectre suddenly shouted in a voice as deep and wide as thunder. The room seemed to grow darker, and Spectre seemed taller and more ominous than I had ever seen him. A storm seemed to appear around us, and the room was thick with tension.

The ghost jumped back, then vanished in a whiff of smoke.

It was a moment before Spectre could compose himself enough

to speak to me.

"What's going on?" I asked as calmly as I could.

Spectre sat down, shoulders slumped with a weight I couldn't see or understand. He held his pipe aloft and leaned back in his chair.

"I'm sorry you had to see that, my boy. Sometimes I can… argue with myself."

"We all do it," I said encouragingly.

"For most people, it's not quite such a display."

"No," I agreed. "What's going to happen to the dragon now? I mean…I'm guessing you don't have a stray dragon department."

"Well, actually we do."

I should have been expecting that. "Of course you do."

"But this dragon is not a stray," Spectre added.

"He's not?" I asked. "His rider is dead, isn't he?"

"Oh, yes. Very. No more living for that human being, who is now more of a human-not-being. Human *been*, I suppose. Quite dead."

"So...? How does it work then, when a dragon rider dies?"

"When a Vector dies, its dragon is, like you say, a stray for the rest of its days. However, as I stated before, a dragon and its Vector are linked. Once its rider dies, the dragon has very limited time left."

"What do you mean?" I asked.

"A dragon will live an unnaturally, almost immortally long life. As will its rider."

I waved my hands in front of my face as if to stop an advance of mosquitos. "Wait, wait, wait. What?"

"A Vector and its dragon are linked in the sense that so long as one of them is alive, the other will remain so. I am one thousand and nine years old. My dragon is still alive, and so am I. If my dragon were to die, however, the years would catch up on me and I would be dead, at my age, most likely within a week."

I stared, open-mouthed like a guppy.

"Likewise, if I were to die, my dragon would die also. Since they are much larger creatures, it would take him longer, but most likely, within three months Pilar would be dead, too."

"Are you telling me that I'm…*immortal*?"

"Sort of. Basically. Yes. But you *can* be killed. So can your dragon."

I waited a full minute before speaking. "So, you're saying that this dragon, the one from today, is going to die in a few months?"

"Normally, yes. But now that dragon is no longer a stray."

"What is it?"

"Angus, that dragon…is *yours*."

"Mine? How can he be mine? I thought there was only one dragon for every rider."

"There is. However, one gift can change this. You are the bearer of that gift. You can 'steal' another person's dragon. This happens when you touch the dragon while your gift is activated. Which is what you did. I would have mentioned this to you if we were not interrupted today."

"So, I can take other people's dragons?" I asked.

"Yes," he nodded. "But you must never do this."

"What about today? Is everything going to be okay?"

"Everything will be fine. You are linked to both dragons now, but your length of life is only connected to your original dragon, unless you change this. We'll get into that later. This dragon's owner is dead, so it's fine, but you must never ever do this to a dragon whose rider is alive. You could kill the original rider, unless you return it immediately. In this case, there is no one to return the dragon to, so you are free to keep him."

"Like…forever?"

"Yes," he answered. "Though, he will remain in medical for quite a while, no doubt. Dragons heal quickly, but his injuries were severe. You will not be able to see him, Angus. I mean it. Leave them to do their work."

"I will." I paused, still shocked. I had gone from no dragon to two in barely any time at all.

"Angus, you must understand the gravity of what you have done. There is a time and a place for this ability. Remember to never touch a dragon while Blinking if the Vector is still alive. *Never.*"

"What happened to me earlier?" I looked away from Spectre and into the flickering flames in the fireplace. "I thought I was going to die. You didn't really seem to care, and then it just, I don't know, stopped."

Spectre looked burdened with the knowledge crammed into his mind. "You are not linked only to Merry, anymore. You are also linked to this dragon. While Merry's death is the one for which you must be most concerned, it does not mean that this dragon will not affect you. What you were feeling, my boy, was the dragon's pain."

"Like I was feeling what he was feeling?" I asked.

"Yes."

"That doesn't seem like a good design feature," I sighed.

Spectre laughed. "It's not. It doesn't happen to everyone, and you will grow more tolerant, capable and resilient as you grow alongside your dragons. You are a very special Vector, Angus. You are one of the Shadowing."

I screwed up my nose. "That sounds a little off-putting."

"It is an elite Vector who—"

The door opened and the longwinded groan of the hinges cut Spectre's words in half. Cyrus walked inside, waif-like and nonchalant as if nothing had happened. Before he was like a soldier, now he was placid and featureless like it had never happened. I wondered what was going on outside. What was going to happen with the dead riders? What was the protocol for this kind of thing?

"What is it?" Spectre asked.

"A call for you, sir," Cyrus droned.

"Take a message, please," Spectre instructed.

"It is the Ascensor, sir," he replied.

Spectre's eyes went wide enough to assure me the Ascensor didn't make a habit of calling on a regular basis to chitchat.

"Read through this," Spectre said, dropping a hefty book into my lap. Dust exploded into the air and tickled my nose. In one lithe movement, Spectre was out the door.

afterboom

My eyes were bleary and red, but the sun on my face started to bring me back to life. It had been the longest day. I was still having trouble accepting that what I had seen – death, blood, mayhem – was real. It already felt like a week ago, but it was mere hours. I flopped down on the grass, as far from anyone as I could possibly manage, and Merry curled herself up beside me, staring at me with her large, unusual eyes. There was something penetrating about her gaze, like she was trying to communicate with me, or as if she was ready, at any given moment, to respond to me.

Slowly, her eyes grew heavy, and she drifted off to sleep. As I watched her sleeping peacefully, her chest rising and falling, I felt a bone-deep tiredness creep up my spine.

I closed my eyes, but in an instant, it all replayed in surround sound in the cinema of my mind. The rider falling to his death, his bones shattering on impact. The dragon, bleeding and broken, crumpled at the bottom of the stairs.

The bloodied note, the handwritten script – *don't blink.*

I shuddered involuntarily and opened my eyes, once again in the safety of the grassy knoll, instead of the chaos of the day. I could feel a wave of anxiety about to crash on top of me like waves on the shore. I took a moment to ground myself, focusing on what I could see, touch, hear. As I scanned my surroundings, I noticed that Merry was awake and staring at me. Her head was high, her eyes wide, staring directly into me. She knew.

I tucked myself in beside her, resting my back on her chest. She tightened her limbs around me protectively. I felt her warm body rise and fall beneath me with each of her gentle breaths and felt calm.

When I was sure I was steady once more, I allowed myself to wonder. What was going to happen now? Was everyone just going to pretend that it didn't happen, or were things going to change? Were we going to have to go home?

My phone buzzed in my pocket. I pulled it out and saw it was Mum calling. I drew in a shaky breath, debating whether to even answer. I swallowed hard and answered the call.

"Hey, Mum," I tried to sound cheerful.

"Angus Cillian Finch!"

I flinched at the sound of my middle name.

"Were you ever planning on speaking to me again? Thirty-one hours of labour and sixteen years of raising you, doesn't warrant regular phone calls?"

"Sorry, Mum. It's been…" I tried to search for the right word, "mayhem."

"I'm worried sick here. Your grandfather has positively slumped into a stupor. Even your dog is depressed. You don't have to stay there you know."

"I… I belong here. There's a lot of important stuff going on here right now."

"A lot of schoolwork, is there?"

"Uh, yeah. Heaps."

I could hear the sound of Mum sniffling through the phone, and I knew she was crying. "You study hard, then."

"I will, Mum."

"Make me proud."

I sighed, wanting nothing more at that moment than to be at home. It would be so easy just to leave, and go back to my normal life, forgetting everything that had happened here. I closed my eyes against the onrushing images of the day. I felt Merry tighten against my body, protecting me, and knew I had to stay. "I'm trying, Mum."

I hung up the phone and drifted into a dreamless sleep.

dismissed

Spectre wasn't happy with my single martial arts lesson per week. I had to train every day.

I tried not to dwell on my concerns about being so brutally forced into martial arts training. Often fears came calling, reminding me that the training was preparing me for physical confrontations that were, no doubt, coming my way. I would quell my fears with the knowledge that I was in good hands.

"Han and Angus, please," Spectre called. "You're up next."

I groaned internally. This had to be some sort of cosmic joke. Getting into the ring with Han Kang? I'd rather get into the ring with a tiger that hadn't been fed in a week. Unwilling to allow a crack in my resolve to show, I stepped up first, throwing myself into the ring a little too eagerly.

I raised my hands to cover my face and set my legs apart so I wouldn't lose balance. Han appeared in front of me, looking entirely unfazed. Loosely, he held up his hands.

I wasn't sure what happened, but I didn't get a single punch in before I was lying on the flat of my back, staring up at the ceiling, almost certain my lungs were full of blood, or my heart had been ripped from my chest, or all my ribs were broken. Surely the damage had to be that severe.

Han looked down at me with disdain and I gritted my teeth. How I wanted to punch him. But, as I had just discovered, that wasn't a possibility.

"Thank you, Han," Spectre said, helping me to my feet. "Next group, please."

I watched the others perform better than I had. When the lesson was over, Spectre instructed me to stay behind. My embarrassment wasn't complete apparently. I wasn't done yet.

There was a very bizarre youthful energy about Spectre. He never acted the age he appeared. He taught me countless moves someone of his age should have struggled with, yet he never appeared to tire or feel injured.

"To control your body, you must learn to control *yourself*," Spectre said, pinning me to the floor. "If your mind is noisy, your body will rebel."

I struggled against his vice-like grip. He loosened his hold, and I slipped out from underneath him. I held my fists up in front of me, my jaw set into a hard line.

"You are angry," Spectre chastised.

"Yeah. I am," I answered.

"Control it," he responded.

"I can't. I don't even understand what all this is for."

"Control it," he repeated.

I closed my eyes and let time wash over me. I blocked out Spectre, and the knowledge of what had been and what was to come. My heartbeat thrummed like a steady drum in my ears. I took a deep breath and took a mental tour of my body, unclenching every muscle and sinew. I focused on the smallest details, like the feeling of the padded mat underneath my feet. The sound of the wind rustling the leaves of the trees outside.

I opened my eyes and threw my fist out. Spectre seemed taken by surprise, but only for a moment. Punch after punch, he blocked, dodged and returned. I managed to avoid being hit for about forty-five seconds, which was a personal best. Then I was on the flat of my back, looking up at the aged wooden beams supporting the roof above me. A view I was getting all too familiar with.

Spectre appeared, standing over me. He grinned.

"Good job, my boy."

"Whatever," I groaned.

Truthfully, in some quiet, hidden part of my mind, I took comfort in the fact that Spectre was good at everything. It made me feel safe. Like, if everything went badly, as I was told it *would*, everything would still be all right. Spectre would protect me, and everyone else at Everwood. Is this what it felt like to have a father?

Feeling battered and bruised, I headed for the dining hall. I took my usual seat with Artie, Hana and our other friends.

"You look like crap," Nolan said.

"I feel like it, too," I replied.

"Spectre killing you in there?" Hana asked.

I tried not to show my embarrassment at having my rear end handed to me by an old man, but had a feeling I didn't succeed. "I don't know how he does it," I said. "It's like he's not even human."

"We're not sure he is," laughed Artie. "The whole school is taking bets on whether he's an Elf or something."

"I don't think I can handle any more imaginary beings coming to life," I moaned, picking at my food absentmindedly. "This whole place is weird."

"You know what's weird?" Nolan pushed his tray of food away, as if in disgust. "It's weird that everyone is acting like nothing happened. Like people didn't die right in our front yard."

The others nodded and voiced their agreement. I snuck a quiet look at Hana. She looked worried, but even so, it was startling how beautiful she was. Her eyes seemed darker today, her hair a shiny curtain separating her private thoughts from the rest of us.

She looked up suddenly and met my eyes. I smiled and looked away. We hadn't had a chance yet to talk about our conversation in the library.

The hum of talking in the background suddenly dissipated. I looked around to see what was going on. Cyrus and a few other faculty members I didn't yet know walked into the room and commanded everyone's attention.

"Students in Class A," Cyrus began, "please note that after lunch you will all be required to report to the assembly hall. Please disregard your current timetables."

He let the words hang in the air for a moment, surveying the students. He looked waifish and ethereal to me, tall and stooped at the same time. Fragile and unbreakable.

"That will be all," he sighed. "Please resume your current activities."

I turned back to everyone. "What was that about?"

"No idea," Artie replied. "But Class A, that's us."

"Maybe things aren't quite going back to normal," Kit said.

The bell sounded, and Hana was the first to stand. I quickly followed suit, catching up to her as she stacked her tray. "Hey," I said.

"Hi." She smiled a little and started walking.

I followed along beside her. "How are you feeling about all this?"

"By 'all this' I'm guessing you mean the dead rider who fell from the sky?"

"Uh, yeah," I laughed humourlessly. "That's right."

"I saw it," she answered.

"So did I. I didn't see you out there, though."

"I was at the window." She tucked a strand of her behind her ear. "I saw him fall. It was… awful."

"I'm sorry you had to see that."

"You had it worse. I saw you on the step," she said.

"Yeah, it was pretty gruesome."

She stopped suddenly.

"I also saw Spectre hand you a piece of paper from the rider."

I wasn't sure what to say. I looked away, trying to figure out how I should respond, but before I could she spoke again.

"Don't worry. I haven't told anyone. But something tells me that there's more to you than meets the eye, Angus Finch."

She held my stare for an age, and all words turned to ash on the end of my tongue. I couldn't think about anything but her face. I was stuck, captive to her stare.

Until someone slammed into my shoulder and broke my reverie.

I looked over and saw Han walking away.

"I think I'm growing on him," I quipped.

Hana laughed, and we walked together until we reached the hall and took our seats. A few minutes passed before Spectre walked onto the stage. His face was grave, and his shoulders were stiff. We waited anxiously for him to speak.

"You have been summoned here today because of your standing within the Academy," he began. "Each of you are members of Class A, meaning, of course, that you are at the top of this school in knowledge and abilities. Some of you bring a high level of intelligence to the table, while others are here because of their unique and powerful gifts. Others still are here for their exceptional abilities in warfare. No one is here by mistake."

I looked at the students surrounding me, trying to read each of their faces. Who were they? What were their gifts?

My eyes fell on Han, and I quickly looked away.

"Many of you were witnesses to the unfortunate events that have unfolded over the last few days," he continued. "I am aware that no one has been given any information regarding these events, and that is why you are here. This information is for Class A students only. In fact, while we are in here, each and every other student of Everwood Academy is being packed up and sent to the French Academy for their safety."

Loud murmurs echoed off the walls as the fifty or so remaining students of Everwood Academy digested the news.

"I am afraid," Spectre said in a raised voice to hush the grumblings, "that things have taken a turn for the worse, and it is now on your shoulders to defend not only Everwood Academy, but each other, and the very culture instilled in us by our heritage. It is my unfortunate task to inform you all that the Rebels have declared war."

The room became impossibly loud as students threw themselves into an uproar. It was at that moment that there was a painfully obvious split in the room, and I could tell into what category each student fell.

Some were concerned, looking from side to side, voicing their opinions to neighboring ears. The warriors were standing, shouting their allegiance to Everwood Academy and their willingness to die to protect it.

Then there were the students with the gifts. They remained in their seats, unmoving and unspeaking. They were either confident in their gifts or waiting for more information.

I felt a chill go down my spine.

"Quiet!" Spectre shouted. As he did so, seven ghosts on either side of him shot out across the floor, in a straight line. Each ghost echoed the word he had exclaimed in anger, and the noise was far louder than the students. As quickly as the ghosts had arrived, they disappeared.

The room fell into silence.

"Each of you is required to commit themselves to the cause of defending Everwood. We have received word from our spies that the Rebels intend to move in two weeks. You have until then to be prepared.

'You will be separated into groups. Those with unique and powerful gifts are with me. Those with high intelligence are with Cyrus. And those who specialise in warfare are with Sensei Hiroto." Spectre paused and surveyed his students. His words hung heavy in the air, and I could almost hear every heart pounding. "Dismissed."

gifted

Artie, Hana and I followed Spectre to an enormous hall dubbed the Theatre.

Along for the ride was Han, and fifteen or so others I didn't know. I was glad for Artie's company; glad, too, that I no longer felt like I was hiding something. If everyone knew the Rebels had declared war, then the only thing I had to hold back was my gift…

… which would be interesting, considering we were all going to be training together, and everyone thought my gift hadn't manifested yet. There were going to wonder why I was here.

Artie seemed twitchy and nervous as we piled into the Theatre and took our seats. The Theatre reminded me of the Colosseum in Rome – not that I had ever been, but I'd seen enough pictures to get a bad feeling in the pit of my stomach.

Hundreds of seats stretched up high on an angle, row after row. The seats looked down on a massive, wide-open, barren space that was circular in shape. It looked open, vulnerable.

The Theatre was a fitting name. If you stood on that floor, all eyes would be on you, like you were an actor on a stage.

"You okay?" I asked Artie, who fidgeted beside me.

"Yeah," he breathed. "Just nervous."

"It'll be all right," I said in what I hoped was an encouraging voice. I wasn't sure if I believed myself.

Spectre stood in the very centre of the floor. Even in such a large space, he still looked big and tall. I started to tap my foot on the ground, anxiously awaiting instruction.

"Thank you for coming," Spectre said, as though we had had a choice in the matter. "We will be undergoing intense training, enhancing each of your gifts. When you are not sleeping, or eating, you are to be in this room. You will come to know every crack and crevice in every wall of this room over the coming days. You are to focus the entirety of your energy on training, and nothing else. Not only your own life, but the life of the person sitting next to you, could be at stake. You are no longer students of an educational academy – you are now, until all of this is over, soldiers of the Draco Exercitus – the Dragon Army. You will be *treated* like soldiers, and you will *act* like soldiers." Spectre surveyed the faces of the young people inside the room. Something told me he hated what he was saying, and I felt certain that if there were any other way, he would take it. It was at that moment that I realised the true gravity of what was at stake.

"Now, I would like to begin with a display of each of your gifts, so that everyone knows what to look out for during training. I will call you out, one by one. Starting with…" he looked down at his chart, "Angelique Thomasson."

A girl who I could only assume was Angelique Thomasson, stood to her feet as Spectre gave her a wide berth. I watched as she took her place in the centre of the room and waited, curious as to what would happen.

Other than Ghosting, the only other gift I had seen in action was Han's, so I was eager to see what another looked like. I had heard the most common gifts were enhanced vision, enhanced hearing and ultra-speed. Beyond that, Spectre was yet to find time in his busy schedule to explain any others.

Angelique stood still, eyes focused on the stone floor below her feet. She was very thin, with white-blonde hair and crystal-clear blue eyes. She wore a sundress that was hemmed just above her knees. Her bare arms were bony, and I wondered what damage this unintimidating girl could inflict.

A sudden chill filled the room, and I shivered. It was as though the temperature dropped by ten degrees in mere milliseconds. When our teeth started to chatter, we realised something very peculiar was happening.

White droplets fell from nowhere, landing gently all about us. I looked down at my knees, now covered in white specks, and realised they were snowflakes.

I let out an incredulous laugh and watched the flakes melt away as the temperature in the room suddenly increased. The air grew thick and heavy, and I felt as though I was breathing in soup. The muggy room suddenly felt like a stormy summer's day.

As a bead of sweat dripped down my face, a flash of light appeared, striking the stone ground with immense force. A deafening snap echoed off the walls. Gasps escaped our lips as thunder rumbled effortlessly throughout the Theatre. We were all sufficiently impressed. This tiny girl had created weather – out of nowhere.

The room's temperature quickly returned to normal, and the thunder ceased. All the snow had melted, and no more flashes of light erupted out of thin air. All was calm.

Angelique looked to Spectre for approval, then, when he nodded, she walked across the floor and back to her seat.

"Next is Reid Seaver," Spectre chimed, without comment on the display that had just occurred.

I watched as Reid took centre stage, and her entire body exploded into flickering lights, spitting sparks out like she was a sparkler at a New Year's Eve party. With a forceful extension of her hand, she threw a ball of white-hot light out of her fingertips and it crashed against the wall like a flash grenade.

After Reid was a boy named Landon who didn't look much more than twelve or thirteen years old. He wore a shirt with a flaming tractor on it and jeans that were torn at the knees. All I could think was that he should be at home with his parents. He was too young to be here, in this room, facing an uncertain future.

I was comforted when he completely disappeared.

A moment later, a student's hat in the front row was plucked off his head by an unseen force. Everything became clear when Nicholas placed the hat atop his own head, causing it to vanish as well. He reappeared, turning visible again, and returned the hat to the student.

At least, if everything turned sour, he could turn invisible and hide until it was over.

What followed was an insane display of abilities that were as incredible as they were unnatural. I began to realise that I was in a room full of people who were very dangerous. Even *without* their own pet dragon.

Artie left my side when his name was called and chose to explain his gift, rather than display it. "If I just start," he began, "you'll have no idea what I'm doing. So…it works like this. I can read radio waves. Radio waves linger, they never disappear. Inside this room, bouncing around all the walls, is every single conversation ever had within this room. I can read them. Or hear them, or however you prefer me to explain it. So, yeah."

"Would you like to explain why this is a gift that warrants you being in Class A, Artie?" Spectre asked.

"Well, it has a lot of real life uses – if someone says the code to a safe out loud in the room, I can tell you what the code is. That kind of thing."

"Very good, thank you, Artie." As Artie took his seat, Spectre added, "Before any of you get any bright ideas, Artie has been utterly forbidden to use his gift at school, for any reason. However, his gift will come very much in handy if we need to know the Rebels plans."

He then called out the next name, and I watched in awe as student after student demonstrated their gifts, then took their seats again as though they had simply stood in class to read out an essay.

When Hana was called to the front, I sat forward in my chair with eager anticipation. What was her gift?

Hana walked into the middle of the room and sat down. It was completely silent. Everyone seemed to hold their breath as we watched and waited.

Then there was a loud bang at the closed door of the Theatre. The another, and another. The door started to buckle under the pressure of the force outside and with one final smash against the wood, the door gave way and a red deer, with enormous antlers, walked into the room. He was followed by a fox, and three small rabbits.

The animals made their way over to Hana, who was still seated on the ground, and stood beside her protectively.

Where did these animals come from?

Before I could think another thought, Hana held out her hands, palms up to the roof. I watched in abject terror as snakes and spiders crawled out of her hand, breaking through the surface of her skin without tearing or blood.

Students who, like me, did not know of Hana's gift, gasped as the creatures crawled out of her body. Hana turned down her palms and straightened her chest, sitting tall and rigid. Silently, slipping through her like it was walking through a curtain, a tiger slunk out of her chest. It stood in front of her and roared mightily, before turning away from us and taking its place behind her.

The only one who didn't seem in awe of Hana's gift was Han. He sat motionless in his chair, arms folded, watching the spectacle with only one emotion on his face. Was it…pride?

Hana stood to her feet and as she did so, each of the animals dropped down until they were lying flat upon the stone surface.

Spectre walked over to Hana and placed a kind hand on her shoulder. "From the look on your faces, I can see that an explanation is needed. Our dear Hana has a very strange, very beautiful gift. Not only can she summon and control animals in the wild, but as you saw, she can also manipulate her cells at an unbelievably fast rate, and create animals from *within.* These 'animals' she has created, are not real animals. They have no heartbeat, no digestive system. They could not survive on their own, as they are a part of her. Though they are lethal when required, these animals are similar to my Ghosts, in that they are simply parts of her body that she can cause to form any animal's shape and send forth as I do my Ghosts. Everyone understand?"

The room was silent.

Spectre smiled. "Good. Thank you, Hana. You may take your seat."

The animals that had come out of Hana's body, disappeared in a cloud of grey smoke, and the animals she had summoned headed for the door. She walked back over to her seat and sat down.

One thing was for certain. This was a very different school, filled with very different people.

But a fear was growing inside of me. Spectre had already told me it was imperative that no one knew anything about my gift. So, what was going to happen when he called my name? *Was* he going to call my name? If he didn't, what excuses would I make?

There were only two students left who hadn't displayed their gifts – myself, and Han.

Han looked calm, prepared. I felt anything but.

I swallowed hard as Spectre prepared to speak. "I'm afraid we've taken a little too long getting through everyone, so those who have yet to display their gifts will, unfortunately, have to wait until we have a moment another time."

I blew out a sigh of relief as he continued.

"This will be your training ground. Each person will be allotted a section of floor big enough for your gift. Training with dragons will take place outside. I will assign a ghost to each of you, so that you are all receiving one on one instruction. Please take your places now."

Spectre exploded into multiple versions of himself, shattering and fracturing skin cells, bone and muscle, forming perfect copies in an instant. We were each accompanied by one of them to a space of our own on the floor.

I got the original.

flame

Since no one would know I was doing it, I attempted to Blink, only to fail miserably. Watching everyone else succeed around me, as I sat there stupidly Blinking my eyes like a moron, was definitively humbling. Two hours later, Spectre led us outside to work with our dragons.

But outside wasn't much better. I sat facing Merry, who looked up at me with eager eyes, filled to the brim with expectancy and loyalty. We hadn't moved in at least an hour. While everyone else seemed to be getting along very well with their own personal Spectre, I was nowhere further ahead than I had been three hours ago.

Spectre wanted me to learn about her as a Glitch and solidify my bond. Instead of giving me any instruction on how to do this, or even exactly what being a Glitch meant, he had insisted that I sit down and get to know my dragon.

So, I sat down, and after petting her, and inspecting each different facet of her body, we were reduced to a staring competition. What did he mean? I knew Merry. Of course I knew her. We spent every day together. How many times had I ridden on her back now? What was this all about?

She was so much bigger now than when she had first hatched out of her strange, unique egg. She was a lot taller than me. Every day, she seemed to grow a little more.

Her colours were brighter today than they were yesterday. The red and green shades that flittered across her scales seemed almost alive in their own right. Her skin flowed and glowed, ebbing back and forth with colour, like waves coming in and out of shore. Her eyes were always on me. She was constantly waiting, expecting, watching. I was pretty sure I was boring the crap out of her.

Not lost from my mind was my other dragon, recovering in Medical. I had heard from the veterinarians that he was still in critical care, and, as Spectre had instructed, I had not been allowed to visit. Not that I'd had the time, even if I had been allowed. A declaration of war really zaps your free time.

"You're getting nowhere, I see?" Spectre couldn't hold his tongue any longer. Honestly, I was impressed he'd said so little in the last hour.

"Oh, now, I wouldn't say that. I've won three rounds so far."

"Of what?"

"Staring competition."

"I see. Important breakthroughs, then."

"Of course."

"Angus… do I need to remind you of why you are here?"

"No," I groaned, frustrated. "You don't. That's why I'm so mad at you."

"You're mad at me?" Spectre seemed hurt. "I was unaware."

"Yeah, well, now you are aware."

"Might I inquire as to why you are mad at me?"

"Because you've got me sitting here, doing nothing, while everyone else is busy. Can't you just explain it to me? She's a Glitch,

I understand. What I don't understand is exactly what that means."

"I can't explain it to you, Angus. Every Glitch is different. I have absolutely no idea what Merry's Glitch is."

I deflated. "Oh."

"But, if it is an example you seek, allow me to demonstrate. Han, will you please join us?" Spectre called over his shoulder.

"Han?" I said quietly. "Why are you calling him over?"

"Han is the only other student in this school whose dragon is also a Glitch."

"Of course he is," I sighed.

The solemn, tall figure of Han Kang appeared in front of me. He seemed eternally shadowed, overcast by something that haunted him.

His dragon was beside him. It was easily three times the size of Merry.

His dragon looked like he did; sinister and angry. It was a bright blue, indicating to me that it was actually a *she*. As she stopped in front of me, I noted a second colour that glistened across her scales. A river of white snaked up her spine, starting at the very tip of her tail and ending on the edge of her nose, where it formed the shape of a bell.

She was quite beautiful, I had to admit.

Spectre glowed at the sight of her. "This is Jia. She's a Glitch, just like Merry. Han, please show us something unique that Jia is capable of because she is a Glitch."

Han nodded and stepped in front of his dragon. He started speaking to her, so quietly I could barely hear him.

Even though he was speaking in Korean, it didn't take me long to understand what he had said. As the words parted Han's lips, Jia became entirely engulfed in flames. Her body, from one end to the other, emitted thick orange flames, busting out of her like she had suddenly been turned into a miniature sun.

I jumped back, and Merry immediately threw herself in front of me, taking a protective stance. With another quiet word, Han put an end to the flames and the dragon once again became a pool of blue and white.

"Well…" I said, nodding slowly. "Cool."

"Han is a very talented Vector," Spectre said kindly. "He has spent a great deal of time training Jia, and as you can see, it has paid off."

"Thank you," Han responded.

"So, Merry can explode into flames because she's a Glitch?" I asked.

"Heavens, no," Spectre seemed amused by the idea. "Every Glitch has a completely unique gift. They say only point one per cent of all dragons are Glitches, so the fact that Everwood Academy has two is, well, very prestigious. Unheard of, even." He gave himself a smile that seemed to infer he himself was responsible for the two animals.

"You must learn to speak to your dragon," Han said. His voice was hard, angry. He reached up and stroked Jia behind the ear. "You have to listen to what she has to say, and she will tell you what her Glitch is."

With those last parting words of wisdom, he turned and went back to his corner, his dragon following along behind him, her tail swooshing back and forth.

I stared after him, feeling lost and inadequate. What kind of nonsense was that? *Learn to speak to your dragon. Listen to what she says.* I was trying. And getting nowhere.

I felt more deflated than ever.

"Angus," Spectre began, seeing the look of misery on my face.

"It's no use!" I snapped. "I can't do this. Not this quickly, at least. There's too much pressure, and I have no idea what I'm doing. And, no offence, but you're not really helping."

Spectre sat down beside me. He didn't speak straight away. Instead, he sat there with me, as I drew patterns in the dirt. Finally, he spoke, his voice low and quiet. "Remember when you first found her egg? I told you that egg had been lying dormant for an age. All that time, she has been waiting for her rightful Vector. You, Angus. There is something very special about Merry. There was a good reason her egg was separated from all the others. She's different. She's old…much older than any of the other dragons here."

I watched as Merry curled herself into a ball in front of me, her back pressed up against my shins so that she was touching me.

"I wish I could tell you everything now, Angus," Spectre continued, "but I can't. The right time will come, and all will make sense. Until then, you must trust me. I truly have your best interests at heart. And *hers*," he gestured to Merry. "I believe you are destined for a greatness you cannot yet imagine. But you are right, none of that can be sped up. It must take its natural course. But I am also right when I say that there are people who pose a great threat to you. To the Academy. They are gathering forces as we speak, and you must be prepared. This *is* your natural course. Your road. You must follow it, if you can."

I shook my head. "I can't do this. It's too much. I wish I never came here. If I didn't, none of this would be happening. No one would be in danger. No one would have to fight."

"Those who seek war will always find a reason to fight. The catalyst can take many forms, but it is rarely in itself to blame. You are no more to blame for this than the sun is to blame for its warmth that can be used to burn."

The dragon rider, plummeting to his death, the rider bleeding out in front of me – it replayed in surround sound. They were dead because of me, and nothing would be able to change that. Not even Spectre. "I never meant for any of this to happen." My voice was just a whisper.

"That is how I know you are worthy of the gift you bear."
Spectre placed a hand on my shoulder. "Come with me."

He didn't give me a chance to respond before he stood up and walked away.

long way down

"Uh, what are we doing here?" I asked, peering cautiously over the edge of the cliff.

I couldn't tell how far down the drop was, because about a hundred feet below me, the fall was cut off by thick swirling mist.

It was cold out, and the sky was overcast with blackened clouds that hung low above my head, threatening a storm. I was being peppered by raindrops, and not the pleasant *Singing In The Rain* kind of raindrops. It was the sharp kind that stung when they hit your skin, like little bullets whizzing down at you from an angry vigilante hiding behind the clouds.

"Your dragon is your better half. The relationship between you and her is much deeper than you yet realise. Your genetics are linked, bonded. To even begin to fully open up what this connection means for you both, you must learn to call her."

"Like… like calling for your dog?" I asked.

"Were you not listening? What part of anything I just said indicates your relationship with her is even remotely like the one that exists between man and Rover? No. You have to call her in a more metaphysical sense. She needs to feel that you need her and go to your aid."

I looked to Merry who sat down beside Spectre. "Uh, how?"

"I would love to give you all the time you need to learn at your natural pace, but I can't. You have to be ready. So, I'll leave it there."

"Leave it wh-"

Before I could finish my sentence, Spectre's hand slammed against my chest and I began to fall.

There was a moment of disbelief. Surely, Spectre, my mentor, had not just pushed me off a cliff. But as the wind blew forcefully past my face, and I felt my stomach roll, I realised there was no mistaking it. I was falling to my death.

I started to scream. Panic was setting in as I rushed further and further towards the ground. I was going to die. Just like that, my short life was over. What would my Mum think? Would she know what happened to me?

At least the war would be over.

My heart was racing, my throat thick. I screamed louder, but I realised that screaming was achieving nothing. I had to focus. There was only one way out of this, and that was Merry. What had Spectre said? *Learn to call her.*

I closed my eyes and tried to reach out to her. I was going to die if she didn't save me. I suddenly felt wet and cold and realised that I was now falling through the mist. How much further was there until I hit the ground?

I tried harder to call out to her, but nothing was happening. I couldn't do it. I wasn't ready.

I braced myself for the impact. Any second now I would hit the ground and every bone in my body would shatter, and my organs would rupture, and I would die a horrible, squelchy death.

My body slammed hard against the feeling of stone. I prepared to die, but I didn't. My body ached all over and my bones felt weak, but I wasn't dead. I was, however, no longer falling. I was moving upward, back towards the top of the cliff, at a ridiculous speed.

What was happening? Had I successfully called Merry? My body hurt too much to move to see whether it was Merry that was carrying me.

Suddenly I was at the top of the cliff, but I wasn't placed gently down by whatever carried me. I was ejected, like a pilot out of a crashing plane. I flew through the air and landed solidly on the ground at Spectre's feet.

When I felt I could successfully move my neck, I peered up at him. His lips were pursed, and a look of dissatisfaction was on his face. Merry sat still beside him. I looked behind me, slowly so as not to further stress the bones in my neck. Hovering in the air was Spectre's dragon, Pilar. I recognised him from the first time Spectre had put me in a life threating situation. This was getting to be a habit.

While I was grateful that Pilar had saved me, I was furious that Spectre had literally thrown me off a cliff.

"You threw me off a cliff!" I rasped, my heart still pounding violently.

"Yes. I did. I really thought it would work too." He bent down and helped me to my feet.

"You threw me off a cliff!" I said again, this time my tone more aggressive. Apparently, I was unable to say anything else. He seemed to be missing the point, that throwing me off a cliff was a Bad Thing to do.

I leant my hands against my knees trying to catch my breath.

"We've already covered that, Angus. Keep up. You need to learn, and like I said, I don't have time for you to take the long way round."

"But…you threw me off a cliff!" Maybe this was all I would ever say again. I was a broken record.

Spectre sighed. "Yes."

The second the word yes was out of his mouth, his hands were on my chest again, knocking me off balance and down I went once more, tumbling off the side of the cliff and beginning another freefall.

freefall

I felt that familiar drop of my stomach as I started to fall. Spectre had just pushed me off the cliff *again*. What kind of training method was this?

My time with Spectre had been nothing short of mystifying. I was constantly in a state of terrified, or angry, or confused. Normal life was so long ago, it was like I had never lived it.

But this time I didn't scream. I focused. In the corner of my eye, I saw Pilar shoot down, his body tucked in tight, his wings flat beside his ribcage. He fell fast and I knew he was trying to reach the bottom before I did.

With the confidence that Pilar would catch me, I put everything I had into calling Merry. My hair blew around my face, whipping my skin. The mist rose around me. I focused harder.

I hit hard against Pilar once more as he flew up to meet me, matched my speed, caught me and carried me upwards. The sense of failure hit me harder than my anger at my deranged mentor. Pilar threw me into the air, and I landed on the ground again, rolling to an undignified stop at Merry's feet.

My body ached as if I had been in a car accident. I waited, eyes on the sky, while the world stopped spinning and I stopped coughing up my insides. I lifted my hand to my head, ensuring my face was still intact and not sliding off my skull as it felt like it was. Slowly, I let my arms fall, stretching out on either side of me along the ground. Pain surrounded me. Merry tilted her head as I looked up at her. Her eyes sparkled, her face open and calm. "Isn't this a team effort or something? Maybe she's the one not pulling her weight," I rasped, my breath ragged in my burning lungs.

Spectre chuckled. "I'm afraid not."

I stood up on shaky legs and gathered whatever was left of my resolve. "Any tips?"

"She needs to feel that you need her," Spectre replied simply.

"I'm falling off a cliff, right in front of her!" I snapped. "What, does she think, that *I'm* the one with wings?"

Spectre just shrugged and shoved his hands out, ready to push me again. I stepped to the side and avoided his blow. "Thanks," I muttered. "But I've got this."

I turned to the cliff, and without looking over, jumped.

Now, I had just thrown *myself* off a cliff. Who does that? What kind of world was I now a resident of? Somewhere in the back of my mind, I knew I should be more afraid than I was. But life like this was becoming addictive. Something I needed. Something I craved. I would never go back to normal, no matter how hard things got.

I must have been missing something. What did it mean to need her? If falling to my death wasn't enough, then there had to be a piece of the puzzle I hadn't placed yet.

I thought about my family and how I needed them. Not because I would die without them, but because I loved them. Maybe that was it.

Did I love Merry?

I thought about the day she came into my life, and how even though it had barely been any time at all, she had become like an extension of me. I felt incomplete without her by my side. Like I was missing an arm or a leg.

As the wind blew past my body and I fell deeply into the mist once more, I thought about my future and what I wanted it to look like. When I pictured it, I saw Merry there. But what if I failed at training and war came to Everwood? What if I lost her? A grim image of a future without her drilled a hole in the pit of my stomach.

I absolutely loved her. And I truly needed her.

A red blur shot off the cliff like a bullet. The figure made itself smaller, to fall faster and faster. Would it be fast enough? I was certain that I was falling further than I had before, which meant that the ground couldn't be far away. If I hit it, I would die, no question. My body would be crushed, organs splitting into pieces as bones punctured them, and I would drown in my own blood.

I tried not to panic, and instead, to trust. Merry would save me. I knew she would. I watched her fall, because that's what she was doing. She wasn't flying. She was dropping like a rock, heading towards the ground as fast as she could. I watched her flatten her wings against her sides, her eyes narrow, focused on me.

I held her gaze.

She had come to me. I had called her, and she had come. Without a word, she had known I needed her, truly needed her, not just to save me from the ground rapidly approaching, but to save me from a life lived without her.

She was right above me; she shifted her vision from me to the ground and back again. She tightened her body even further. I watched her eyes become slits as she tried to increase her speed.

Was she going to be fast enough?

I kept my eyes on hers. I didn't need to twist to see how far away I was from the ground. I knew it would be close. If it came to it, I could always try to Blink to give her more time. But I wouldn't. I would trust her. If I Blinked now, all it showed was that she wasn't enough. And I hadn't perfected my skill yet. What if I couldn't do it?

I watched her adjust her body so that her feet were outstretched in front of me. She wanted to grab me with her claws and stop me from falling. But if she did that it would break my back, snapping it like a matchstick.

The second that the thought came into mind, she moved again, as if I had said the words out loud. She had to match my speed then slow me down or come up from underneath and reach me at the same speed I was falling, and slow that way. Any other way would kill me in an instant.

I heard a loud shriek, then Pilar appeared behind Merry, dropping fast like a stone in a river. He stretched out his gargantuan wings and pushed himself closer towards the ground. He looked like an athlete swimming the butterfly. His wings pointed directly in front of him, then scooped the air back towards his tail to propel him forwards. His mouth was open, and a deafening screech shattered the air.

That was the moment I realised I was going to die.

I drew in a deep breath and slowly released it.

Come on, Merry. Come on.

She let out an almighty roar, her jaws opening so wide I thought she was going to snap into pieces. The sound was like nothing I had heard before. Pain stabbed at my ears, and my chest vibrated with the sound. I saw her teeth, thick saliva strands stretching from the bottom jaw to the top. Her eyes were dark. She was afraid. Truly afraid.

And then my body came to an abrupt halt.

thievery

My body was frozen, suspended in mid-air. No dragon had caught me, and I had not Blinked. Merry still rushed towards me, unaffected by whatever had frozen me in time. Beyond her, Pilar was paused in an anguished, somewhat mangled position. His wings were splayed out behind him, his body contorted strangely. His mouth was open in rage, his skin curled back over his teeth, each one longer than my hand. His blood red gums were vibrant with fear.

What was going on?

Moving my hands through the air, I could see smudged ink trailing behind them. My body felt strange, like I was moving in water. The sensation was as familiar as breathing. But I hadn't Blinked. I knew I hadn't. Then… had Merry?

Merry flew down to meet me and placed herself delicately on the ground. I looked to the side and noticed I was just a few feet from death. I could see the pile of rocks that waited for me, just a couple of feet away.

I couldn't believe I hadn't Blinked. Why hadn't I even tried? Had Merry become so important, so vital to me, that I would die like this?

I waited for regret to come, but it didn't. All I felt was exhilaration.

Merry dropped her head and nuzzled herself underneath me, until I was situated on her back. I rolled over, and sat upright, in time for Merry to gently stretch her wings and float off the ground.

Then, suddenly, time caught up. Pilar had to catch himself, roll tightly and fly back up to the top of the cliff to avoid crashing into us. I felt the rush of the wind from his wings blast across my face and I held on tight to Merry to avoid being blown away.

Merry flew slowly, methodically, towards the top of the cliff. I rested my head against the back of her neck and stroked her chest. I could feel her heart racing, pulsating against her scaled skin.

Spectre came into view. His expression was indecipherable. Merry landed softly on the ground, as Pilar thudded down beside us. I slid off her back and stared at her in awe.

"What happened?" Spectre asked.

"I was going to ask you the same thing," I replied. "It was…it was almost like she Blinked. I didn't do it. I wasn't going to, even if it killed me. She needed to know I needed her, or all of this is pointless and I'm dead anyway. So, I…I waited. She caught me just a few feet off the ground. I froze in the air, like I was floating on a bubble."

"That is interesting. Perhaps the most interesting of all of the interesting things that I've ever thought to be interesting." He placed two fingers on his chin as he mumbled to himself. "I wonder if that means what I think that it means. Of course, it certainly means one of the things that I think that it means, which is that Angus is much more fascinating a character than I, at first, assumed."

I watched him as he started to pace. Had he forgotten I was here?

"To not even try to Blink when he knew that it would save his life, well, that's really something," Spectre muttered. "Something stupid, possibly, but something none the less."

"Indeed, it is something!" A second Spectre appeared, joining in the conversation. "The boy nearly died, and still he chose not to call on his abilities that would have allowed his dragon to catch up to him."

"I know!" The original exclaimed. "Let's not forget that he now has a *second* dragon. We should do some investigating to see if there is anything special about it. It did come from the resistance, after all."

"I agree. Though, of course, coming from the resistance isn't necessarily a guarantee that this dragon is special."

The first Spectre paused, and a sentimental smile spread across his face. "I think all dragons are special in their own way."

"Well, of course they are," the other said, with a wave of his hands. "But back to this dragon. Merry. Do we think that she has the ability to copy gifts?"

"Well, she certainly has the ability to copy Angus's gift. Whether or not she can copy another's is yet to be seen."

"Even if she can," the ghost added, "it doesn't mean he knows her well enough to be able to bring it out of her."

"This is true, this is true. Though, with Angus's current Blinking ability, he can only slow time down, leaving his dragon unaffected. He can't put her in a stasis field, which is practically what Merry just did. She warped time around him, leaving him aware, unfrozen, yet still safe from the impending few seconds. Angus hasn't scratched the surface of what his gift is." Spectre laughed, mirthlessly, like he knew a grave secret and took great delight in it. Was this the original Spectre, or the ghost?

"Very true. He has no idea why Blinking is the most powerful gift."

I was starting to get dizzy. Watching Spectre pace around, having the most bizarre conversation with himself was making me woozy. "Can you both just stop for a minute?"

The two Spectres stopped and stared at me. "Is everything all right, Angus?"

"Uh, let's see. You threw me off a cliff."

"That wasn't me," the ghost said. "That was him."

"Fink," the original retorted.

"You are him!" I yelled. "You both threw me off a cliff – twice – then, for some insane reason, I threw myself off a cliff. And I nearly died!"

"That's what we were just discussing! Utterly marvelous!"

"No, not utterly marvelous!" I said, accentuating the words in a mocking tone. "Terrible!"

"But you discovered your dragon's Glitch, and you figured out how to call her. This is a wildly successful day, Angus."

"I nearly died!"

Spectre looked at me, sudden compassion in his eyes. The ghost faded away and the original knelt down in front of me. His incredible height meant that, even kneeling, he was only just shorter than I was.

"Angus, my boy," he said quietly. "That is the very message I have been trying to get through to you. Your very life, indeed, the lives of everyone here, are on the line right now. There is much to achieve in a very small amount of time. You are the newest student, and, given your gift, the one who is most in danger. Very clearly, they know about you, Angus. That was made evident in the note we found. I don't know how they discovered you. I haven't even informed the Concilium about you yet."

"Why?" I asked.

"Well, they have a lot more important things on their minds right now than the gift of my brilliant new student."

"What do you mean?" I asked.

Spectre sighed. "I didn't want to have to tell you this, but I fear it will be the only way you understand. None of the other students know about this; only me and a selected handful of the academy's administration."

"Just tell me," I urged.

"In cases like this, where there is a threat to an Academy, protocol is to alert the Concilium and they will, in response, send help in the form of their best riders. When I alerted the Concilium that we have received a very credible threat against Everwood, they informed me that each and every other Academy has also received a similar credible threat. They must disperse their riders among all the Academies, to ensure that each have at least some back up. This, unfortunately, means that we will be receiving only two riders to come to our aid. I suspect they will be here in the coming days."

"Two?" I questioned. *"Two?"*

"Now, don't go panicking, Angus. I am relying on you here. I haven't told any other student, and I will hold you to the promise that neither shall you. I need you, Angus. I need you to keep your wits about you. Make no mistake, these two riders are simply superb at what they do. And," he smiled proudly, "I'm not so bad myself."

"Why only two?" I pressed.

"There are limited numbers, Angus. It was all they could spare. Particularly since they must leave enough men behind to guard the Concilium on the off chance that this is all some rouse and distraction, and the rebellion's true target is not us, but them."

"You mean they're protecting their own hides first?" I snapped.

"Angus, you must understand. If the Concilium were to fall,

chaos would take over. They must be protected."

I shook my head and raised a hand to my brow. "This is insane."

"A little, yes."

"So, what do you need?" I asked.

Spectre smiled and stood up, towering over me once more. "That's the spirit, my boy."

Spectre's ghost popped out again. "I think this will be a job for both of us."

Merry wandered over and began to sniff the first Spectre curiously, then the second. She then sat down on her back legs, and I watched, stunned into silence, as her body split in two, and a second Merry appeared.

Delighted with her progress, the two Merry's began wrestling each other playfully.

I turned, opened mouthed, to Spectre and his ghost.

"Well," the original said. "I suppose that answers that question, now, doesn't it?"

released

"No strenuous flying, no rich foods, no rough-housing and no licking his stitches."

The nurse did not seem thrilled to be releasing the dragon into my care, and given our last encounter, I wasn't thrilled to be in the same room as the nurse, so we were even.

The dragon was much larger than Merry. Double the size, at least. He was chocolate brown, with gold eyes and intimidatingly large horns. His wings were curled up to his side, and his scaled body was rough to the touch.

"Does he have a name?" I asked.

"What do you want, a dog tag? Pick a new name. Now go."

"Thanks," I muttered.

There were huge barn-like doors at the back of Medical, for large dragons to move in and out. I gently steered my new dragon towards them, and we walked out into the sunshine. Merry was waiting for us. She perked up when she saw us, and started clicking and rumbling.

"I hope you guys get along."

Merry approached the larger dragon, and rubbed her sides up

against him, like a cat would. He didn't seem to mind. As I watched them get acquainted, I tried to figure out what to call him. Nothing really seemed to suit. Naming a dragon wasn't exactly like naming a dog. Nothing seemed powerful or regal enough.

When I was about to give up and name him Rover and call it a day, Hana appeared behind me.

"Who's this?" she asked.

"Uh," What was I supposed to say? Was anyone allowed to know? I finally decided to just go with the truth. "He's my new dragon."

Hana's eyes went wide. "You have another dragon?"

"Yeah. I accidentally stole him. It's a long story. But the rider's dead. Like, I didn't just take it from someone. But he's mine now. I can't think of what to call him. I don't know what his name was."

"I knew there was something different about you, Angus Finch."

I shrugged uncomfortably. "I really wish there wasn't."

Hana stepped up and touched the chocolate-brown dragon's face soothingly. She traced her hands from the tip of his nose down to the stitches on his side. "Don't overthink it," she said.

"What?"

"All of it. The name for the dragon, your gift… your secret." Her eyes flashed as they met mine. "Me."

My face grew hot.

"You don't have to carry it all alone, you know," she continued. She walked the length of the dragon and stopped in front of me. I could smell the strawberry scent of her shampoo. "How about Ransom?"

"What?"

"For the dragon. Ransom. It's simple. Strong."

"Sure. Ransom." I would have named it whatever she wanted if she just kept looking at me like that.

She smiled and walked away.

I stared after her, quite confident I was already completely in love with her.

"How's he settling in?"

I jumped and groaned when Spectre appeared beside me out of nowhere. I was getting pretty good at telling when it was a ghost or the original.

"Fine, I think," I answered. "His name is Ransom."

"Excellent, strong name," he replied.

"I thought so," I smirked to myself.

"They seem to be getting along well."

I watched them rotate around each other, investigating the other with growing interest.

"Looks like it."

"Perhaps you should take him for a bit of a spin." Spectre winked, then vanished in a puff of smoke.

The nurse said no strenuous flying, but surely that didn't mean no flying at all. I slowly approached him and hoisted myself up onto his back, sitting squarely between his shoulder blades. I wasn't sure what to expect. They had said that the owner takes on the traits of its rider – if one is evil, the other is too, but Ransom seemed calm and kind. He began lumbering forwards, as if he already knew I wanted to fly.

Merry followed along. It felt like riding an elephant. With each footstep, I rocked back and forth as he thudded along.

When we reached a clearing big enough for him to spread his wings and take off, he shot off into the air much faster than I had expected. His was like a lightning bolt. Walking had been slow and laborious, but this was nothing like that.

"Whoa, whoa, whoa! Slow down!"

Merry appeared beside us, a red and green blur. As they started to dart back and forth, teasing each other, I realised that this was their flight, and I was just along for the ride.

I spent as much time with Ransom and Merry as I could. When I was with them, it was easy to forget about everything else. It was natural, and fun and peaceful. I would fly a lot at night, alternating riding on Merry and Ransom. We always flew together, the three of us, and there was a part of me that wanted to escape it all with them. I could just take them and fly away, leaving the fear and chaos behind. But I would never let everyone at Everwood deal with this on their own. I couldn't.

Things were tense at the Academy. Spectre was always on the move. There were dozens of him walking around at any given time, and I couldn't help but think about how every mother on earth must wish they had the same ability to be in two places at once and juggle as many things as he did.

I was spending more time with Hana, but there was a frigidity in the air that had everyone feeling off. We were scared, even though we didn't want to admit it.

I didn't envy Spectre. He had to defend the Academy with two elite Vectors, a couple of security Vectors, and a bunch of teenagers. Training was intense, every day. Martial arts, flight, boxing, and using our gifts. I was *finally* getting good at Blinking, and I could freeze time at will. I now understood how to intentionally start it and stop it, but keeping my secret was difficult, since everyone was working hard to get ready to protect the Academy. It looked like I was a useless tag along, with nothing to bring to the table. It made my interactions with Han worse than ever.

Mealtimes were silent, some people opting out of meals altogether. I couldn't help but feel guilty - this was all my fault.

I walked into the dining hall, which was somber and quiet, just as it had been the night before last, and the night before that.

I saw Hana sitting alone, a book stretched out lazily on the table. I walked up to her, the familiar sensation of nerves making me lose my appetite.

"Good book?" I asked.

She looked up and smiled. "Hi. You look…"

"Great?" I finished for her, then laughed. The truth was, I looked terrible. I was exhausted. Sleeping wasn't something that came easily to me lately. I was training all the time, and my body burned all over.

Hana laughed. "How did you know what I was going to say?"

I sat down, my aching body enjoying the chance to rest, just as the doors to the hall opened with an ominous bang.

a familiar face

They walked into the Academy in slow motion, the ground thudding under their heavy footsteps. They were dressed similarly, in leather boots, rising to their knees, black floor length coats, and black linen shirts.

Spectre stood at the front of the dining hall and waited for them to stop in front of him. We all sat waiting anxiously.

"Welcome to Everwood," Spectre said in a deep, resonate voice.

The first rider nodded. The two guardians were intimidating to say the least. There was a man and a woman. The woman had impossibly long hair, draped down her back in an intricate plait with black leather bands twisted through the strands. Both sides of her head were shaved short, and her hair was so blonde it was almost white. Her eyes were clear blue, but there was a darkness that fell across her face when she turned to observe us all.

There was something oddly familiar about the man. He had short hair, cropped tightly against his head, and a ragged five o'clock shadow across his face. He was tall, solid. His nose was narrow, with a ridge in the middle, and his jaw was square. He had a tattoo that started at the base of his ear and disappeared down the collar of his shirt. It was just like the tattoo I had seen on the back of Spectre's neck the day I arrived.

"These two riders are here to join us in our efforts to defend Everwood Academy," Spectre said. "You can be confident their skills far surpass your own. This is Vice and James. They were both students of this fine establishment and have returned to protect it."

James. *James.* It suddenly struck me why the rider looked so familiar. My eyes widening, I scrutinized his face. It was definitely him. I hadn't seen him since I was four years old, at my grandmother's funeral, but there was a photo of him on the mantle above the fireplace in our living room. He was younger in the photo – less imposing. But that intense stare was the same.

The rider here to defend us was my uncle.

I shot out of my seat in shock. All eyes turned to me. James's eyes met mine. They flashed briefly with recognition, then his face grew hard again.

"Is something wrong, Angus?" Spectre asked.

I froze, not sure what to say. Would James even know who I was? Everything made sense now. This was why Uncle James was a constant feature of family debates and arguments. He was a Vector. An important one, by the look of it. Would I end up just like him? Leaving my family behind, incapable of being a part of a normal society?

Spectre cleared his throat. "Angus?"

"No," I said quickly. "I… I just… wanted to say thank you. Thank you for coming."

The guardians nodded and turned their attention back to the rest of the students. I sat down slowly. Spectre kept his eyes keenly on me. He nodded knowingly.

James was the first to speak. "I don't know what Spectre has told you, but the threat against Everwood is real and you are all risking your lives by staying. Anyone who does not wish to be a part of this should leave now, though I cannot guarantee your safety outside the walls of this Academy any more than I can inside it. At least here, your families are safe."

James was silent, allowing time for any students to stand up and leave. If anyone was considering fleeing, the last thought hanging in the air made it impossible. There was no way any of us would put our families in danger.

"Then let's move on. Continue your training, get plenty of sleep and wait for instructions." James turned to Spectre, nodded curtly and strode out of the hall, with long, sure steps. Vice followed closely behind him.

Spectre smiled at us all gently. "I have the utmost confidence in you all. Rely on your gifts and on your dragons. Rest assured, I will keep you all safe. Even if it kills me." Silence hung in the room.

"You are to focus on training. Your studies, needless to say, have been put on hold. Please, enjoy your meals then promptly retire to your rooms."

Spectre left quickly. My eyes followed him until he disappeared behind the heavy wooden doors that led out of the hall. Slowly, people started to rise and head over to collect their evening meal. I wondered how they had any appetite at all.

"Well, they look friendly," Artie joked, appearing beside me. "You gonna grab something to eat?"

"No," I said, shaking my head, "I'm not really hungry. I think I'll just head to bed."

"More for me," Artie laughed, slapping my shoulder. As he walked away, I wondered how he could keep so positive. Then I remembered no one had been told quite as much as I had. I was glad Artie was in the dark. Part of me wished I was, too.

a family matter

I had no intention of going to bed early, despite what I told Artie and Hana. I slipped out of the dining hall without drawing any more attention and headed down the ancient hallway.

I checked Spectre's office, but it was empty. Every classroom I passed was the same – there was no one in sight. I headed for the library, and as I pushed open the door, I knew exactly where they would be.

The library was silent, empty, ghostly. I hurried to the back, where the private room I had visited countless times waited. The door was slightly ajar, warm glowing light spilling out across the old wooden floors.

I could hear their voices, but I needed to get closer. I crept quietly towards the door and rested my back against the wall.

"Does he have any idea?" James asked, an edge of anger in his voice.

"No," Spectre answered, "and I intend to keep it that way for as long as possible."

"You don't believe he has a right to know?"

It was a woman's voice, so it must have been Vice.

"I will keep him shielded from it for as long as I can. It is too great a burden for him to carry," Spectre replied.

Who were they talking about? I leaned forward to hear better.

"You're making a mistake," James insisted.

"I don't make mistakes very often, boy," Spectre snapped. "And last I checked, I am still headmaster of this Academy, and the decisions within these walls are mine alone."

"He could destroy everything!" Vice shouted.

I jumped at the sound of her voice. She was angry. What was going on?

"I believe in him," Spectre replied calmly.

"You're a fool," she snapped.

"Maybe so," Spectre answered wearily, "but why change my ways now? I've often found the most foolish of things can put the wisest to shame."

"He will be your undoing," she spat.

"So be it," Spectre replied, without hesitation.

"You are condemning us all!"

"Vice," James chided.

Silence lingered for an age. When Spectre spoke again, his words were heavy, aged. "Angus is capable of more than you know."

My stomach lurched. They had been talking about *me?*

"That's what concerns me," James replied. "I warned you not to bring him here."

"I cannot allow an unrevealed Vector to remain idle, without ever knowing their purpose. It is against the code." Spectre's voice was hard. "It was simply out of the question. I didn't know he could Blink. There was a chance, of course, but there hasn't been a Vector who could Blink in two hundred years."

"His ability to Blink is only the beginning of our problems," James returned.

My chest heaved up and down with ragged breaths. What was happening? They couldn't be talking about me. I was a nobody. My hands trembled by my sides. I felt like I was going to be sick.

"Angus is not a commodity to be used or spared," Spectre retorted. "He has his own mind, and I think… I *believe*… with the proper guidance, his allegiance will lie with the correct side."

"You're willing to put the fate of this school in his hands?"

"I will tarry under the burden alongside him. There hasn't been a Vector like Angus Finch in generations. I will not leave him." Spectre stood, the chair scraping against the floor. "Frankly, I'm disappointed in you, James. He is your family."

"This isn't personal," Vice retorted.

"How can it not be? It's personal to Angus!" Spectre argued.

"Yes, he is my family," James replied, "but I left that thought behind the second I walked through the Academy doors. I'm here to protect this school, these students. And if I have to protect them from Angus, I will."

I couldn't handle it any longer. I burst through the doors, breathless. They turned to me, startled, eyes wide with shock. James clenched his jaws, and anger flashed across his face. Vice stepped back, like I was wielding some sort of weapon.

Why were they so afraid of me?

Spectre walked towards me, hand outstretched. "Angus," he breathed, "how long have you been listening?"

"Long enough," I replied. I turned to James. "How could you think I would ever hurt anyone here? What do you think I am, some kind of monster?"

"Angus," James began, but I cut him off.

"And you," I snapped at Vice, "I don't even know who you are, but you sure seem to think you know me. But you're wrong. It's you two who are the real monsters here."

"Angus!" James snapped.

"What?" I yelled. "You abandoned your family. Your father hasn't heard from you in years. Do you even know what Mum has had to go through because you disappeared?"

"Enough," James said, holding up his hand. "You don't know what you're talking about."

"What I don't understand is what *you're* talking about! You think I'm going to go crazy and kill everyone here? You think I'm some kind of danger?" I slammed my fist against the wall. My breath was catching in my lungs. My heart was racing. The room started to tilt on an angle. Rage boiled through me, but this was something else. Sweat beaded on my forehead and dribbled into my eyes. I blinked away the salty liquid and that's when it happened.

The room smudged and smeared in front of me, like Van Gogh's rejected painting. I felt like I was falling, but my feet were on the ground. The faces of the people looking at me dripped and slid, like thick icing slipping off a cake.

My heartbeat was thrumming in my ears; my limbs were heavy, as if gravity was baring down on me with excessive force. Spectre, James and Vice started to move. Their bodies jolted from one position to another, and all I could do was stand there, watching in horror.

What was happening? This was different – this wasn't the Blinking I had experienced before. I had to stop it. I blinked aggressively, but nothing changed.

I was afraid now. The room looked like an electric current was passing through oil paints smeared on a canvas. How did I stop it?

I groaned in pain. An ear-splitting ringing reverberated in my ears, slicing through my head like a meat cleaver. I covered my ears as a guttural shout escaped my mouth without my consent. "Stop!" I shouted.

And it did. The ringing was silenced. I looked up slowly, dropping my hands from my ears. James, Vice and Spectre stared at me in surprise. Spectre walked towards me. "Angus," he breathed, "how long have you been listening?"

"What?" I said weakly.

Spectre shot an angry glare at James. "Angus, I'm sure you overheard a lot of things, but you must understand-"

"What are you talking about?" I asked. "We've already had this conversation. I heard everything."

"What do you mean?" Spectre asked.

"When I walked in here before, you asked me how long I'd been listening." What was going on? My head was spinning. I turned to face the doorway, mentally retracing my steps. "I yelled… you…"

Spectre's face grew dark. James shook his head and pointed an angry finger at me. "Do you see?" he spat. "It's already begun!"

"What's going on?" I asked.

Spectre held up a restraining hand to James. "Calm yourself, James." He turned to me, and his eyes grew soft. "Angus, my boy, I need you to tell me everything that just happened to you. Don't miss a word. A word can mean the difference between life and death. Tell me everything."

a twist in time

The fireplace flickered, its warm, ethereal glow casting shadows across weary, worried faces. I sat closest to the fire, but I was shivering anyway. They had been silent for the last few minutes. I had told them everything, but no one had seemed relieved. Spectre sat across from me, a pipe in his hand. He quietly puffed out smoke into little rings, his mind in a place I couldn't hope to follow.

James sat in a high-backed chair, his ankle resting on his knee. His hands were folded across his stomach. His expression was unreadable. Vice stood by the window, as far away from me as possible. Was I really this much of a monster? What was wrong with me? I had lived my whole life thinking I was a nobody, but maybe that wasn't true. Maybe I was something much, much worse.

"I thought nobody knew about my gift," I said to Spectre.

"I said I hadn't told anyone. James already knew. Or, at least suspected. It was confirmed upon his arrival."

"How? I don't understand." My voice was barely more than a whisper. "Please…tell me what's happening to me."

"You need to tell him," James said to Spectre. "He needs to know. If, as you say, his allegiance will be with us, then we can all fight this together."

"I won't betray you," I said to Spectre, my voice fervent. "You're the only person who's ever really seen me for what I am and believed in me. Please."

Spectre nodded slowly, reluctantly. He stared into the fire, his voice hollow and distant. "Your gift, Angus, is incredibly rare. It is rare for a reason. It's unfathomably dangerous in the wrong hands."

"How is it dangerous?" I asked. Then I paused and asked the question I really meant. "How am *I* dangerous?"

"What you just did was bend time," James interjected.

"Bend time? What's the supposed to mean?" I asked.

"You rewound time," Spectre clarified. "You literally turned back the clock, my boy. You remember walking into this room and arguing with us, but we never experienced it."

Surely I hadn't heard that right. "I turned back time?"

"Yes." Spectre didn't look as jovial as he normally did when he was discussing my gift. "And I'm afraid you're only just scratching the surface of your ability."

"I don't understand. I didn't mean to. I don't even know how I did it."

"When you are just beginning to learn about your gifts, it can be easy to set them off. You're triggered by heightened emotions and senses. When adrenaline is coursing through your veins, or anger is flooding your body." Spectre seemed to have forgotten about the pipe in his hand. His eyes were trained on me; wide, dilated, focused.

I tried to steady myself. My knees felt weak beneath me. "But that's not all, is it? There's more?"

"A lot more," James answered. "Your gift will continue to develop at a rapid pace."

I clenched my jaw and looked at James. I couldn't figure out what he was thinking. I didn't know why he was looking at me like that.

We were family, weren't we? How could this be my fault? I had no idea about any of this. All I wanted to do was help. I finally felt like I was a part of something, like I mattered just for being here. And now everyone was looking at me like I was the enemy. "And that's why everyone's so afraid of me?"

The room fell silent.

"I don't understand," I stood up, shaking my head. "How is this so terrifying? So, I could turn back time by, like, thirty seconds. Why does that make me such a villain?"

"You're not a villain, Angus. Not at all," Spectre said.

"Tell that to them," I argued, waving my hands at Vice and James.

James adjusted his weight. "It's not your fault, Angus. No one is looking at this personally. You're a good kid, I know."

"Then why are you afraid of me?"

"Because you could defeat us all," James said quietly. "With your gift, you could take over and destroy everything."

"But I won't!" I shouted.

"You say that now," Vice scoffed.

"What is your problem?" I snapped at her.

"You," she hissed.

"Enough!" Spectre shouted. His voice was deep and dark, and the room shadowed over. James jumped back, and Vice took three steps closer to the window.

Spectre seemed startled by his own reaction, as if a part of him he tried to bury had resurfaced. He breathed slowly and spoke as calmly as he could. "I will not allow you to besmirch Angus in this manner. He is not personally responsible for his gift, or for the sins of others. Perhaps if you looked in front of you, instead of behind you, you might see what's been before you the entire time. Behind you is never the place to look to see ahead and looking ahead is the only way to move forward, and forward is where we must go."

"The only way you're going to know that I won't betray you is if you give me the full story," I said. "Tell me why I'm such a danger to everyone. The truth."

Spectre rubbed a hand across his forehead, wearied. "His name was Silas," Spectre began. "He was the first Vector to Blink in 490 years. I was young when I met him. Young by my standards, anyway. I hadn't been headmaster of Everwood for more than a year or two when he arrived. He was brilliant, really. Smart, too smart. He took to his gift with frightening speed. I could see how it was changing him, but I thought I could handle it. I couldn't. I was wrong. The first time I've ever been wrong. The *last* time."

I remembered the day I arrived here, when Spectre promised he wasn't wrong about me. I belonged here. I had a dragon. *I've never been wrong, Angus. Well…once, with disastrous consequences…*

"What happened?" I asked.

"He began to question the entire system we're built upon. He believed the Concilium was evil; working against us, trying to destroy us. All of this was a cover for what he really wanted, which was power. More power. Always more. He, like you, Angus, had the most powerful gift, but it wasn't enough for him. He wanted control. He left the Academy, and the Rebellion was born. It all started right here, under my roof. I should have stopped it before it got so far, but I… didn't. Couldn't."

Spectre took another puff of his pipe. His face flashed with pain. He cleared his throat. "Silas accumulated a following of like-minded Vectors, and the Rebellion grew. People were dying. It was war. Silas had a plan – he was going to take control of the Concilium. He needed to be stopped. I…" Spectre's voice caught in his throat. "I had to stop him. I used our friendship to get close to him and I… I killed him. Just as the Concilium ordered me to."

I sucked in a breath. Spectre closed his eyes and steadied himself. "His dragon died, as well."

The room was silent, the air heavy. Finally, Spectre continued, his face drawn and gaunt. "As you must already have deduced, the Rebellion didn't end with Silas. He had a son, who carried on his legacy. I've mentioned him before."

"Grayne," I guessed.

"Yes, that's right," Spectre nodded. "As you may be able to imagine, it's no surprise that Grayne's hatred of me grows stronger every day. He wants to finish his father's work, but he wants to destroy me, too."

"I won't let that happen," I answered.

"There's more, Angus," James added.

How could there possibly be more? "What is it?"

Spectre hesitated, not sure how to start. He stood to his feet and walked over to the fireplace. With his back to me, I had to strain to hear his words.

"Angus," Spectre said quietly, "Silas was your grandfather."

My brows furrowed together, my head spinning with this new information. "But… if Silas was my grandfather, that would mean…"

"Yes, Angus," Spectre nodded, "Grayne is your father."

The Man.

The words hung in the air, bloated and fat with fear and disbelief. No. That couldn't be right.

"What?" I croaked. "What did you just say?"

"Grayne is your father, Angus."

"That's…" I paused, words falling off the end of my tongue and into the abyss.

"It's true, kid," James grunted his agreeance.

"That's not possible," I said, in almost a gasp.

"I'm afraid it most certainly is," Spectre replied.

"Does my Mum…" I couldn't finish my sentence.

"No, Angus," James answered, knowing the question that faltered on my lips. "She doesn't know. About any of this."

"Shouldn't she?"

"I'm afraid not. She isn't a Vector, and since your parents aren't together anymore, and were never married, the laws are quite clear."

"Laws?" I scoffed. "Who cares about laws? This is my life!"

They stared back at me with sympathetic expressions, and it made me want to scream. All my life, I had wanted to know who my father was. For him to know who I was. I had spent countless hours wondering about what he must be like, who he is, what he did. When I was a kid, I used to imagine he was a spy, with powerful enemies and that's why he couldn't be a part of my life – to protect me. I breathed out half a chuckle when I realised that I wasn't that far off. He did have powerful enemies, but he hadn't stayed out of my life to protect me. He had stayed out of my life because I would get in his way. He had stayed out of my life because *he* was *my* enemy.

"So, you're afraid that because he's my father, I'm going to help him?"

James, Spectre and Vice were silent. James looked down at his feet and Vice stared out the window. Only Spectre met my eyes.

"This is what you meant, isn't it? About blood?" I said quietly. "Earlier, you said to me, sometimes blood overcomes even the clearest and most solid of intentions. I never forgot that. I didn't know what you meant until now. It is in my blood to betray you. My grandfather, my father. Now me."

"Angus, no one is saying-"

"Yes, you are," I interrupted Spectre. "You're all afraid that I'm going to do exactly what they did. But I'm not. Why would I side with someone who abandoned me? Who never let me even know his name?" I stood up and started to pace. "This is the first..." my words got caught. I cleared my throat. "This is the first place I've ever felt like I really belong. You..." I looked up to Spectre, whose wide child-like eyes kept his whole face looking young. "You're the... I mean... I've never had a father. But I feel like I know what it feels like to have one. Because of you. I wouldn't betray you. Not for him. Not for anyone."

Spectre walked up to me, closing the gap in a few long strides. He clasped his enormous hands over my shoulders and shook me gently. "Of course, you wouldn't. Never doubted it."

He turned to face James and Vice, wrapping an arm around my shoulder protectively. "There. I believe you've heard everything you need to hear. I shall take full responsibility for Angus. Perhaps instead of worrying how Angus could be used against us, we should start to consider how Angus could help us."

James hesitated. I could almost see the thoughts spinning around in his mind. Finally, he nodded. "All right. If you're going to help us, you'll need this."

James walked over to the table and picked up a thin file. It was crumpled and stained. The file was old. I took it from him and opened it. There, staring back at me, was a picture of a man I'd never seen before.

"Who is this?" I asked.

"It's your grandfather, Silas," James replied. "This is everything we know about him, and his ability to Blink. You're the first one since him."

"It's thin," I noted.

"He was elusive," James explained.

I flicked through the file, trying to add the story together, piece by piece. I paused when I reached a section titled *Blink*. It was a definition of sorts; everything they knew Silas could do with his ability.

"To understand your own ability," Spectre said, "you need to understand his."

I skimmed through the pages of eyewitness accounts, things that people had seen Silas do, or heard from his own mouth. "You're saying," I started, looking to Spectre for guidance, "I'll become like this?"

"Yes, Angus. Your gift will only grow." Spectre smiled a small, sad smile.

"Here," James said, passing me another file. "Take this one, too. You might find it an interesting read."

I opened the file and saw my father's face staring back at me. Guilt gnawed at me.

"That's your father," James said.

"I know," I answered.

"I didn't think you'd ever met him," Vice said.

"I… I hadn't." I looked up at Spectre. He looked at me with a disappointed, knowing expression. "When I went home to visit my Mum, he found me. He can ghost, like you can. He cornered me on the street. I didn't know what to do."

"Tell me what he said to you, Angus," Spectre said quietly.

"Nothing that made a whole lot of sense. He knew I could Blink. He told me not to. He said I can't trust anyone. That I can't trust you." I felt guilty just saying it. Why hadn't I told him earlier? Maybe I could have prevented this. "I didn't believe him. I trust you. I do."

"Then why didn't you tell me?" Spectre asked, his voice barely above a whisper.

I didn't want to answer, but I had avoided this long enough. "I thought you wouldn't trust me anymore."

"What else did he say, Angus?" James asked.

"He said that I was in danger. That something was coming. That's it. He didn't give me any real details. It was all a blur, really."

"You should have told Spectre," James said angrily. "He should have known.

"I'm sorry," I said. "But you've got to understand how insane it all was for me. I'd never met him before. Never. My own father. Then he appeared like a ghost. Out of nowhere. I just wanted to forget it happened."

"Your father is the leader of the Rebellion! He has killed our people!"

"I didn't know that!" I shouted. "He didn't exactly broadcast it! And no one told me!"

Spectre stepped in between us. "I think that's enough for one evening. Take that with you," he gestured to the file, "and we'll talk again tomorrow."

"This isn't right," I said angrily. "I didn't mean to-"

"I know, Angus," Spectre said, gripping my shoulders. "It's all right."

Spectre led me to the door and closed it behind us.

"I'm sorry. Really," I said, my voice empty and hoarse.

"There's nothing you could have done to change what has happened, Angus." Spectre kept his voice low, so James and Vice couldn't hear through the door. "There's so much you still don't know."

"That's what he said," I replied. "This is all about me, isn't it? The other threats are a bluff. The Concilium isn't in danger. It's *always* been about me." I had thought this before, I knew, but there was something so finite about it now. Something so true and raw. It was sinking into my marrow. This was all my fault, and I felt it in a way I never had.

Spectre knelt down beside me, his expression sympathetic and hesitant.

"What if I just forgot?" I asked. "You said there was a pill I could take, and I'd forget. Then they'd have no reason to come for me."

"Angus the gift is in you. Forgetting it's there won't erase it. They'll simply drag you back into this world."

"Then what can I do?"

"Is it true? Do you trust me?" he asked.

"Yes," I said. "Of course."

"Then trust me to keep you and this Academy safe. Don't worry, Angus." He drew back and smiled warmly. "You must be tired. Go."

I nodded wearily. I couldn't help but feel like I was still being left out; there was more I didn't know. But I was tired. Bone tired. My legs felt numb and weak, and my mind was clouded in a fog that I couldn't lift. I wanted to stay and learn more about myself and the family I never knew, but whatever I had done to rewind time had drained me.

I stumbled my way down the hall until I found my bed and I disappeared into unconsciousness.

no rest for the weary

I couldn't have been asleep for long, before my eyes snapped open. I thought I heard someone calling my name. An uneasiness swept over me. I felt cold, colder than I should. I rolled over and tried to go back to sleep, dragging the blankets up around my neck.

"Angus!"

I opened my eyes again. I definitely heard my name.

I sat up. Artie was sleeping soundly. I threw the covers back and stood up. Opening the door, I peered down the corridor. Everything was silent, the halls were dark.

I spun around, a familiar feeling sinking into my stomach. This had happened before.

"It has begun," the voice whispered.

I closed the door quietly and leaned against the wall. My heart was racing in my chest so fast my head was pounding. I shook my head, as if it would somehow shake out the voice.

This was all about me. I was bringing this on everyone. This was my fault. I had to do something. What kind of person would I be if I let everyone protect me, defend me, sacrificing themselves while I cowered in hiding? It was pathetic.

Anger coursed through my veins, pulsating beneath my skin. The two dead Vectors, the oncoming war, it was all about me. How many people were going to die for this? Could I live with myself if even one more person's heart stopped beating? I had no idea what was coming for us, but I knew one thing for certain – it was me they were after, and if I wasn't here, the Academy would be safe.

I reached under the bed for my bag and started stuffing clothes into it. I knew what I had to do.

I had to leave.

I couldn't go home, couldn't risk harm coming to my family. I just had to disappear, go as far as I could. I had to leave everything behind.

Slowly, I let my mind take me through the front doors, winding me through the halls, into the library. I let every corner sink in, every sight, every shadow. I knew I wouldn't be coming back. This was it. It was surprising to me how important this place, and all these people, had become to me. I wasn't sure who I was going to be without it.

I shoved my phone into my pocket, slipped its charger in the bag and slung it over my shoulder. I dressed quickly with the clothes I had left out and shoved my feet into my shoes. The Dragon Dial was in my bedside table. I slipped it into my coat pocket.

I took a last look at Artie to make sure I hadn't woken him, then slipped out of the room.

Heading down the hallway as quietly as I could, I wound my way through the Academy until I reach the doors that led to the courtyard. Outside it was dark and icy cold. The moon was directly overhead, its light earie and melancholy. There were no stars tonight. Thick clouds moved in the wind, illuminated by the white light glowing steadily from the moon.

Silently, I moved across the courtyard towards the stables. I snuck in as quietly as I could and stopped at Merry's stable.

She was waiting for me; aware I was coming. Beside her, Ransom was alert and ready, like a sentinel. Other dragons watched us in silence, while still others slept on, without fear of impending danger.

I reached out and stroked Merry's head. Ransom stared at me with solemn eyes, like as if he already knew what I was going to do.

I could see the Academy through the stable windows, and an ache filled my stomach. It was home. It felt like a place of belonging. But that's why I had to leave. I couldn't let them fight a battle that wasn't theirs, couldn't put their lives in danger.

If I left, there would be nothing here to fight for.

Merry pushed gently against the gate.

"I'll be back," I whispered to Merry, pressing my forehead against hers. "I'll come back for you. Somehow. Wait for me just a little longer."

I pulled back and touched Ransom's rough jaw. "Take care of her."

As I turned to leave the stable, I heard Merry's soft groan, calling after me. I didn't look back. It hurt too much. It was like cutting my heart in two. Instead, I hurried into the darkness.

I wanted to take them with me, but how was I supposed to keep two dragons out of sight? If we got caught, they'd spend the rest of their lives in a cage, getting poked and prodded and tested. They would be a spectacle. I couldn't risk that.

My feet were almost silent on the dewy grass. I headed for the mirror with renewed urgency. I had to take myself out of the picture – for days, weeks… years. Whatever it took. I had to protect the Academy.

I could see the mirror ahead. I would slip through, then disappear. I'd find a way to let Mum know I was okay, but I knew it would be too dangerous to see her. I quickened my step, afraid I would lose my nerve if I thought about it too long. As I reached the mirror, I put my hand into my pocket to retrieve the watch, but before my fingers brushed its metallic surface there was a sharp pain in my neck. I heard the unmistakable sound of Merry and Ransom roaring and then everything went black.

taken

Hours or days could have gone by, and I never would have known.

As my mind started to awaken, I felt cold all over my body. I couldn't move my fingers or toes, and my head throbbed. I felt dizzy, and my stomach was taut with acid.

My eyes fluttered open. Where was I?

I scanned my surroundings. The room was small, the walls a pale cream. I was on a bed, with a yellow bedcover mussed underneath me. Curtains that seemed to match the bedcover hung from the large window to my right and to my left was a bathroom that looked just big enough to fit one person.

The air was musty and there was a small kitchenette in the corner of the room.

I could tell almost immediately that I was in a hotel room. Albeit not a very nice one.

The most captivating feature of the room was a man seated on a chair covered in plastic, positioned in front of the window with his back facing me.

"What do you want from me?" I asked.

"Interesting question. Most people would start with, where am

I?"

"I know where I am," I replied calmly. "I'm in a hotel room. A pretty crappy one."

"Yes, this is true. But you're missing something rather important."

"And what would that be?"

"*Where* are you?"

I didn't understand. The man stood to his feet and drew back the curtain.

My stomach dropped. Outside the window was a busy, neon light-filled skyline. One I had never seen before. We weren't in England anymore.

I tried to remain calm. "Who are you?"

There was a moment of silence before the man turned around. I recognised him immediately.

"Felt like some father-son bonding time, did you?" I asked my father, who stood in front of me, with a weary expression on his face. "Do I get a copy or the original?"

"I'm really here," he confirmed, walking over to the bed. He sat down on the end and sighed. "I didn't want it to be like this."

"Then why did you kidnap me?"

"It was the only way."

"For what?" I asked.

"For you to see. See the truth. What you know isn't all there is, Angus. There's more to any of this than you could possibly understand."

"I'm getting a little tired of hearing that. *And* being left out of the loop. I know more than you think I do. I know who you are. Grayne, the leader of the Rebellion. Son of Silas, betrayer of the Concilium."

"Yes, I suppose that's all factual," he replied. Grayne stood up and started to pace. "Tell me what you know."

"I know that you're leading a massive rebellion against the Concilium and that you're responsible for a lot of deaths. I know that you sent people to get me and take me out of the Academy so that you could fill my head with whatever crap you can to get your agenda across. I know that you're a liar and a thief and that you want to overthrow the Concilium. What I don't know is *why*."

"Would you like to know?" Grayne asked.

"Honestly, I'm not sure."

"Why is that?"

"Because just a few months ago, I was a normal kid. And now I've been kidnapped, and I'm supposed to be saving everyone one day, and I don't know how. But mostly because I won't believe you even if you tell me, because, frankly, why would you tell me the truth?"

"Because I have nothing to hide. I have done terrible things, yes. But it was all for a cause. A cause I deem worthy."

"Control." I spat. "That's your cause."

"In its crudest term, yes."

"Well, then, I guess I know why."

"You don't know why I want to control the Concilium, Angus. If you did, you would help me."

"I doubt that very much."

"I don't."

"Well, it's good you have confidence. Confidence is key."

Grayne chuckled. "You're funny. I like you."

"Bully for me." I let out a deep sigh. "What do you want with me?"

"I want you to help me. I want you to join me."

Grayne's face was calm and flat, and showed no hint of humour.

His skin was olive, his eyes a dark brown. His brow was furrowed with creases that showed years of concern, but despite that he didn't look much older than forty.

"You can't be serious," I responded. "I mean, I know you're serious, but you can't honestly expect me to join you. You can't really think this is going to work."

Grayne shrugged. "I'm hoping that it will. I need you."

"I know a little of what it's like to need someone. I needed you my whole life. If I knew what I was missing out on I think I would have made Mum hang up the phone on the rare occasion you called."

A hint of pain flashed across Grayne's face. "It was always to speak to you. She would never let me."

"You know what they say. Mother knows best."

"Angus!" Grayne shouted. "This is no joking matter. This is war! There are lives at stake. You have no idea how powerful your ability is. You have no idea how valuable you are to them. To *me*."

"I am not your weapon," I hissed, standing up. My legs were shaky but I held firm.

Grayne was frustrated. His brows furrowed in annoyance and exasperation, and he ran his fingers through what little remained of his tightly cropped hair. "Do you have any idea how long they have been waiting for you?"

"Who?"

Grayne sighed, and held his hands out in front of his body, as if to steady himself. He took a few deep breaths and when he spoke again, he was calm. "There's only one family line with the genetic ability to Blink, Angus. Your family line. My family. But the ability to Blink skips a generation, which is why I can't do it. I'm sure you've already been told that a Vector's life is connected to their dragon, and dragons live an extraordinarily long time. Silas was old, very old, before I was born. He was the only Vector who could Blink for hundreds of years, but he chose to go against the Concilium. I never meant to have a child. I knew that child would inherit the ability to Blink, and I didn't want my son or daughter to be caught up in this world. But then I met your mother, and she was… like no one I had ever known. When I found out she was pregnant, I left. I thought that if I wasn't around, that if I wasn't a part of your world, I could spare you from this. I tried to hide you from the Concilium, but… here you are."

My head was dizzy with new information; information I wasn't sure if I should believe. It all seemed a little too convenient, a little too good of an excuse for abandoning me and my Mum for sixteen years.

I shook off whatever emotions were trying to get a grip on me, and walked over to the window, determined not to be affected by Grayne or his story. Instead, I tried to focus on the skyline and decipher where in this world – or another – I could possibly be.

The skyscrapers were bright with lights, the world outside cloaked in black night. That meant one of two things – first, that I wasn't far from England, since it was night when I was taken from the Academy. Second, that I was on the other side of the world, and I had been unconscious for long enough that it was now evening here, and daylight in England.

I scanned the world, as it unfurled before me like a crumpled blanket. It was ablaze with light and colour. Rugged mountains pierced the horizon beyond the chaos of the city. Winding streets zigzagged through the cacophony of noise and people. That's when I noticed none of the signs were in English.

They were written in Korean.

seoul searching

"What are we doing here?" I asked.

"Here in Seoul? Or here together in this room?"

"Both," I replied, turning from the window to view him.

"We're here in this room, because we're waiting for some friends of mine. We're here in Seoul *because* of those friends of mine."

That's when I remembered Spectre telling me about Jun-Ha, and his sister, Ji-Ha. They were Grayne's right and left hand. Spectre told me how dangerous they were. My brain started to feel hot. But there was one glimmer of hope in all of this. If I was here, then the Academy was safe. I felt relieved. It was strange to be standing here, in a country as far from home as possible, kidnapped and in danger, yet feeling thankful. If was here with them, the Rebellion had no reason to attack the Academy. Spectre, Hana, Artie… they were all safe.

A sinking realisation washed over me like waves dunking me at the beach.

"This was your plan all along, wasn't it?" I breathed.

There was a knock at the door.

Grayne turned from me and headed to the door. He stepped aside to allow who I could only guess was Ji-Ha and Jun-Ha inside.

They walked in like apparitions, soundless and quick. They were tall and lithe, and I could see the relation as obviously as I could see the neon lights outside. I wasn't sure why, but they weren't what I was expecting. Jun-Ha wore a tailored black suit, looking more like he stepped out of a boardroom than off the back of a dragon.

Ji-Ha had long hair, as red as fire, tangled in intricate plaits. She was dressed entirely in black, with a leather jacket that fell to her knees, and a scruffy scarf wrapped loosely around her neck. I noticed she carried a laptop under her arm.

Perhaps the most startling feature the two shared was how shockingly beautiful they both were. That, and the fact they walked in almost complete silence.

"Hello, Angus," Ji-Ha greeted me, without the hint of a tone. She swept into the centre of the room, to set up her laptop.

Jun-Ha eyed me suspiciously as he followed her. "Are you sure he can be trusted?" he asked Grayne, as if I wasn't standing right there.

Grayne didn't reply. He stared coldly back at Jun-Ha until he turned away, letting it go.

"Excuse me," I said, piping up, "it's not like I asked to be here. In fact, I'd like to go now. I think I can say without a doubt that no, you cannot trust me."

Ji-Ha was already tapping away at her keyboard. "I've removed your entrance into South Korea from all databases, so there's no evidence you were here."

"Excellent," Grayne said.

I watched them all with total lack of confidence. What was I going to do? It wasn't as if I could climb out the window and scale down like a superhero. We were at least thirty storeys high. Why was I here? Were they going to kill me?

"No," Ji-Ha answered.

I looked around. No one had spoken.

She looked directly at me. "Yes, I'm talking to you. And the answer is no."

"I didn't say anything," I replied.

"Not out loud."

Spectre had told me she could read minds, but even with everything I had seen, it was almost too unbelievable to experience it. *Can you hear me?* I thought.

"Yes," she answered, only this time the voice wasn't audible. I heard it in my head, like as if she had taken up residence there.

A shiver ran down my spine. I wished now more than ever that I had Merry and Ransom here. I couldn't believe that I had been so stupid, as to fall into his trap. This is what he wanted all along. But I would have to protect my thoughts now, and rely more on instinct. I was alone – truly alone.

"If in some alternate reality I agreed to help you, what is it that you want from me?" I asked.

Grayne looked at me with surprise in his eyes, feeling more confident that I would side with him. "We would help train you, perfect your skills. There's only so much Spectre can teach you, Angus. He can't Blink and he didn't know Silas the way I did."

"And then?"

"And then you would help us overthrow the Concilium."

"How exactly?"

Grayne laughed. "I don't think so, Angus."

"Nice try," Ji-Ha added. Jun-Ha just stared at me the same way he had done since he walked in.

"You think I'm going to tell you my whole plan so you can tell Spectre? I don't think so, Angus. You have no idea how long this plan has been in motion, and you have no idea how important you are to its execution. Don't worry. We're not staying in this hotel room. We'll take you somewhere much more comfortable."

"Where are we going?"

Grayne smiled. "Home."

compound

Outside, the air was fresh and colder than I had expected. Seoul was alive with light and colour, and I was certain I would have loved it under different circumstances. People didn't even seem to notice us as we walked towards a long black sedan, with heavily tinted windows. I tried to get someone's, *anyone's*, attention, but they didn't even look at me. It was like I didn't exist.

What's going on? I thought to myself.

Ji-Ha didn't need to be a mind reader to know what I was thinking. Neither did Grayne. "She's very useful in a situation like this," he said. "It's not just hearing people's thoughts. She can project thoughts, block them, infiltrate them. No one is even registering your presence, Angus."

Deflated, I felt anger grow inside me. "You do realise I'm your son, don't you? Or does that mean nothing to you?"

"Of course it does, Angus." Grayne opened the car door and gestured for me to get inside. "You're here for your own protection just as much as you are for my purpose. Now get in the car."

With little other choice in front of me, I slid into the backseat.

For over an hour I sat in the back in silence, while we wound through the streets of Seoul. We turned off the main stretch and onto a long winding road that seemed never-ending. Thin trees with spindly branches stretching out over the road like an old woman's fingers arched above us. Moonlight flickered through the leaves. Finally, we pulled up in front of a gated compound, with enormous traditional rooftops poking out over the top.

There was a guard posted at a small building right outside the gates. Grayne wound down the window, and upon seeing him, the guard quickly buzzed open the gate and waved us through. I turned around and watched the gate close again, clinking shut with an ominous thud.

In front of me, perfectly manicured gardens were flooded with enough light to convince you it was daylight. There were men posted everywhere, armed and intimidating.

The compound was quite beautiful. There was one large main building that looked like an ancient Korean palace, and then several other small buildings, some attached by undercover walkways, and others separate. All were traditionally built. Perfectly trimmed grass spread across the undulating gardens. Trees and flower beds framed the scene, and it would be, in any other circumstance, a tranquil place to be.

The car stopped and once we got out, I was shown to my room, which was far nicer than I had been expecting. There were no locks on the doors, and that confirmed to me that there didn't need to be – I couldn't leave this compound if I tried.

Grayne lingered in the room, as I stood in front of a neatly made bed. Despite the traditional architecture, the room was modern and sleek. Spotting the dresser beside the bed and the lounge in the adjoining room, I got the distinct impression I was going to be here for a long time.

"What is this place?" I asked.

"Home. My home. Yours too, if you want it to be."

"This is all yours?" I asked.

Grayne smirked. "I was born here actually. Silas had close ties to the headmaster of the Seoul Academy, and when he chose to go against the Concilium, she was right beside him."

"She?" I asked. "Ji-Ha? Is she your…"

"I can't tell whether you're going to ask if she's my mother or my partner. Such is the world we live in. But the answer to both is no. She's also not the headmaster I was talking about."

"Who, then?"

"Her name was Kang Jan-Di. She was your grandmother."

Grayne couldn't have known it, but he had just answered a question I had toiled with my entire life. What was my story? What was my heritage? What gave my eyes that colour, my skin that tone? What made me look the way I did? I had always wondered and now I knew.

The moment the words left his lips, I felt like a piece of me fell into place.

I cleared my throat to shake myself loose from my reverie. "Grayne doesn't sound like a very Korean name."

"It's not," he answered. "It's not my real name either."

"So," I said, clearing my throat. I wasn't going to let Grayne in on the revelation I just had. He hadn't earned that right. "You live here?"

"Yes. Silas passed it down to me. I've lived here most of my life."

"I guess I'm not leaving here any time soon?"

Grayne didn't answer. Instead, he turned to leave. "Get some sleep. We have work to do tomorrow."

He left without another word, leaving me to dwell in the silence that followed. I dropped my bag on the bed and sat down. I supposed there were worse places to be held captive, but knowing I couldn't leave was making me sick to my stomach. How long had I been gone? What would Spectre think? Would he think I had betrayed him?

I checked my pocket for my phone, but of course, it was gone. The Dragon Dial wasn't there either. I tipped the contents of the bag out on the table, just in case I had put both somewhere else, but there was nothing but a few clothes and a couple of books.

I threw the bag on the ground, anger seeping into my bones. I finally had a relationship with my father. It just wasn't the kind I was hoping for.

I flopped down on the bed and stared at the wall opposite, with no idea what I was going to do next.

temporary allies

I must have fallen asleep at some point, but when I was woken up by Grayne sliding open my door and splashing a bucket of water in my face, I was tired enough to know it couldn't have been long ago. I didn't have long to think about why I was now soaking wet, because I was yanked out of bed and practically thrown outside, in nothing but a thin pair of linen trousers.

The morning was ice cold, and if that wasn't enough, water was thrown at me again. Drenched and on the verge of hypothermia and a mental break down, I spluttered. "What is going on?"

Grayne stepped up to me, looking remarkably dry and warm. "It's time for training."

"What kind of training do you call this?" I asked.

Someone I didn't even see coming hit me in the stomach with a bat. I gasped for breath, buckled over in pain. When I could finally breathe again, Grayne stepped in front of me, his eyes drilling into me. "The real kind."

The same bat, or maybe it was a different one – I couldn't tell – hit me in the back and I dropped to the ground. I grasped at the cold earth, begging it to save me. Is this what life was like now? I gritted my teeth and tensed as another blow landed on the backs of my legs.

"What are you doing?" I shouted. "Stop!"

"Up until now, your training has been pathetic. You aren't being prepared for anything. You couldn't hurt a mayfly."

"I don't want to hurt anybody," I groaned through the pain. "That's not a weakness."

"What you want has nothing to do with it. Skill, strength, ability, power, these are the things that will protect you and those you love. Your body is *weak*, your skills are *weak*, your mind is *weak*."

Someone kicked me in the gut and I flew to my side, clutching my ribs.

"We will beat the weakness out of you and replace it with a strength you never knew was possible."

A bamboo bar with two large pails of water tied to either end was placed in front of me. "Pick it up. Run fifty laps around the compound. If you spill a drop, you start again."

I got to my feet, still gasping for breath and wanting to retch. But I picked it up, and placed it on my shoulders. It dug into the back of my neck.

"Go," Grayne growled.

I ran. I didn't know how long I was going to be here. How much pain was I going to have to endure? I wanted more than anything to go back to the safety and comfort of the Academy. But no matter how much it hurt, no matter what he did to me, one thing was for certain – I was never going to let him see me break.

The following days could have been weeks or months for all I knew. One brutal day blurred into the next. Grayne was a fierce teacher, but despite it all, I could feel myself growing stronger. My thin arms stretched to accommodate muscles, and ridges and valleys appeared across my stomach and back as strength made its way through me like a poison.

I didn't give him the credit for this. I gave it to myself. I was the one who refused to let him break me.

I didn't know how long I was into the torture Grayne called training, but at some point, I realised that if what everyone had been saying was right, if I *did* have the most powerful gift and I did have the protentional to bring danger to the Academy or even the Concilium, then surely I had the potential to get out of here, if I could truly learn to harness my gift.

That's when I decided to throw myself into training with abandon. I didn't need to be woken up in the mornings with an ice bucket anymore. I was awake and training on my own before the sun was up. Grayne had to come looking for *me*.

One of the smaller buildings in the compound housed a dojo. I spent nearly every waking hour in there. I didn't want to just improve my ability to Blink. I wanted to become a master at hand-to-hand combat. I wanted to know that being taken, being held against my will, would never happen again.

Grayne seemed impressed with my drive to train, confusing my desire to beat him with a plan to help him. That was fine with me. I would let him think whatever he wanted if it meant I could learn to harness my gift enough that I could crush him and get out of here. For now, we were temporary allies in the fight to train me.

As time wore on, there was a quiet voice in the back of my mind that wondered if this was the place I really belonged. And if not for everything that Spectre had told me about my father, I probably would have wanted to stay. He wouldn't have had to kidnap me – I would have come of my own accord. All I had ever wanted was to know my father and find a place that I felt like I belonged. I thought

I had found that at the Academy, but it would have been easy to find my place here, if I thought for a moment Grayne was on the right team.

The truth was, I *wanted* to belong here. I wanted to embrace my identity, my purpose… my father. I wanted to be a part of this place, and I had to remind myself daily that Grayne was the enemy.

The training, the early starts, the pounding I gave to my body every day, secretly I was starting to relish it. I could feel my body growing stronger every day, and I liked it. Not long ago, I had been the kid Neal Bateman beat up every couple of days. Now, if I were to see him again, I knew the tables would be turned.

I liked that I was becoming strong, and I liked that I was learning more and more about my gift. It was easy now for me to stop and start time, to rewind it, even. I was able to go further and further back, and I had even started to learn to fast forward again, back to the present. On one evening, two cups of steaming tea in front of us, Grayne told me that one day, I would be able to fast-forward into the future.

"How?" I asked. "Show me."

"I can't. Not yet. You're not ready."

"I can do it," I insisted.

"I have no doubt you have the heart," Grayne replied. "But your body and your mind must be prepared."

When he saw my discouragement, he was quick to offer comfort with an easy laugh. "Don't worry, Angus. That's why you're here. I can show you things Spectre never could."

I felt a stab of guilt at the name as it hung in the air like a puff of smoke, but it vanished when Grayne stood to his feet and walked to an intricately designed cupboard. I watched as Grayne unlocked it, and retrieved a thick book. It was old, that much was obvious.

Grayne walked back over to me and placed it in my hands.

"What's this?" I asked.

"This belonged to Silas. He wrote it. It's the only copy in existence. It's everything he could do, and detailed techniques on how to do it. You won't be able to do all of it now, even if you tried, but your time will come."

"It's thick."

"He also wrote his thoughts and agendas. Why he disagreed with the Concilium and ideas on how to fight back."

"Why are you giving it to me?" I asked.

"I thought maybe it might help you to understand. Why we do what we do. Why you are so important."

I ran my hands across the surface of the book and wished I could absorb it all by osmosis, just by holding it in my hands.

"It mustn't leave this room, Angus. You may read it, but you must do so in here."

I nodded.

Grayne smiled at me. It was a warm smile, and I could almost convince myself that it was the kind of smile he would have given me growing up, when I made him proud in little ways, like learning to ride a bike, or doing well on an exam.

I was starting to get worried. In that moment, I knew beyond a shadow of a doubt, I wanted to see that smile again.

lessons learned

The book was weighty, filled with information I desperately wanted to know. I started at the beginning, where Silas broke down the different facets of his gift. He wrote it when Grayne was born, as a way to ensure that his child would know the answers to the questions that would no doubt arise. Silas's grandfather had died long before Silas could learn from him, and being the only person in the world who could Blink had been a lonely experience. I knew the feeling. If anything happened to him, Silas wanted the answers to be available. I was thankful he had had the foresight.

Spectre had always insisted there was so much more for me to learn, but it had to come later. He'd only given me a thin folder on Silas that had been more about his crimes against the Concilium than anything else. Everything about his ability to Blink was from eyewitness accounts, and none of it ever explained *how* to do it. I hated not being privy to information about *my own* life. I was grateful to have a book full of the knowledge I had been seeking right in front of me. This was my life. My gift. For better or worse, I was the only one alive who could Blink, and that meant I needed all the support I could get. Reading the words from my grandfather, who knew firsthand what this gift was and why it was so important, was invaluable to me.

Spectre meant well, and Grayne had been helpful, but both of them could only take me so far. Neither of them could Blink, no matter how much more experience or knowledge they had. I found myself struggling with the realisation that the man who wrote this was really my grandfather, and he was dead because of Spectre. I had trouble reconciling the image of Spectre killing my grandfather with the same man I had come to know and, honestly, love. I tried to shuffle out of the uncomfortable thought and focus on the book in front of me. The book that was the closest I would ever get to the grandfather I had never known.

The book began with things I already knew, like the first manifestation of the gift is freezing time. I read his description with fervor, like a lost letter from an old friend.

It is like the end of a dream, when one is starting to wake. He wrote. *The world is a blur, still, yet moving, slowly, lethargically, as if the hold of sleep is still strong. I can move, but my body is smeared like paint, as if I am moving out of step with time, which desperately seeks to take hold of me.*

Daylight was fading outside, and I had spent the majority of the day here, reading, just as I had done the day before. How long had I been here now? A month? Two? Six? I missed my dragons like a drowning man misses air. Every day when I woke up, I had to realise all over again that my dragons weren't here, and it felt like dying a little bit each morning. I wondered how they felt. Would they forget me? Their absence caused a constant sense of nausea right in the pit of my stomach. I had never wanted to leave them, and I never would have if I didn't believe that I was the reason everyone was in danger. It was a sacrifice I had to make. My pain for their safety.

My mind constantly flicked back to them and I wished they were here. But dragons mean freedom, and I wasn't free.

Somewhere in the back of my mind, I wondered what Spectre thought about my disappearance. Did he know I was with the Rebellion? Did he think I came here of my own accord? I wished I could call him and tell him that I wasn't betraying him. But I knew I was more than a captor now. I was stuck here, of course, but I needed the chance to learn. Grayne was right. He could take me further than Spectre, if for no other reason than his access to this book.

The thought of calling Spectre reminded me of something else, and I was instantly gripped with fear. I snapped the book closed and ran to find Grayne.

The halls were wooden, but I wore socks, so I ran silently and quickly. I found Grayne sitting in the courtyard, alone.

He turned to face me, surprised at my state.

I don't know what happened to me. It was like my brain shut down and I forgot about everything but this place, this world. How selfish could I possibly be? I began to understand the seriousness of my situation, and the responsibility that fell on my shoulders, juggling my ability to Blink and the rest of my life.

"I have to call Mum," I said breathlessly.

"Why?" Grayne asked.

"Why do you think?" I spluttered. "How long have I even been here? She's probably alerted Buckingham Palace by now!"

"Don't worry, Angus," Grayne said, shaking his head. "It's been taken care of."

"What's that mean?" I asked. "Mum's all right, isn't she?"

"Of course she is, Angus. You've called her multiple times, and she's excited you're doing so well in your studies."

"What?"

Grayne tipped his head to the left. I followed his nudge and saw

Ji-Ha and Jun-Ha walking down the covered walkway connecting the main building with another. They were talking quietly to each other.

"Oh," I said, "She can change her voice?"

"No, her abilities are strictly in the mind. Ji-Ha has been having weekly conversations with your mother, and simply altering the voice your mother hears in her mind."

"It's like I've been deleted from my own life," I said quietly.

"Not at all Angus. You've just been given a new one."

"I'm not going to abandon her the way you and James did," I argued. "I want my Mum to be a part of any life I lead."

"She will be Angus. This arrangement is temporary."

"The arrangement where I'm trapped here and can't leave? The arrangement where I'm separated from my dragon?" I made sure to keep the existence of Ransom to myself. "Did you think I had forgotten I'm a prisoner here?"

"You're not a prisoner, Angus. You're here for your own good."

"Yeah, sure. I just can't leave."

Grayne looked amused. "I never said you can't leave."

"What?"

"You're free to leave any time you like." He threw something at me and I caught it reflexively. It was my pocket watch, the one I used to get to the Academy.

I rolled it around in my hands, surprised he had given it back. "To go back to the Academy?"

"I would rather you didn't, of course." His voice was clipped. "And I have a feeling that's not where you want to go, anyway."

"You know me, now, do you?" I asked.

"I like to think I'm getting there."

"Try me then," I prompted.

Grayne smiled and stood, folding his book and placing it on the table beside his pot of tea. He walked to me slowly, circling me like a shark. "You've just discovered a part of yourself you never knew existed. Your father, your Korean heritage, your grandfather – a kindred spirit of sorts. You've had time to adjust to your awareness of me, and your knowledge of your grandfather and his gifts has done nothing but grow. But your heritage… that's yet unexplored. You haven't seen more of this country than the skyline and my home. If you were to leave, I know exactly where you'd go." He paused and I was surprised at how easily he read me. "You would go into Seoul. You would connect with your history."

I was silent, unwilling to confirm his suspicions.

"You see, Angus, you and I are not so different. You belong here. You just never knew it."

Spectre's face flashed before my eyes. I gritted my teeth to remember my goal. *Learn. Grow. Train.* Then beat Grayne and return to Spectre. But Grayne was right about one thing. If I could leave the compound, I wouldn't run back to the Academy. After all, I left the Academy for a reason. If I went back, all I would do is bring the Rebellion to them, as they hunted me back down. And they had already made it quite clear that finding me was easy, and taking me was even easier. I wasn't strong enough to overcome Grayne yet. Not by a long shot. No. I had to stay here, and take the Rebellion down from the inside. I wouldn't go back to the Academy. I would go into Seoul.

"Let's go then." Grayne's voice snapped me back to reality.

"Go where?"

"Into Seoul."

"What? Now?"

"Why not?"

"Okay," I nodded.

A man dressed in black walked up to Grayne and spoke softly, leaning in close. I couldn't hear what was said, but Grayne looked pleased. He clapped a hand on the man's back and gestured his thanks.

"Come with me," Grayne said, taking me by the shoulder. He led me across the courtyard.

"What's going on?" I asked.

"Our transport has arrived."

We walked through the gardens, out onto a large clearing. "What are we doing here?" I asked.

It was windy, the air rushing around my face. It took me a moment to realise it wasn't the wind tousling my hair. I looked up and saw the underbelly of two enormous dragons. My mouth fell open when they landed, and I realised it was Merry and Ransom. Two other grey dragons hovered in the air, watching as Merry and Ransom took stock of their surroundings, before they rushed over to me.

It was like a piece of my chest just slotted back into place and I was whole again.

I threw my arms around Merry's neck. I couldn't believe how much she had grown. She nuzzled me with her huge head, and snorted excitedly in my face. Ransom was more solemn; he lowered his head slowly and pressed his nose up against my chest, and let out a low, sad grumble. I rubbed his head and shot Grayne a look of thanks, though how he knew about Ransom was beyond me.

Grayne's face was expressionless. "His name is Bleu."

"You know him?" I asked.

"I do. His rider was one of my men. His name was Luc."

I remembered Luc's death as if it were yesterday. The smell of blood in the air, the feeling of terror, the crumpled note.

"I was there."

This was news to Grayne. He looked at once both shocked and apologetic.

"He died in pain," I said. I said it not to punish Grayne, but to honour Luc, by telling the truth. "He had a note. It said, *don't blink.*"

"I sent him," Grayne said quietly. "That note was for you."

"Spectre said it was a threat."

"It was a warning."

"For whom?"

"For you."

"Why?"

"Because the Concilium would use you as a weapon against me if they found out you could Blink."

"Spectre said he didn't tell anyone else."

"If that were true, I doubt it's the case anymore. Not now that you are gone from the Academy."

"Where do they think I am? What do they think happened?"

"With me, no doubt. They probably think that I kidnapped you."

"Which you did," I confirmed.

Grayne breathed out a laugh. "Only in the technical sense. Though I know the truth."

"What truth?"

"That you were leaving anyway." Grayne walked up to Bleu and stroked his face, from the tip of his head to his flaring nostrils. "Why?"

I took a moment to answer, not sure if I should tell the truth or not. "To stop this," I finally answered. "To stop you attacking the Academy."

Grayne tilted his head to the side in surprise. "Attacking the

Academy? What are you talking about?"

"Spectre told me. He said the rider, Luc, told him that more were coming. He said that you were coming to attack us in a few weeks."

Grayne shook his head. "That's not possible."

"Don't lie to me. You even said that things were coming. Spectre said that the rest of the Academies had similar threats posed against them, and that's why only two riders could come to our defence."

"Was one of the riders your uncle? Was one of the riders who came James?" Grayne asked, his voice growing more enraged.

"Yes," I said, confused. Nothing was making sense. Grayne had to be lying. Spectre wouldn't have lied to me. There's no way he would have made this up.

"Angus, think about this. Why would I attack a school? A school full of children?"

"To get me."

"I did get to you, Angus. And I did it without a war."

I was starting to feel sick. "Why? Why did you take me?"

"To protect you. From the Concilium."

"If that's the case, why did you let me go in the first place? That was you on the street that day. You told me to trust them, to go with them!"

"Yes. Your dragon was waiting for you there. You had to go."

I leaned up against Merry, feeling weak. "None of this makes any sense."

Who was I supposed to trust now? Nothing felt right, and somehow I was right in the middle of it. The only soul alive who could Blink. A commodity both sides wanted. My father on one side, Spectre on the other.

"But… why would he say that?"

"I don't know."

I was starting to feel dizzy. Merry, sensing my discomfort, took a protective stance around me and started to growl. I couldn't think clearly with Grayne right here. I had to park my panic and change the subject. I was either being told the truth or fed lies, and honestly, I didn't know which I would have preferred. "How did you get them?" I asked. "Merry and Rans…Bleu." I guessed I was going to have to get used to that.

"Same way we got you. Only the dragons came willingly, since they knew you were with us."

"How?" I asked.

"They communicate. Plus, we took some items of clothing as proof."

"Thank you," I said, really meaning it. "I… I haven't felt complete without them."

"I know. I'm sorry it took so long, but security has increased at the Academy since you left."

"Is Spectre…"

"He's fine. I know you care for the old man."

"I don't want him to get hurt. If your issue is with the Concilium, you can leave him out of it. He's never done anything to me but help."

"Are you sure?"

I stayed silent, not sure what to think or believe anymore.

"You know Spectre is a member of the Concilium, don't you?"

I wasn't sure why, but this news hit me like a punch in the stomach.

"Ah." Realisation spread across his features. "He didn't tell you."

I shook my head. "No, no. I knew," I lied.

Grayne didn't look convinced, but he let it go. He shook free of the serious nature of the conversation and smiled, as his dragon loped up to him. It was red and black, two tone like Merry. Did that mean she was a Glitch, too? "Let's go. Time for a little sight-seeing."

sight seeing

I was quietly confident Grayne was trying to do something nice for me, but I couldn't really let myself relax. I had to remember that there was something bigger than my twisted relationship with my father at stake here.

I had expected we'd be seeing Seoul from the ground, but soaring high above it, with Merry and Bleu, was the perfect way to see the bigger picture. It was strange to think that this was my heritage. This country was a part of me.

The aerial view was expansive and beautiful and chaotic. The city gave way to the countryside, and when I thought it couldn't possibly get any more breathtaking, the night took over and Seoul was ablaze with light, as if it was a reflection of the starry night above.

It felt tranquil up here. Like everything was right again, now that I had my dragons. As the wind brushed through my hair, Merry pushed her translucent wings through the air and kept us gliding peacefully through the wispy clouds. I finally felt like I could breathe. I had needed to escape the tumultuous thoughts that ravaged my brain. Who was I supposed to trust? I knew one thing for certain – I wanted to know the truth, whatever that was. One way or another, I was going to figure it out.

I needed to know why Grayne hated the Concilium so much, and what he had done to try to overthrow them. I needed to get back to Silas's book. Grayne told me that Silas had mentioned things about the Concilium in there, reasons why he was going to fight against them. I had been more interested in reading about Silas's abilities than his beliefs. But with everything Grayne had told me, I knew this had to be more than political differences. It had to be deeper than that.

When we got back to the compound, I was going to get the answers I needed and choose a side for myself.

"Angus!" I turned to Grayne expecting him to point out another site, but his voice was anguished, and his face was twisted into an unreadable expression.

What was wrong?

Ji-Ha appeared beside us, and Jun-Ha wasn't far behind. "What's going on?" I shouted.

"They've found us!" Grayne called.

I looked around. At first, I couldn't see what Grayne was talking about, but then I spotted them, circling us like piranhas.

They had come for me.

Spectre, James and others. They were here.

I should have felt good, relieved. But instead, I felt afraid.

What was going to happen?

In the last conversation I had with Spectre, he told me he had killed my grandfather, at the command of the Concilium. Would he hesitate to kill my father, too?

Somewhere in the back of my mind, I wondered if one day, I would be next.

damage

The night around me was dark, and it was almost impossible to keep track of the dragons looping around in front of me. I watched in horror as Jun-Ha erupted into flames, moments before a shot of fire from a dragon's mouth collided with him. Where was Ji-Ha? My eyes scanned the sky until I saw her, way below us. A blue light, transparent and reflective, almost like an oil stain, rippled out from her.

It took me a minute to realise what she was doing. She was hiding us from the people below.

Above her, it was a cacophony of chaos. The sky was alight, thick tornadoes of fire thrown forth out of dragons' mouths. The sound was deafening.

"Angus!" The voice of Spectre was unmistakable. "Flee!"

I stared back at him, frozen.

It wasn't supposed to happen like this. They weren't supposed to come for me. They were supposed to stay away. I didn't want a fight.

I felt powerless, drained of life and strength. They were determined to fight, determined to hate each other. My father wasn't going to stop until he had taken over the Concilium, and Spectre would never let that happen; not while there was breath in him.

"Angus!" I looked to the left, and saw Grayne.

I was stuck in the middle, torn in both directions. Stuck between my father and my father-figure. Death on either side of me.

"Stop!" I shouted to anyone who would listen. "Please, stop!"

Merry roared, and Bleu took a defensive position in front of us, flapping his gargantuan wings in front of him, instead of up and down.

James and Vice were attacking Jun-Ha. Their dragons darted at him, in turn, spitting fire and screeching so loud I could hardly stand it.

Jun-Ha's dragon was the colour of midnight. He was lithe and quick, shifting out of the way effortlessly. I wondered how Jun-Ha could possibly hold on.

Pilar, with Spectre holding tightly, flew past me in the blink of an eye. I turned my head to see him push his wings down and throw his claws out, launching directly into the side of Grayne's dragon.

They rolled together like tumble weeds, ear-splitting screams filling the air. "No!" I shouted, my voice lost amongst the noise.

"Get moving!"

I looked up to see Han careening towards me, followed closely by Hana.

"What are you doing here?" I called.

"What does it look like?" Han spat.

"Hana!" I called. "This isn't safe! You need to leave!"

"I don't need your protection!" she shouted back. "But it looks like you need mine!"

"Get out of here!" Han yelled. "Now!"

"No!" I looked back over at Spectre and Grayne. There was no way I was going anywhere.

"What did you just say?" Han spat.

"No," I snarled.

Han's jaw hardened. I couldn't tell if he was impressed or disgusted.

I had to do something. I couldn't just sit here, watching it all unfold. This was all because of me. I had to stop it.

Fury was raging inside me. Anger was growing in a way I could hardly control. Why did they have to fight? Why did it have to be one or the other? What was this really about? My breath was catching in my throat, panic taking over. I needed more time. Time to think.

I Blinked.

Time slowed to a crawl. Merry and Bleu remained unaltered, hovering in the air as the world around them came to a sudden stop. I drew in shaky breaths and bathed in the quiet, in the pause and stillness that came from stopping the onrushing train of life. The sound of Merry and Bleu's wings beating rhythmically through the air was a comfort and balm to my soul. I needed to get a grip. I took a minute to assess what was happening around me. James's dragon was frozen in the air, a ball of fire with wild tongues of flame exploding like a dying star paused halfway out of his mouth. Beside James was Vice, her lips curled into a feline snarl, arm raised in anger, about to strike.

Hana and Han were on either side of me. Why were they here? Why had Spectre allowed them to come? To defend the Academy from incoming danger was one thing. To go out in pursuit of it was another. *Why*?

Below us, the blue telepathic wave was still there, suspended like an acrobat's net high above the audience below. Ji-Ha was safe atop her dragon. No one seemed to be paying her any attention.

I finally allowed my eyes to find who I was really looking for.

Spectre and Grayne were mid-fight, and it was a sight to behold. Both Spectre and Grayne could ghost, and it was like the night of the undead, like graves had opened and spirts had come to life once more. There were a dozen carbon copies of them launching midair at each other, suspended in time and space. Ghosts, faces gnarled and angry, fought to the pointless death on either side.

This had to stop. Lives were on the line. For what? Politics? Power? What was the point in power if there was no life, no love, no friendship, once you reached the pinnacle? What was the point in supremacy if the cost was your soul?

We moved over to them, and Merry did her best to position herself in between them. Bleu took up position beside me, facing Spectre.

I drew in a slow breath.

I Blinked.

Time restarted with a vengeance. "Stop!" I shouted, with enough force and volume to burn my throat.

Spectre and Grayne, who were heading directly for each other, had to deflect quickly to avoid hitting me. To them, not a second had passed. I was over there one moment, and between them the next. I watched them circle back and hover either side of me, their ghosts vanishing like puffs of milky smoke.

"Enough!" I shouted again, with the same fervor.

"Get out of here, Angus!" Spectre bellowed.

Pilar roared, his mouth opening wider than I was tall. I could see down the back of his throat. His lips curled over his teeth, saliva dripping from his pointed fangs. The lining of his throat was red and pulsating. Breath blew across my face like wind, but I was too angry to be afraid.

Merry shrieked back at him, and immediately she ghosted,

dispersing into a dozen versions of herself, each angrier than the last. Bleu roared, his head twisting like a cobra before it strikes.

Pilar wouldn't back down so easily, but his eyes darted from each copy of Merry to the next.

As I looked from Spectre to Grayne, I could see Grayne's astonishment at Merry's Glitch. He tried to recover quickly.

"Move, Angus," Grayne growled.

My breath was ragged in my chest. "Get out of here! Both of you!" My voice was foreign to me, as if it belonged to someone else. My eyes couldn't focus; everything was shaking.

"Angus, my boy," Spectre said, looking almost afraid of me. "Calm down."

"Calm down?" I could barely believe what he had just said. "Calm down? How can you tell me to calm down! Look at what you're doing!"

"Angus," Grayne's voice was trembling with adrenaline. "Spectre is right. You need to calm yourself. Find your centre." He held out a hand to me, like I was an escaped zoo animal that he was trying to usher back into its enclosure. But I was done being caged.

I was incapable of calming down, and saw no reason why I should.

"End this now!" My voice erupted from my throat, and in that split second, reality felt as if it closed in on me. The world faded to black for just an instant before re-emerging. Everything was transformed.

skip

I wasn't in between Grayne and Spectre anymore. In less than the blink of an eye, I was beside Jun-Ha, who was injured and bleeding.

It took a second for my mind to catch up and figure out what had happened. I hadn't lived it, but I knew what had happened. I had read about this in Silas's book.

I had just skipped forward in time.

Breathless, I tried to get a hold of myself.

I hadn't managed to fast-forward time before, but I had read about Silas's experience. He started skipping forward by just a minute or two at a time, but in the end, he could go forward by a few years. The movies call this kind of thing time travel. Silas called it skipping. Unlike the cinematic version, when Silas skipped, he remembered *everything* that happened in between. He didn't bypass it, he just sped it up.

It seemed to be working the same for me. I knew exactly what had happened. Vice had been hurt badly, and she had no choice but to retreat. The commotion had been enough of a distraction for Grayne and Spectre to shift their attention to them. When Vice slunk away, Jun-Ha had stopped, satisfied that that was enough – the bloodshed didn't need to continue.

But James was in a rage. His body was contorted in a twisted ball of anger, while his dragon screeched defiantly.

Thick black smoke-like whips shot forward out of his hands, like something from the underworld. They snaked through the air, heading towards Jun-Ha, at frightening speed. Without warning, a pointed tendril of black ooze stabbed into Jun-Ha's chest. His breath was caught in his lungs and blood bubbled out of his mouth.

"No!" Grayne bellowed.

Merry sensed the horror rising within me, and she flew over to Jun-Ha's aid, which brought me to the precise moment that time caught up with me.

"Are you okay?" I asked, uselessly, pointlessly. "What can I do?"

To me, it didn't matter about sides. Life was the only thing that mattered. Was whatever they were fighting for worth killing over? Why did people always have to die? Why was death the currency of power?

Jun-Ha was a fighter. He spat blood and wiped his mouth. "I'm fine," he answered.

"You need to get out of here!"

"No," he replied, gritting his teeth. "I'm not leaving."

I watched blood seep from the wound in his chest, sweat glistening on his forehead. I truly grasped how unaware I was. What was so important that it was worth this sacrifice? Worth dying for? There had to be more than what I had been told, and I resented the fact that Spectre and Grayne had kept vital information from me. Was the aim merely to conquer the Concilium? If so, what made their cause worth their lives?

James was circling back around, cloaked in a cloud of smoke. I knew beyond all doubt that he was coming back to kill him.

Han and Hana arrived beside us, appearing out of nowhere.

"What can we do?" Hana asked.

I hadn't been expecting their help. Why did they care? Wasn't defeating the Rebellion why they were here?

"What are you doing?" I asked.

"What does it look like?" Han shot back.

"We're here for *him*," Hana replied.

The roar of a dragon made me look up. James's dragon was coming fast.

"You need to go!" I shouted to Jun-Ha, but he kept a steady gaze on James.

"I told you," Jun-Ha grunted through the pain. "I'm not going anywhere." He raised his hand out in front of his body and balled it into a fist. It erupted into flames and bile rose in my throat as Jun-Ha pressed his fiery hand against his chest to close his wound. He shouted in pain, his jaw stretching to capacity.

Han and Hana shot each other a glance, and a glance was all it took. In a synchronised motion, they swung around us and took a protective stance between Jun-Ha and James. James's dragon slowed, and I could see confusion and hesitation flash across his face.

"What are you doing?" James spat.

"He's injured. This isn't why we're here," Hana replied.

"He's the enemy," James growled. "He deserves to die!"

I struggled to accept that James was my family. How could we possibly share any blood? My blood rushed through my body so quickly that I felt chilled. Then, without warning, James slowed. His expression changed dramatically, and he hunched over as if burdened by an invisible weight.

What was happening?

At first, he was silent, his eyes wide and wet. Then came the screams. "No!" James shouted, shaking his head. "No, no!"

It was as if he was gripped with insanity. He clawed at his hair and cried out, like he was begging to be rescued.

There was something familiar about this scene, and I was taken back to the day I had almost died. Han had stood over me, reducing me to a shaking, shivering mess, incapable of speech or clear thought.

I looked over to him and saw his body was rigid, his face a dark mask of concentration.

I shuddered.

I was impressed with Grayne's and Spectre's gift. I was *terrified* of Han's.

A strange sound tore my attention from Han and gave it to Hana. Birds, hundreds of them, were pouring out of her body. With her arms stretched wide to either side, enormous winged creatures, unlike any kind of bird I had ever seen, stretched out of her skin, bursting forth into the night.

Their wings spanned eight feet; their bodies were like the bodies of eagles, but the resemblance to a bird ended there. Talons like daggers were at the end of scaled feet, and fanged faces, more comparable to a feline, hissed and screeched.

The birds encircled James and he swatted away at them, to no avail. They clawed at him and shrieked.

"Get away from me!" he screamed like a madman.

The birds were more than he could handle. His dragon turned and flew away with astonishing speed.

Open-mouthed, I stared at the siblings who were more powerful than I could possibly imagine.

The birds turned back around and headed straight for Hana. They flew directly into her, absorbing back into her body as if they were never there.

Yeah. I was definitely in love with her.

A roar of pain made me whip my head to the side. Bleu roared and Merry shrieked. I watched in terror as Grayne's dragon arched back in agony, and Grayne fell, plummeting towards the earth below.

choice

I stared after him in shock, my chest heaving with disbelief. My father was falling to his death.

I couldn't be losing him. I had only just found him. I felt Spectre's eyes boring into mine. I looked up to meet his gaze. His face, his kind face that I had come to know and trust, was foreign to me in that moment.

This must have been what it was like to have an out-of-body experience. I couldn't quite comprehend what was happening to me. All the training, all the pain and hard work, none of it had prepared me for this moment. It struck me, somewhere in the back of my mind, as my father fell to his death, that now Spectre would have killed both my grandfather and my father.

There was a dark irony buried deep in that notion, and I wondered if things between us could ever be the same.

My father's death would either end or severely harm the Rebellion, and it would be a monumental victory for the Concilium. I would go back to the Academy and continue my training as a Vector, and life would continue. I hadn't known my father long, after all. Just a few months. It wasn't as if he had been a huge part of my life.

The Concilium would say Grayne deserved it. They would call Spectre a hero. The feud would end, or at least be wounded enough that the Rebellion posed a threat no longer.

It would be easy to let it happen. Easy to do nothing. After all, it wasn't long ago that I didn't have any gift at all. Under normal circumstances, there would be nothing I could do to save him anyway.

But there was nothing normal about this at all.

If I saved him, my new life could be over before it even really began. It didn't know what Spectre would do, but I was confident nothing would ever look the same again. Would I be welcome back at the Academy? Would Spectre ever speak to me again?

It occurred to me then that the answer didn't matter.

Not more than a second or two had passed. I had to snap out of it. He wasn't dead yet.

"Go," I whispered, my voice barely above a whisper. A whisper was all she needed. Merry plummeted towards the earth in a free fall, her wings folded tightly against her body. I clung to her with every ounce of strength, my hands gripping her horns, my legs pressing against her as hard as I could. Ghosts emerged before her, then more ghosts appeared further ahead, creating a line of Merry's rushing towards the ground.

"Bleu!" I shouted. "The dragon!"

There was no way Merry could help save Grayne's dragon. She was far bigger and heavier than anything Merry could handle. She needed Bleu.

Bleu needed no further instruction. He shot down, heading towards the dragon, who was dropping like a cannon, wrapped and tangled in her own wings. I couldn't watch to see Bleu. My eyes were focused on Grayne. His arms were raised, a reflex to reach for anything that could save him. Our eyes were locked; he knew I was coming. I stood on the back of Merry and launched towards the ghost in front of me. As my body flew through the air, Merry roared.

I landed solidly on the back of the dragon in front of me, but I didn't rest long. I stood and threw myself across the cavernous divide and landed squarely on the back of the next ghost.

I wasn't fast enough. I watched Grayne slipping further and further away. He was going to die.

I Blinked.

Time froze. Bleu and Merry kept moving, her ghosts keeping in time with us. Grayne was still, his body warped into an unnatural pose, his arms and legs above his head. His face was peculiarly serene, as though his imminent death came as no surprise.

If that was the case, I wasn't sorry to disappoint.

I had a choice about who I wanted to be: the kind of man, the kind of Vector, the kind of son.

I didn't want to be the person who chose to let someone die, no matter the cause. I wouldn't be that person. Not now. Not ever.

Merry screeched, and I turned my head to face her. She was faster than her ghosts, faster than I had ever seen her. This wasn't normal. She wasn't this fast. She was Glitching again. She flew down beside me, and I jumped.

Like a smeared smudge of oil and water, the air around me parted as I soared through the air, nothing below me but the Seoul skyline. I stretched out my hands and gripped her horn. My body swayed fiercely, but Merry didn't falter. She was solid beneath me as I threw myself on her back. We reached Grayne, and Merry slowed.

Bleu roared, hovering around Grayne's dragon. He was ready.

I had to do this carefully. Merry floated beside Grayne's motionless body. She gestured to me she was ready, with a shake of her head. I restarted time, and we began to fall with him.

Merry slid beneath him. I gripped his chest, my fingers tightly clutching the fabric of his shirt. I pulled him toward me, and Merry gradually slowed until we were no longer falling.

My head snapped up to Bleu. He was under Grayne's dragon, trying to slow their fall, but he wasn't enough. Grayne's dragon was immense. They were still falling.

"Merry!" I shouted.

Immediately, her ghosts sped forward and encircled Bleu and the wounded dragon until I couldn't see them at all. I held my breath and watched. Merry roared. The ball of red and green started to rise. They were no longer falling.

The relief was heavy in my bones. Grayne was okay. His dragon was okay.

I was immensely glad in that moment to be a nobody who had managed to be a somebody who could save another's life.

answers

I stared ahead in disbelief. Of all the things I had seen so far, the sight before me was the most unbelievable.

Merry had flown us directly back to the compound. Heavy rain had started hammering down on us, soaking us in an instant. I had wanted to see Hana and Han, if for nothing else than to thank them, but I had to get Grayne away from Spectre. We dropped directly into the clearing in the middle of the grounds. Landing softly on the grass, Merry held on until we had stepped off her, then she collapsed.

Her ghosts were lowering Grayne's dragon to the ground, but when she fell, they disappeared in a smokey haze and Bleu and the wounded dragon fell the last few feet to the earth, splashing water like a fountain.

"Merry!" I pressed a hand against her face, as her eyes rolled back into her head, and she surrendered to unconsciousness. Grayne headed for his dragon. I tried to wipe the rain out of her face, but it was so heavy there was no point.

"Don't worry, my boy. She's just worn herself quite thin. She'll be fine. Grayne's dragon, too."

The voice was instantly recognisable.

I turned to see Spectre approaching.

I didn't have time to think of what to do, or how he had found my father's compound. Instead, I threw myself between them, hands extended either side.

"Don't!" I shouted. "Don't come any closer. Both of you, stay back."

Spectre paused.

"I know there's a lot I don't understand," I said, my voice desperate and cracking. "But, please… don't do this." I turned to Spectre. The rain was intense. I had to shout just to be heard. "I know you think I let you down, but how can killing him be right? He's… he's my father. For better or worse, he's part of me, and I can't let you kill him. I don't know what's right or wrong anymore, what the right team is, who's telling the truth. But I can't… I can't let you do it." I shifted my gaze to Grayne, who was back on his feet. "Spectre has been like a father to me. When *you* weren't. Please. Please don't do this."

The silence lingered between us for what felt like an age. The rain sent a chill down my spine, but I wouldn't budge.

"I'm sorry, Angus," Spectre finally said. I could tell in his voice he really meant it. "I had to be sure."

"What?" My head flicked from Spectre to Grayne.

Spectre approached me slowly, and Grayne followed suit. "I don't understand."

"Angus," Grayne said calmly. "We need your help."

"We?"

Grayne took his eyes from mine, and looked over my shoulder. I turned to follow his gaze. Han and Hana were standing under the covered walkway. Beside them was Ji-Ha and Jun-Ha.

"We," Spectre confirmed.

"I don't… I don't understand."

"I had to know what you would choose, Angus," Spectre said, gripping hold of my shoulder. "As did your father."

"Choose? What do you mean?"

"Angus," Grayne pressed a hand against my chest. "We need to take down the Concilium. You have to understand. They're dangerous. It's not about mindless power and control. You're right – people are dying. But not at the hands of the Rebellion."

I spun around to face Spectre. "But you're… you told me he was the enemy. You're a part of the Concilium."

"Yes. I did. And yes, I am."

"Then… then…"

Spectre's eyes were warm. A small, compassionate smile stretched his lips. "Your father and I are working together, Angus."

I turned to Grayne for confirmation. "But he tried to kill you."

"We needed to know. I'm sorry, Angus," Grayne replied. "We needed to know what you would do."

"It was all… a test. Everything?" I asked, breathlessly.

"No, no. Not everything," Spectre replied. "The Academy is real. I am the headmaster there, and everyone you met, including James and Vice, are squarely in the corner of the Concilium. With, I should mention, the rather obvious exception of Han and Hana. They're with us."

"But you told me the Rebellion was killing people!"

"That's the line the Concilium touts, of course. I couldn't say anything else. I'm sorry, Angus. There was no other way."

The rain was finally starting to ease. I stood between them, drenched and confused, and starting to shiver. My head was swimming.

"The Concilium is corrupt," Grayne began. "They've been

running the Vector world, and even the world you came from since time began. They control and manipulate and kill to have their will be done. It's so much bigger than you can imagine. The Rebellion aren't evil, Angus. We're fighting to overthrow the Concilium to save our people."

I looked to Spectre. "It's true, Angus. I'm sorry for everything. I really am. But we need you. You're the first Vector to Blink since Silas. One day, Angus, you could be more powerful than any of us. Your father and I… we can't do this without you."

My shoulders rose and fell with quick breaths. "So, you're… working together. To take down the Concilium?"

"Yes," Grayne nodded.

"And you want me to help?"

"Yes," Spectre agreed.

"How?" I asked, looking over at Hana and Han. I could almost see Hana smile.

"Well," Spectre beamed, gripping me by both shoulders. "That's where it gets complicated."

"You're soaking wet. Come on. Let's talk inside." Grayne brushed past me and started walking towards the main house. He paused and called over his shoulder. "Oh, and Angus?"

I sighed, wondering what else he could possibly say. My eyes fell on Hana, and everything I felt for her seemed suddenly so much more confusing. If she was involved in all this, she had lied to me as well. And I was sick of being lied to. I tore my eyes from her and set my mouth in a hard line. "What?"

Grayne smiled a small, satisfied smile. The glint in his eyes was unmistakable. "Welcome to the Rebellion."

Angus Finch will return.

About the Author

P.M. Bloomfield is both a novelist and screenwriter. She can almost always be found with a tea in her hand, her nose in a book, and a dog on her lap.

Acknowledgements

I wouldn't be where I am today without my family, so thank you. Special thanks to everyone who made this book possible. Thank you to all who pick up this book and dive into Everwood. I hope you feel at home within its walls. Thank you most of all to Jesus, for being so good to me.

www.ingramcontent.com/pod-product-compliance
Lightning Source LLC
Chambersburg PA
CBHW020606310726
48979CB00008B/1368/J

* 9 7 8 0 6 4 8 7 6 9 4 5 3 *